HER FINAL
CONFESSION

BOOKS BY LISA REGAN

HER FINAL CONFESSION

LISA REGAN

GRAND CENTRAL
PUBLISHING

New York Boston

Copyright © 2018 by Lisa Regan

Cover design by Elizabeth Connor. Cover photo of figure © Rekha Garton/Arcangel. Cover copyright © 2022 by Hachette Book Group, Inc.

Grand Central Publishing
Hachette Book Group
1290 Avenue of the Americas, New York, NY 10104
grandcentralpublishing.com
twitter.com/grandcentralpub

First published in 2018 by Bookouture, an imprint of StoryFire Ltd.
First Grand Central Publishing edition: September 2022

Grand Central Publishing is a division of Hachette Book Group, Inc. The Grand Central Publishing name and logo is a trademark of Hachette Book Group, Inc.

The publisher is not responsible for websites (or their content) that are not owned by the publisher.

The Hachette Speakers Bureau provides a wide range of authors for speaking events. To find out more, go to www.hachettespeakersbureau.com or call (866) 376-6591.

LCCN: 2021952442

ISBN: 9781538706213 (trade paperback)

Printed in the United States of America

LSC-C

Printing 1, 2022

*For Helen Conlen, for showing me
what it means to be extraordinary.*

CHAPTER 1

Seattle, Washington

JUNE 1992

Billy was coming out of the store, a bag containing two pints of mint chocolate chip ice cream slung over one wrist, when he stopped to light a cigarette. He inhaled deeply and checked his watch; he could have two cigarettes and still be home in time for dinner. His wife didn't like it when he smoked.

In his periphery, he saw a woman heading over to her minivan. The flash of her silver hair in the sun as she stumbled through the parking lot caught his eye. He watched her walk in a full circle before fumbling with her keys. Maybe she was sick; maybe she was drunk; maybe she was just old, or mad, or both. His gaze drifted once she got into the van and started it up, distracted by the rattle of a motorbike engine.

He couldn't believe his luck as Lincoln Shore roared to the front of the store and parked his bike. Even outlaw bikers had to eat, he guessed. The truth was that Billy knew Linc frequented this grocery store and a few other places in the area and had been hoping he'd run into him. He was already well-known to a couple of Devil's Blade members but had yet to capture Linc's attention. Billy lit his second cigarette from the end of his first one and flicked the butt to the ground as Linc heaved himself off his bike. Billy felt the heat of his gaze. Then heard his gravelly voice. "You're that hang-around, aren't you? The one who's been sittin' at the bar lately."

"Yeah," Billy answered, "I—" but his words were swallowed up by sounds his brain couldn't quite process right away. A rush of air, a squeal of tires, the screech of metal against metal, and the howl of an engine being pushed to its limits.

He had a split second to react, and his instincts took over. From the corner of his eye, he registered the minivan trampling shopping carts and clipping a parked car. Other shoppers jumped out of the way of the speeding vehicle.

Billy barreled into Linc, throwing all of his weight into the burly biker and sending them both flying through the air. Concrete rushed at them. Linc's body cushioned Billy's fall, and his leather jacket kept him from losing generous strips of skin as they skidded across the ground. Behind them, the minivan crashed into a parked car, pushing it into two other nearby cars before finally coming to a stop. Its engine continued to rev, its front tires screaming against the asphalt. The driver slumped over the wheel. Red blood stained her silver scalp. As the other patrons in the parking lot rushed toward the minivan, Billy stood and extended a hand to Linc, pulling him to his feet.

They stood silent and staring at the trail of damage the minivan driver had left behind her. Linc said, "Thanks, brother."

Billy smiled. "Anytime," he replied, and because he didn't want to press his luck, he started walking away.

"Hey," Linc called after him. "What's your name, hang-around?"

Billy turned back. "Benji," he said, using his undercover name. "Benji Stone."

CHAPTER 2

Denton, Pennsylvania

PRESENT DAY

Spread out on the kitchen table before Josie was a vast array of brochures advertising home security systems. It had been six months since her life was turned upside down by the woman Josie had thought was her mother. The assault on Josie's life and sanity had included a home break-in, and for months she'd been trying to select a home security system advanced enough to keep her anxiety at bay. Twice she'd had the representatives out to the house to install the systems but changed her mind at the last minute when she discovered a hidden flaw or outrageous additional fees.

From the pile, she pulled out a colorful brochure from Aegis Home Security. SPECIALIZING IN HOME SECURITY FOR OVER 20 YEARS. They were one of the few companies transparent enough to put their full pricing scheme in their promotional materials. She flipped it open and looked at the options. She wondered if a dog would be a better way to go. A big dog. But her work schedule could be crazy. As a detective for the small city of Denton, Pennsylvania, her cases often kept her away from home for days, even nights. Sometimes she only returned long enough to shower, change, and head back out to work. If she owned a dog, she'd have to hire a dog walker. Then she'd worry about whether the dog walker was trustworthy. Josie sighed. Too many complications. She would just have to bite the bullet and spend a small fortune on a security system if she ever wanted to feel safe in her own home again. Her fingers hovered over a smaller brochure from a different company: Summors Security.

A knock at her front door interrupted her thoughts, and she made her way into the foyer. Through her peephole, she saw that it was Lieutenant Noah Fraley. She opened the door and looked him up and down, giving a low whistle. "Well," she said. "If I knew you cleaned up this nicely…"

He wore a perfectly cut charcoal-gray suit with a tasteful yellow-and-gray striped tie that brought out the hazel of his eyes. When he smiled at her, she felt a slight flutter in her chest. "Very funny," he said, stepping past her and making his way back to the kitchen. "You're not ready. You're not even changed."

Josie looked down at her jeans and faded Luke Bryan T-shirt. "It'll only take me a minute."

"Isn't that what all women say before they spend an hour on hair and makeup?"

Josie raised a brow. "Watch it. I don't *have* to bring a date to this dinner."

"Kidding," Noah said. He looked around the kitchen. Then he walked back out to the foyer, poking his head into the living room. Returning to the kitchen, he asked, "Where is everyone?"

Josie had recently been reunited with a biological family she had no idea she'd been separated from at birth. She was still getting used to calling Shannon and Christian Payne "Mom" and "Dad." She ticked off her fingers as she spoke. "Shannon and Trinity are out shopping. They'll meet us at the restaurant. My dad and brother are coming in from Callowhill. They'll also meet us there. My gram is back at Rockview since I needed the spare bedroom for Shannon, and Mrs. Quinn is on babysitting duty for little Harris this week."

Noah moved around the table, drawing closer to her until the backs of her thighs were up against the table's edge. He leaned in, pinning her there, his hands finding her hips and his lips grazing hers. "Do you mean to tell me that we're actually alone for once? Really and truly alone?"

Josie laughed and slipped her arms around his neck, drawing him down for a kiss. It was true that since the end of the Belinda Rose case, they hadn't had a moment to themselves when they weren't working or too exhausted to do much of anything. With an entirely new family in her life, Josie's home had seen a constant influx of guests in the last six months. Her real mother, Shannon, had stayed with her for several weeks, trading off with Lisette, Josie's grandmother, when Shannon had to return home for work. Josie's arm had been in a cast for nearly two months after the attack, and the help was welcome. Occasionally, her sister, Trinity, came from New York City, where she worked as a national network news anchor, and spent the weekends with Josie. And a few times, Christian and her teenage brother, Patrick, had stayed with her.

Josie had lived alone for some time. It was difficult at first being surrounded by people at every moment. The first time she had gone into her refrigerator to find that her half-and-half was gone had been frustrating, as had the first time she'd found her bathroom devoid of both towels and mats because Shannon was washing them. Her carefully ordered world, the sanctuary of her home, was being turned on its head. But, she reminded herself, family was more important than any household item or habit she had become accustomed to over the years. The Paynes wanted to swoop in and reclaim the last thirty years in only a matter of months, but for Josie, it was going to take longer than that.

Then there was Misty Derossi, the woman Josie's late husband, Ray, had been seeing before he died. Misty had given birth to Ray's son after his death, and the two women had struck up an unlikely friendship. Baby Harris was almost a year old, and Misty had stopped stripping and gotten herself a job at the mayor's new women's center doing intake for domestic violence victims, which meant that Josie's occasional babysitting duties had become routine. Now traces of

Harris's place in Josie's life were scattered throughout her home—a high chair at one end of the kitchen table, baby gates, sippy cups, a bin of toys, and a rocking chair in her living room. It was easier for Josie to keep some things at her own house rather than ask Misty to lug everything back and forth each time she brought the baby.

Noah's lips moved to Josie's throat. His hands cupped her bottom and lifted her up, setting her onto the table. Reflexively, her legs wrapped around his waist. She threw her head back. "Your suit," she breathed.

His hands traveled up, under her shirt, to the clasp of her bra. "I don't care about my suit."

She could feel the frenetic energy building between them, and she knew that if she gave in to it, there would be no turning back. The tension between them had been building for so long, it felt like a volcano about to erupt. She had told him when the Belinda Rose case ended—after their first kiss—that she needed to move slowly, and he had respected that. Josie had a bad track record with relationships, and she didn't want Noah to be another casualty of her horrible upbringing and all her personal baggage. She wanted it to be right. Or maybe she was just afraid...

"Is this how you want to do it for the first time?" she asked. "On my kitchen table?"

He scooped her up off the table as if she weighed nothing. "We'll go upstairs then."

Her mouth opened to protest, but as her body melded to his, every inch of her skin burned to know what was hidden beneath that suit.

They'd made it as far as the bottom of the stairs when the muffled beat of a cell phone sounded from within his jacket pocket, then from her own somewhere on the other side of the house.

Their bodies froze. Josie broke their kiss first, her head turning toward the sound. She'd left her phone in the living room. Neither one of them said it, but they both knew that there was only one reason both their phones would be ringing so close together. It had to be work, and it had to be serious. Although many of Denton's twenty-five square miles spanned the untamed mountains of central Pennsylvania, the population was large enough to give the police department about a half dozen murders a year and enough other crimes to keep the police department staff of fifty-plus fairly busy. In recent years, the small city had seen a couple of cases so shocking that they had caught the attention of the entire nation. She and Noah had both been deeply affected by those events, and Josie knew he was feeling the same sense of trepidation that spiraled up from her core. If they were both being called in on their day off, it must be big.

Slowly, Josie unhooked her ankles from Noah's waist, and he lowered her to the floor. His phone stopped, and Josie's began again. She straightened her clothes and walked into the living room to answer it. Denton chief of police Bob Chitwood wasted no time getting to the point. "Quinn. I need you and Fraley on the street right now. We got a homicide."

"Sir," Josie said, "we were—I—"

"I know. I don't care. Get your asses out to the scene right now." He rattled off an address that sounded familiar to Josie.

Chitwood's voice was so loud, it carried across the room to where Noah stood in the doorway, his suit wrinkled, one eyebrow raised. He mouthed, *Gretchen?*

Gretchen Palmer was another detective with the Denton Police Department. Josie said, "Detective Palmer is on duty tonight. She can handle it."

Chitwood made a noise of exasperation. "I'm aware of who's on duty, Quinn. But I can't get hold of Detective Palmer."

"Did you try her—"

His voice rose to a shout. "Dammit, Quinn, I don't have time for twenty questions. I've got a dead body, a crime scene, and no detective. Now one of you get over there." He spat out the address again, and it was then that Josie realized why it was familiar.

It was Gretchen's home address.

CHAPTER 3

"Slow down," Noah said.

Josie glanced over at him to see one of his hands tightly gripping the door handle of her Ford Escape as the city of Denton flashed past beside him in a blur. "There's a homicide at Gretchen's house," she reminded him.

"And we know it's not Gretchen, because if it were, the responding officers would have made that known," Noah replied.

Josie slowed down, but only fractionally. "Text her."

"I already did," Noah said. "And I tried calling her while you were changing. It goes straight to voicemail. No response to my texts. But I called the station, and dispatch told me that Gretchen was last seen there, about an hour before the body was found. We don't even know she was at her house when this happened."

"But we don't know that she wasn't. An hour is plenty of time for her to have gone to her house."

"While on duty?"

"Maybe. I don't know. We don't have enough information."

A sinking feeling spread through her stomach. It was unlike Gretchen to disappear and not answer her phone or texts—particularly in the middle of a shift. Josie's foot pressed harder on the gas once more. "Dispatch couldn't raise her?" she asked.

"No," Noah answered. "They're checking the MDT now to see if they can locate her car."

Gretchen usually drove a department-issue Chevy Cruze that was outfitted with an MDT, or mobile data terminal, a computerized mobile device that not only allowed Gretchen to communicate with the department's dispatch, but also allowed dispatch to locate her vehicle.

"I want to know the moment they've found her," Josie said.

Noah nodded silently. When Josie chanced a quick glance at him, she saw a muscle in his jaw tick, his gaze set on the scenery flying past his window. Nestled in one of Denton's quiet, middle-class neighborhoods, Gretchen's home was a detached two-story redbrick craftsman. It sat on one acre of land with a long, straight driveway leading from the street and running along one side of the house to a garage in the backyard. A tall white fence ran the length of the driveway, cutting off the neighbors on that side. Towering evergreen shrubs barred the view of the neighbors on the other side. On any other day, the house looked cute and welcoming, but today it was surrounded by police cruisers and ambulances. Josie and Noah parked across the street and walked to the driveway, edging around an ambulance parked across its entrance. A strip of crime-scene tape kept them from getting any closer to the house. In front of it stood one of Denton's patrol officers with a clipboard in his hands.

"Hummel," Josie greeted him.

"Boss," he responded.

Josie's fingers drummed a steady beat against her thigh, but she managed a tight smile. "Just Detective Quinn now, remember?"

For two years, Josie had served as Denton's interim chief of police but had happily returned to her position as detective once the mayor insisted on replacing her with Bob Chitwood. But the staff still called her "Boss."

"It's a hard habit to break," Noah said, giving Hummel an easy smile.

Hummel nodded as he entered their names into the log. He gave Noah a quick once-over. "Nice suit."

With lightning speed, Josie had changed into her usual khakis and a Denton PD polo shirt under a black jacket, but Noah still looked like something out of a men's fashion magazine. "I was on my way to dinner when I got the call," Noah told him.

Hummel pointed to one of the cruisers parked curbside, its trunk open. "There are Tyvek suits in there."

"What've you got?" Josie asked Hummel.

Hummel motioned toward the house, where members of Denton's evidence response team were working their way across the driveway, yard, and porch, wearing white Tyvek suits. They were busy marking evidence with yellow flags, taking measurements, sketching out the crime scene, and taking photographs. To the left, in the driveway, several yards from the front porch, a white pop-up tarp had been erected. Josie knew that was where the body lay.

Hummel said, "We got one dead body, Caucasian male, gunshot wound to the back, unarmed, no identification. No one else is here, but the front door was open. We tried reaching Detective Palmer on her cell phone, but it goes straight to voicemail. Cap says she's not at the station either. Someone saw her there about an hour before the body was found, but now nobody can find her. Dispatch couldn't raise her. They're checking the MDT now."

"I heard," Josie said. "If she's still unreachable a half hour from now, I want Lamay to check the station's CCTV footage to pinpoint exactly when she left. Who found the body?"

"The house has one of those security monitoring systems. You know, like the kind where if an alarm gets tripped, they send out the police?"

"Yeah," Josie said. "I'm thinking of getting one for my place."

"Well, the alarm for the front door went off. Security firm called Detective Palmer, got no answer. They called 911. We rolled up. Found the dead body. Oh, and there's something else…"

"What?" Noah asked.

Hummel shifted from one foot to the other, his mouth briefly forming a thin, nervous straight line before he answered. "It's best if you just go have a look."

CHAPTER 4

Once they were properly suited up, Hummel let them pass beneath the crime-scene tape, and they made a beeline for the tarp. Inside, they found a young man's body facedown on the blacktop. One of their evidence response team officers snapped photos as Josie squatted down next to the corpse. She immediately saw what Hummel was talking about. The man was dressed in jeans, white sneakers, and a green T-shirt, the back of which was now stained red from a single bullet hole just under his left shoulder blade, near his spine. But what made the scene unusual was that someone had used a safety pin to fix a photograph to the collar of his T-shirt.

"Is that an actual picture?" Noah asked, crouching down beside her.

With gloved fingers, Josie probed it. "Yeah. Looks old too."

It was three and a half by five inches, and it showed a small boy—maybe four or five years old—in profile, running through tall grass. The edges of the photo were yellowed and curled. Even its matte finish seemed faded. The boy was white with shaggy blond hair, and he wore brown corduroy pants and a flannel shirt. His small body was in motion, one arm and one leg raised mid-run when the photo was taken.

"Look at this," Josie said. Gingerly, she lifted the photo without removing it from the pin so that Noah could see the back of it, where faint black print announced: 2004.

"Is that the year it was printed?"

"Not printed," Josie said. "Developed. I think maybe this was taken with an actual camera. Looks like thirty-five-millimeter film. Developers often printed the dates on the backs of the photos."

"Those places are all closed," Noah pointed out.

"True," Josie said. "But I think it's safe to say this photo is from 2004."

"You think it's this guy?"

Josie used her cell phone to quickly snap a picture of the photo. She stood, moving to the man's head. He had landed with both hands up as though trying to catch his fall. A small pool of blood had gathered beneath his mouth. Only one side of his face was visible, but he looked young. Josie put him in his early twenties. Olive skin, curly black hair. His eyes were closed. "Hard to tell. The photo is from the side, so you really can't see the boy's face, but based on skin tone and hair color, my initial impression is no, it's not." Her eyes returned to the bullet wound in his back. "Has someone called the medical examiner?" Josie asked.

Noah nodded. "Hummel did. She's on her way."

"Hummel said he had no ID on him. After Dr. Feist gets a look at him, we'll roll him over and check his front pockets. Have someone check the vehicles on the street. He might have parked nearby—assuming he drove here. Tell me someone's canvassing the neighbors."

"Hummel dispatched a couple of officers to do that as soon as they locked the scene down."

"Great," Josie said. She moved away from the body, heading to the porch and counting her steps as she went. Twelve paces from the dead man to the base of the steps. Climbing the steps, she saw a yellow evidence marker on the floorboards of the porch, halfway between the top step and the front door. As she drew closer, a shiny nine-millimeter shell casing winked at her in the waning sunlight. One of her team members had circled it in chalk. Josie turned back, looking out at the driveway, putting the scenario together in her head. Had the killer stood here, on the top step, and shot the male in the back? While he was walking away? While he was unarmed? A chill enveloped her.

One of her ERT officers, Mettner, emerged from inside the house. "Boss? You okay?"

"Detective Quinn," she mumbled. "Hummel said the front door was open. Unlocked or ajar?"

"Ajar," he said. "No pry marks. The locks are intact. Door's not busted up."

Josie said, "So it doesn't look like this guy broke in." It was odd. Knowing how much crime Gretchen had been privy to in her long career, Josie found it hard to believe she was the kind of person who left her doors unlocked—even in Denton, where petty crime would never rival that of a city the size of Philadelphia. Or had she left the station house and come home only to answer the door when the young man arrived there?

Mettner said, "If he did, it wasn't through the front door."

"So why was the security company notified? What tripped the alarm?"

Mettner motioned toward the doorway. "The door was left ajar. I guess if it's left open for longer than ten minutes, an alarm is sent to the security company."

"Is there a keypad?" Josie asked. "To enter in a code?"

"No, it's via cell phone. So if the doorframe was damaged or the door was left open too long, the security company would send a message to Gretchen's phone. She enters in a code, and they know everything's fine."

"But the door could be unlocked, and someone could come in and out without tripping an alarm?"

Mettner shrugged. "Well, yeah, I guess."

"So we have no idea if the door was already unlocked, or if a key was used to open it and leave it ajar?"

"No, only that it was left open for a long time."

"Any indication the male in the driveway was inside the house?" Josie asked.

"We checked the whole house and didn't see anything that would prove one way or the other if he was actually inside. No one was here when we rolled up. Nothing looks disturbed. I mean, nothing obvious. We called Detective Palmer—she'd be able to tell us if anything was missing or out of place. But she's not answer—"

"I know," Josie said. "I heard. Did you take photos inside?"

"Yeah. Video too."

"Great. I want the downstairs printed, okay?"

"You got it, Boss," Mettner replied. Josie opened her mouth to correct him but changed her mind. She'd been correcting them all for months. It wasn't taking. With a glance behind her to where Noah still stood over the body, scribbling furiously in his notebook, Josie slipped through the door.

Gretchen's living room was sparsely furnished with a brown microfiber couch, a dark wood coffee table, and, across from that, a small pedestal with an equally small television on top. The floors were hardwood, and aside from a few houseplants, there weren't many personal touches. Gauzy curtains hung across the windows. In the dining room was a table with its chairs tucked neatly beneath it. A few bills, balled up receipts, and pieces of junk mail dotted the table's surface. A plastic filing bin sat in the corner of the room. Josie squatted down and lifted the lid to examine its contents. It held only paid bills, homeowner's and car insurance policies, and a file marked Emergency Credit Card.

The car.

Josie knew Gretchen had her own personal vehicle. A Nissan Sentra according to the auto policy. Josie returned to the front door, poked her head outside, and asked Mettner if anyone had checked the garage at the back of the house.

"Yeah, her personal vehicle is in there," he answered.

Noah climbed the porch steps. "Should we issue a BOLO if the MDT doesn't turn her up? Our guys are already looking for it, but we could bring in the state police."

The likelihood of the MDT not locating Gretchen's vehicle was slim to none. Still, Josie couldn't shake the discomfort coming to a boil in her stomach. "If the MDT doesn't turn her up," Josie said, "then do it."

Mettner nodded and pressed a phone to his ear. Noah moved past Josie into the house. "You think Gretchen is in trouble?"

Josie stepped back inside and put her hands on her hips. "I don't know. It's extremely unusual for her to be out of touch like this—or missing."

"Do we know that she's really missing?" Noah asked. "It hasn't been that long."

It hadn't. No more than two hours had elapsed since the body was found in Gretchen's driveway. She'd last been seen at the police station while on shift. There could be a logical explanation for why she wasn't answering any calls or texts—or responding to dispatch. Perhaps her phone had somehow broken. Maybe the car had broken down and she was on foot somewhere.

"You think I'm overreacting by issuing the BOLO?"

"Not if we can't locate her using the MDT," Noah said. "If she's in trouble, it's better to get it out as soon as possible rather than wait. But if her car broke down, or she dropped her phone, and she shows up at the station in the next couple of hours, we're going to feel like idiots."

"Let's be idiots then," Josie said decisively. "I don't want to take any chances, especially if it turns out that she is in trouble."

Nodding, Noah said, "What've we got in here?"

Josie panned the living room once again. "Not a hell of a lot from what I can see. There are no obvious signs of a struggle, but like Mettner said, we really wouldn't know if anything was out of place."

"Except here," Noah said, pointing to one of the end tables. Beside the lamp, a circle of perfect wood shone through an otherwise dusty surface.

"Maybe she set her coffee mug there this morning," Josie said. "Then washed it and put it away before she left."

Noah's brow furrowed. "It could be from a vase or a bowl of some kind."

"Well, when we find Gretchen, we'll ask her about it. Make sure it's been photographed."

As Noah went to find Mettner, Josie moved deeper into the house. She had never actually been inside Gretchen's home. She'd only dropped her off or picked her up for work-related reasons. Now Josie felt a wave of guilt wash over her. Gretchen had been good to her, had understood Josie in ways that other people couldn't—her intense need for privacy and the personal issues that came with being raised by a toxic mother. Perhaps Josie should have made more of an effort to get to know Gretchen better, to get past the wall of strict professionalism Gretchen always hid behind.

When Noah returned, they explored the rest of the house. It was neatly kept, but like the living room, held few personal touches. Only in Gretchen's bedroom did they find some framed family photographs. A 5 x 7 folding frame on top of Gretchen's dresser held two photographs: an elderly man and woman sitting at a restaurant table, and the same elderly couple in folding lawn chairs with Gretchen leaning down between them, one arm around each of them, her face alight with an uncharacteristic grin.

"Agnes and Fred," Josie said.

"What's that?" Noah asked, opening the closet door and peering inside.

"I think these are Gretchen's grandparents," Josie said, pointing to the photo. "Gretchen told me they raised her after her mother went to prison for accidentally killing her sister."

Noah turned toward her. "Jesus. What happened?"

Josie turned away from the photos, an intense feeling of discomfort creeping through her at having to explore Gretchen's private space. But she had to treat this like any other crime scene, and at any other crime scene, they would give the entire house a once-over to make sure nothing important had been missed.

"Gretchen's mom had Munchausen by proxy," Josie said.

Noah used the cap of his pen to scratch his temple. "That's the syndrome where the parents make their kids sick for attention, right?"

Josie nodded. "Yeah. Listen, Gretchen told me that in confidence, so if this all turns out to be nothing—I mean if she shows up in the next half hour with a broken phone and a big apology—please keep it to yourself."

"Of course," Noah said. "But if she doesn't show up..."

"I know," Josie replied. "We have to dig into her private life."

"Yeah, we'll definitely have to track down some family members to see if they've heard from her."

Josie started pulling out drawers and carefully looking through them. In Gretchen's sock drawer, she found a wad of cash inside a single sock pushed all the way to the back of the drawer. Without unwrapping it, Josie counted the corners of the bills. They were all hundreds. About $2,000. She waved it toward Noah so he could mark it down before putting it back where she found it and closing the drawer. In the nightstand drawer was a small glass box with red, black, and silver mosaic tiles forming a pattern of flowers. Josie opened it to find a small collection of jewelry. She had never seen Gretchen wear any accessories, but here was a handful of necklaces, bracelets, and rings, along with her name badge from when she worked for the Philadelphia Police Department. "More valuables," she told Noah.

He took a quick inventory of the box and scribbled more notes. "So this wasn't a robbery."

"No, I don't think it was," Josie agreed. "Mettner said nothing was disturbed, and he was right. Remember when those punks robbed my house? They trashed the place."

"Yeah. This place barely looks lived in."

With a sigh, Josie left the bedroom, glancing into the other rooms as she went. The first was completely empty, devoid of furniture or even a carpet. Hardwood floors gleamed in the faint twilight seeping through the window. The other room was filled with what looked like moving boxes that hadn't been unpacked. Josie's eyes tracked the hastily handwritten labels: KITCHEN, BOOKS, XMAS. Gretchen had lived in this house for at least two years, and yet it still looked as though she had just arrived. Had she not planned to stay in Denton? Josie wondered. She moved deeper into the room, where two boxes caught her attention. One was marked NANA'S KNITTING STUFF, and the other read POP'S TOOLS. Josie frowned. She turned back to the other boxes and took a peek inside the one marked KITCHEN. It was curious that in two years, Gretchen wouldn't have unpacked all of her kitchen stuff. Inside the box was an array of decorative rooster-themed kitchen items: a paper-towel holder crowned by a ceramic rooster head, salt and pepper shakers in the shape of roosters, hand towels, pot holders, place mats. Packed tightly in beside an enormous white rooster-themed cookie jar were two pieces of wall art on distressed wood. One said COUNTRY KITCHEN, and the other said THE ROOSTER MAY CROW, BUT THE HEN DELIVERS THE GOODS.

The floorboards creaked as Noah walked up behind her. "What's with all the chickens?" he said, looking over her shoulder.

"I don't think these belong to Gretchen."

Noah raised a brow. "Yeah, I wouldn't have pegged Gretchen for someone who decorates her kitchen with cute farm animals. What are you thinking?"

Josie pointed to the boxes. "I think this is all her grandparents' stuff. They must have passed away."

"Which is going to make it harder for us to track her down if we have to start questioning family members."

With a sigh, Josie closed the flaps of the box. "Hopefully she'll show up and it won't come to that." But the fizzing in her stomach told her otherwise.

From downstairs, Mettner called, "Boss? Lieutenant Fraley? The ME is here."

CHAPTER 5

Already clad in a Tyvek suit and skullcap, Dr. Anya Feist knelt next to the body, carefully unpinning the photo and depositing it into a brown paper evidence bag that Mettner held out for her. As he sealed it and marked it, Dr. Feist turned back to the body, her gloved fingers probing the jagged bloody circle the bullet had punched into the man's shirt. She didn't look up as Josie and Noah approached.

She said, "Whoever this guy is, he never stood a chance."

Noah took his notebook out and turned to a fresh page.

Dr. Feist continued, "I'll have to get him on the table, but I can tell you right now that the bullet probably perforated his lung, maybe even went through the heart. He was probably dead in seconds, if not before he hit the ground. You guys find a shell casing?"

"Nine millimeter," Josie offered.

Dr. Feist nodded, moving up toward his head, smoothing the curly black hair away from his forehead. "Yeah, nine millimeter will do it. Jesus. He's young." She went back to his torso and slowly curled the shirt up his back to reveal the bullet hole just below his left shoulder blade, an inch from his spine. "I don't see any stippling or tattooing, so this wasn't a contact shot."

"We think the person who shot him was standing on the porch," Josie said. "At the top of the steps."

Dr. Feist looked from the porch back to the body. "Then your shooter is either really lucky or a really good shot. I mean, this kid wouldn't have even had time to cry out. Death was likely instantaneous."

It was only a small relief to Josie that the boy hadn't suffered. Dr.

Feist was right—he was young—and Josie felt the weight of what his parents were about to endure. She didn't need to be a mother to know that the loss of their son would shatter their lives completely. His life had ended, but their torture was only just beginning.

With a heavy sigh, Dr. Feist got to her feet, brushing off her knees. "All right. Get him in the ambulance and bring him over. I'll get started right away. I'll make sure he gets fingerprinted too."

Mettner signaled to Hummel, who let a couple of EMS workers through the crime-scene tape with a gurney. Josie recognized one of them as Owen. He wasn't much older than the dead boy, but Josie knew he had twins under the age of one, and he worked so much overtime that members of the Denton PD were likely to see him at every scene that required an ambulance. He waved at her and Noah as they laid out a body bag next to the boy and then turned him onto his back so that he was lying over the opening of the bag. Noah checked the front pockets of his jeans as Owen and his colleague tugged the flaps of the bag up over the body and sealed it.

"No wallet," Noah groused as the EMTs lifted the bag onto the gurney and steered it toward their open ambulance with Dr. Feist in tow. "You think he was robbed?"

Josie stepped back toward the house. "No. I don't know. We don't even know if he was in the house, and if he was, who else was here. Assuming it wasn't Gretchen."

"An accomplice?"

Josie walked down the driveway, around the side of the house, and Noah followed. "I think we can safely say this wasn't a robbery," she said. "If there were two guys, then what happened? They came here—for what, we don't know—then they turned on each other and the killer shot his accomplice in the back, took his wallet, and left him here with a mysterious old photo pinned to his collar? Again, without taking anything from the house? Without even disturbing the house?"

Noah said, "Maybe once he shot the kid, he got freaked out and took off. Besides that, we don't actually know that nothing was taken from the house. We're just assuming that since the place wasn't trashed, and we found the cash and jewelry in her bedroom. There could have been something else here that was valuable to them that we don't know about. We really need Gretchen to go through and tell us if everything is as it should be."

Josie stopped in front of each window along the side of the house and studied it. None of them looked disturbed, but all of them appeared to have a homemade burglar deterrent on the outside sill. "Look," she said as Noah stepped up behind her. The windowsills were about a foot above her. Nearly a head taller than her, Noah was almost eye level with the sill. He reached up to touch it.

"Careful," Josie said.

"Jesus," Noah said as he extended an index finger to gently touch the sharp point of one of many small nails pointing up out of a strip of wood on the sill. "She's made her own deterrents." He tried to dislodge the strip of wood, but it wouldn't budge. He stood on tiptoe and looked at either end of the strip. "Yep," he said. "She nailed this onto the sill."

"So if anyone ever tried to climb up and break in, they'd take a bunch of nails through their palms," Josie said.

She walked briskly around the house with Noah in tow, noting that every one of the downstairs windows had the same trap. Back inside the house, she pushed the gauzy curtains of the living room windows aside and found wooden dowels jammed between the top of the window frame and the top of the movable window. You wouldn't be able to open the window without removing them. Of course, nothing would stop someone from simply smashing the glass and climbing through. Perhaps Gretchen figured the noise of glass shattering would be enough to alert her to an intruder if she was home.

Beside her, Noah gave a low whistle. "Talk about paranoid."

"Yeah," Josie agreed. "Something's not right here."

"What do you mean?" Noah asked.

Before Josie could answer, they heard Mettner calling from outside. "Boss, we got something."

CHAPTER 6

Josie and Noah followed Mettner beyond the crime-scene perimeter, out to the street, and nearly a block down from Gretchen's house, where a blue Ford Fusion was parked curbside. Mettner stood behind it, fingers flying over a tablet in his hands. "A couple of the neighbors told us they've never seen this car before. It's been here since this morning. We ran the plates. It's a rental," he explained. "I already called Prime rental company, and they confirmed it was rented two days ago in Philadelphia."

"Who rented it?" Noah asked.

Mettner frowned. "They want a warrant to give out that information. I already called Lamay. He's writing one up."

"There's a Prime right outside of town," Josie said. "We might have some luck if we pay them a visit. All we need is a name."

"We'll head over after this," Noah said. Addressing Mettner, he said, "Did any of the neighbors see anything?"

"The lady across from Detective Palmer's house thought she saw Gretchen walking up her driveway not that long ago, but she couldn't say when."

"Walking?" Josie said. "Did she see Gretchen's vehicle?"

"She doesn't remember. The officers canvassing pressed her, but she really couldn't remember anything of use. She also said that Gretchen is in and out all day."

Josie sighed. "So she could have seen Gretchen walking in her own driveway an hour ago or this morning."

Mettner grimaced. "Pretty much, yeah. A couple of neighbors heard the shot, but most of the neighbors who were home were sitting down to dinner or watching the evening news. Plus, between the privacy fence on one side of the property and the bushes on the other…"

"No one can see anything," Josie finished for him, frustration starting a small headache behind her eyes. "All right. I think we're done here. You guys can finish processing the scene. Fraley and I will swing by the station to see what the MDT turned up, get that warrant, and see what Lamay found on the CCTV."

As they drove through Denton to police headquarters—a large, three-story, gray stone building with ornate molding over its many double-casement arched windows and an old bell tower at one corner—the sun sank below the horizon, its last rays suffusing the horizon with a pink-and-yellow glow. Neither of them spoke. Noah studied the notes and sketches he had made at the crime scene. Josie ignored the insistent buzzing of her cell phone—her new family texting about the birthday dinner she was missing. It was her and Trinity's birthday, and this would have been their first family birthday dinner together. Guilt pricked at her, but she couldn't shake the feeling that Gretchen needed her. Josie parked in the municipal lot, and they went in through the front lobby. The desk sergeant, Dan Lamay, gave them a nod and then waved them back to the CCTV room behind the lobby desk.

"Boss," he said as Josie and Noah crowded into the tiny room behind him, "I found what you were looking for."

"It's Detect—" Josie began but stopped. As Lamay settled into a creaky desk chair in front of the large bank of screens streaming various areas of the building, Josie put a hand on his shoulder. "Dan," she said, "just call me Josie, okay?"

He smiled and nodded at her. Lamay had been with the department nearly forty years. He had seen the coming and going of five chiefs of police—Josie included—and survived a huge scandal. He was now past retirement age, with a bum knee and an ever-increasing paunch. Josie had kept him on as a desk sergeant during her tenure as chief because his wife was recovering from cancer, and his daughter was in college. He had been fiercely loyal to her, helping her when she needed it most. Now she was worried that Chief Chitwood would let him go, but so far, he had stayed off Chitwood's radar, performing his duties quietly and efficiently.

"What did you get from the MDT?" Josie asked.

Lamay pointed to a laptop open on one end of the table that showed a GPS map of south Denton. "We lost the signal here," he said, pointing to a thick line that Josie knew represented a bridge that ran over the Susquehanna River.

"Lost the signal?" Josie asked.

"That's impossible," Noah said. "Did you send units out there?"

"Of course we did," Lamay answered. "There's nothing there."

Which meant that someone had tampered with or destroyed the MDT in Gretchen's Cruze. Either that, or someone had driven the car off the bridge into the river. "Was the guardrail still intact?" Josie asked.

Lamay stared at her a moment, chewing the inside of his mouth. "I assume so," he said. "Patrol didn't report anything out of the ordinary."

"We'll take a ride out there before we go to the rental car company. What've you got on CCTV?"

Lamay swiveled the chair to face the large computer screen directly in front of him, which showed the hallway on the first floor. Lamay had paused it. The time stamp in the upper right-hand corner read 3:06 p.m. Standing outside the door to the kitchen was Gretchen, wearing the same uniform Josie wore but with an old, worn leather jacket over her shirt. Gretchen was never seen without it, but no one on the force dared pry into the story behind it. In one hand she held a mug of coffee.

Lamay pressed PLAY. They watched as she walked slowly away from the kitchen, sipping her coffee and running her free hand through her short, spiked hair. Then she stopped and pulled her cell phone out of her back pocket. With a frown, she studied the screen. She seemed to hesitate before answering, her scowl deepening as she pressed the phone to her ear. There was no audio, so they couldn't hear what Gretchen said, but it didn't look good. The conversation lasted about three minutes. Then she hung up, put the phone back into her pocket, left her mug on top of the water cooler in the hallway, and walked out of the frame.

"Where did she go?" Josie asked.

Lamay swiveled in his chair to face another screen, where he pulled up footage of the lobby. "She walked right out the door," he said, playing the footage. Sure enough, Gretchen entered the lobby from the first-floor hallway and strode out the front door without looking back.

"Was that a department phone or a personal cell phone?" Noah asked. "If it's department-issued then we can find out who called her pretty quickly."

Josie shook her head. "It's her personal cell. I gave her the option of having a department-issued phone when she started, and she declined. Dan, when we're done here, write up a warrant for her phone provider. We'll see if we can triangulate her cell phone signal. Can we go back to the other footage?"

Dan turned his chair back to the first screen and queued the footage up again. Josie had him play it three times, but her attempts at reading Gretchen's lips failed. "What is she saying?"

Noah leaned in and took the mouse, resetting the footage one more time. "Right there," he said. "Before she hangs up she says, 'I'll be right there.'"

"Well that doesn't do us any good," Josie said. "We have no idea where she went. Can you figure out anything else she said?"

They watched it twice more, but none of them could make out any more of Gretchen's words. "Where did she go? Did you guys get anything from the MDT?"

Lamay nodded. "MDT tracked her to one block over from her house. The vehicle was there for a half hour, then it traveled south, and the signal disappeared midway across the bridge."

Lamay pulled the laptop toward him and clicked a few times, bringing up a different screen that showed a grid of streets, one of which was the 400 block of Campbell Street. Gretchen's house was in the middle of the block. The icon representing Gretchen's vehicle had stopped on Miller Street, the block behind Gretchen's house. From Josie's calculations, it didn't appear as though she'd parked directly parallel to her own home, but she still could have snuck onto her own property from the back. But why would she? If she'd been headed to her own house, why hadn't she parked in the driveway? If Gretchen had left the station after that phone call and gone directly to her own neighborhood, that meant she'd been at the crime scene. Didn't it? If she had been there, where did she go afterward and why had she disabled her car's MDT? Or had someone else disabled it? Had someone else shot the boy and taken Gretchen?

Noah said, "I'm going to get that BOLO issued."

"Good idea," Josie said, tearing her gaze from the laptop. She patted Lamay's shoulder. "Thanks, Dan. How about that warrant for the rental car company?"

CHAPTER 7

There were two bridges in Denton that crossed the Susquehanna River where it snaked and curved through the outer edges of the city. The bridge in south Denton was relatively small—one lane in each direction—and didn't see very much traffic. On the other side of it lay a network of narrow roads that weaved through the mountains and led to the neighboring county of Lenore and its rolling valleys of farm and game land.

Josie pulled over on the shoulder and got out. Noah followed. "What are we looking for?" he asked.

One car passed by, headed toward downtown Denton. Otherwise, the air was still and quiet, the streetlights overhead giving off a dull yellow glow. Josie leaned over the edge of the guardrail. Below them, the river flowed peacefully. "I don't know," Josie said.

Noah touched a hand to the guardrail. "Well, we know she didn't drive the car off the bridge. Everything is intact. The banks don't look disturbed. If someone drove down one of them, I'd expect to see some flattening of the brush, a tree knocked down."

"Which means whoever stopped the vehicle on this bridge disabled the MDT," Josie said. "And probably threw it into the river."

"You think someone besides Gretchen was driving the car?"

Josie met his gaze. "You think Gretchen was driving? You think she left a dead body in her driveway, drove here, disabled her MDT, tossed it into the river, and then just took off?"

Noah's voice was even, reasonable. He was always reasonable. "Gretchen was at the station. She got a call on her cell phone. She said, 'I'll be right there.' She drove to the block next to her house. Her front door was ajar, and the shell casing found on her porch was a nine millimeter, which is the same caliber that her service weapon takes. Everything we know points to her having been at her house when the victim arrived and probably having shot him. Plus, disabling an MDT isn't as easy as tossing it out of the car. Whoever did it knew what they were doing."

"So maybe the person who shot that boy used Gretchen's gun to shoot him and left him for dead in Gretchen's driveway. Maybe that same person knew how to disable it, or maybe they made her do it." As soon as she said the words, doubt seeped in. If Gretchen were under duress, she would have found a way to leave them a message, a clue. She would have made it look like the MDT was disabled but left the antenna intact so they could find her. Wouldn't she?

"Josie," Noah said. "I think we need to consider that we really don't know Gretchen all that well—not enough to know what she's really capable of."

Josie put her hands on her hips and glared at him. "I know enough to know that Gretchen is not capable of shooting a boy in the back, leaving him behind, and running."

Noah put his hands up in a conciliatory gesture. "Boss—I mean, Josie—I know you have strong feelings about Gretchen, and she's been a loyal, dedicated officer to the department here since she came on, but how much do you really know about her?"

Josie pushed past him on her way back to the car. Over her shoulder, she groused, "Enough. I know enough. Now, let's go to the rental car agency. We need to find out this kid's identity and his connection to Gretchen."

CHAPTER 8

The Prime Car Rental agency was located on a wooded two-lane road at the edge of town, just a quarter mile from the interstate. A large parking lot surrounded the squat, one-story building. Shiny sedans and small SUVs of every color filled the spots. Fluorescent lights glowed through the glass walls at the front of the building, illuminating a small, tiled lobby area with a smattering of vinyl chairs and a table packed with various brochures. Across from the lobby was a high countertop. As Josie and Noah entered, a long, high-pitched *ding-dong* sounded somewhere in the back of the building, and a young woman with black hair piled high on her head in a messy bun emerged from a door behind the front counter. She wore a simple black dress with a gray sweater over top of it. She pulled the lapels close together as she shot them a perfunctory smile. "What can I do for you?"

Josie slid the warrant across the counter to her and flashed her credentials. "I'm Detective Quinn; this is Lieutenant Fraley with the Denton Police."

The girl's eyes widened as she took in Josie's department ID. "Oh my God, I know you!" she exclaimed. "You used to be the chief of police. Your sister is that reporter—"

"Yes," Josie cut in. "That's me. But I'm not here—"

"Oh my God," the girl went on. "I watched the *Dateline* about you. I mean the third one. You solved that case where—"

"I'm sorry, Miss…" Noah interrupted with a megawatt smile, edging in front of Josie. "I know that Detective Quinn is a bit of a local celebrity, but we're actually here about a case. It's really important. We were hoping you could help us out."

She pressed a hand against her chest, and Josie noticed her fingernails were bitten to the quick, and the red polish had faded to jagged streaks. "Me?" she said. "I would love to help."

"Yes," Noah said, tapping a finger against the warrant. "We have a case involving one of your rental cars. This warrant allows you to release the name of the person who rented it."

She picked up the warrant and looked it over, her brow furrowing. Her eyes kept darting behind Noah to Josie. "Is this, like, a big case?" she asked in a hushed tone.

Josie said, "We treat all of our cases with equal care."

"Of course," said the girl. Carefully, she placed the warrant beside her keyboard and began typing. "James Omar," she said. She turned the screen so they could see a copy of his driver's license. "From Boise, Idaho."

Josie would need to compare the license to the body, but she was quite certain that James Omar was the man who had been shot in Gretchen's driveway. His license showed a young, olive-skinned man with curly black hair and hazel eyes. He was unsmiling in the photo, but Josie could see he was attractive. As if reading her mind, the girl said, "He's cute. And only twenty-three."

Josie suppressed her grimace. She couldn't help but think of all the people James Omar would never get to date. What had he been doing there?

"I thought you couldn't rent a car if you were under the age of twenty-five," Josie said.

The girl waved a hand in the air. "Oh, that's an old rule. Not all rental agencies abide by that. Newer companies, like us, lowered the rental age to twenty-one. It brings in a lot more business."

Noah was busy taking down information in his notebook. To the girl, Josie said, "Any chance you could print that out for us?"

She smiled. "Of course!"

A moment later came the sound of a printer whirring from behind the desk. The girl bent beneath the counter and came back up with a sheaf of pages, which she handed to Josie. "His rental agreement is there as well."

"We understand he rented the car in Philadelphia two days ago," Noah said.

The girl turned her screen back and clicked the mouse a few times. "Yep, that's right. At our 3300 Chestnut Street location. Is there anything else I can help you with?"

Josie took a pen from the countertop and marked the address on the top of the sheaf of papers the girl had handed them. "No, but thank you. You've been very helpful."

In the car, Noah studied the printout of James Omar's driver's license. "What is a kid from Idaho doing in Philadelphia?"

"Work? School?" Josie suggested as she fired up the Escape and pulled out of the parking lot, headed toward the morgue.

"He's twenty-three—he was twenty-three. Too old to be a student."

"Not if he was a grad student," Josie pointed out. "Or maybe he took a job with a company in Philadelphia."

"Then what was he doing here?"

"We'll find out," Josie assured him. "Is there a cell phone number on there for him?"

Noah shuffled through some pages. "Yep," he said, pulling out his phone and dialing. He put it on speaker so they were both able to hear it ring once and go directly to voicemail. A young man's voice said, "You've reached James. Leave a message."

Noah pressed the END CALL icon with a sigh. "We'll have to get a warrant for his cell phone provider too. We'll get records for the last week or two and then see if we can triangulate his phone as well as Gretchen's. There was no phone on the body or in the rental car."

Josie nodded. "We'll do that. Let's get a positive ID first."

Denton's city morgue consisted of a large windowless exam room and one small office presided over by Dr. Feist. It was housed in the basement of Denton Memorial Hospital, an ancient brick building on top of a hill that overlooked most of the city. The smell hit them before they even entered the exam room—a strange mixture of stringent chemicals and decay that Josie never quite got used to. With a pang, she remembered standing in the exam room beside Gretchen, who had been completely unaffected by the odors of the morgue—or its sad and often gruesome contents.

The boy lay naked on the examination table, a large circular lamp blazing down into his face. Josie could see that he was lean and muscular, with a runner's physique. His chest and legs were thick with dark, wiry hair. A tattoo of a wolf's head sprawled across his left upper arm, its gray eyes penetrating. Dr. Feist's back was to them as she organized her instruments on the counter. She had on navy blue scrubs, and her silver-blond hair was tucked up beneath a matching cloth skullcap. She turned when they entered, offering a grim smile. "I hope you've got something for me."

Josie handed her the copy of James Omar's license. Dr. Feist studied it, her smile fading. "This looks like a match if I ever saw one. Of course, when we get in touch with the family, verification of the tattoo will seal the deal."

She walked over to the exam table and held the license photo up next to the boy's head. Josie and Noah crowded around and stared. For Josie, death always seemed to steal something essential from a person's physical appearance so that they no longer resembled the person they'd been in life. It was the same for Omar. The thing that made him James Omar was gone, leaving only a lifeless shell behind. Still, the bone structure, hair, and eye and skin color were all identical.

Noah let out a heavy sigh. "That's him."

Dr. Feist held up the copy of his driver's license. "Can I keep this?"

"Of course," Josie said. She took out her phone and snapped a picture of it.

Standard protocol when an out-of-state murder victim was found in their jurisdiction was for the medical examiner's office in Denton to contact the medical examiner in the county and state where the victim resided, and then that office would make the death notification and put the family in touch with Denton's police department.

Dr. Feist said, "I'll ask the Boise medical examiner's office to contact you once they make the notification. I expect you'll want to talk to his family."

"Yes," Josie said. "We've got a lot of questions for them."

CHAPTER 9

Seattle, Washington

MAY 1993

Clarity came in pieces. Luisa Munroe didn't understand what was happening at first. She didn't even realize something was happening at all. Arriving home from her three-to-eleven shift at Northwest Hospital, she was more concerned with the ache in her lower back than the fact that the porch light wasn't on. She let herself inside and through to the darkness of the living room.

"Josh?" she called.

She flicked the light switch next to the front door. Nothing. A tired sigh escaped her. *How long has the power been off?* she wondered. Long enough for all the food in their freezer to have gone bad? Throwing her purse onto the couch, she made her way to the kitchen, where a slant of light cut across the room, illuminating the space in a dim glow. Luisa looked left toward where her neighbor's backyard floodlight shone, as it always did, through their kitchen window. She'd been nagging Josh for months to put up miniblinds, since the jerk next door refused to turn the light away from the side of their house.

"Josh?" she called again.

She crossed over to the back door, upsetting the hot-air balloon–shaped wind chimes that hung over the door on the back porch as she opened it. She peered outside, noticing for the first time that lights glowed from the windows of the neighboring houses, meaning it was only their power that was out. Heading back inside, she noticed the drawing stuck to the front of their refrigerator. A slip of white paper with awkward stabs of color that jerked back and forth across it—a child's rudimentary drawing of a red house, complete with a clunky yellow sun and four stick figures.

"Josh!" This time, Luisa's voice held a tinge of panic.

They didn't have children. They didn't have friends or coworkers with children. None of the neighbors they were friendly with had small children. They didn't even have any nieces or nephews. One of the things that had drawn them together and solidified their commitment to one another was their decision *not* to have children. They were happy. They had enough. It was a decision most people couldn't understand, but it made sense for them.

Luisa worked in the ICU—where it was painfully apparent just how fragile life could be—but more importantly, she had no contact with children unless you counted the adult children who sometimes lost their parents. Josh worked as an auto mechanic, and he was usually under a vehicle, not out dealing with customers—or their kids. Staring at the drawing, Luisa racked her brain for a scenario in which her husband might receive a drawing from a child—and then hang it on their fridge.

The drawing—wherever it had come from—did not belong to them.

Suddenly she heard the silence of the house like a thunderclap. Racing to the bedroom, she threw the door open. She had a split-second glimpse of Josh on his knees at the foot of their bed, the naked skin of his back, his hands bound behind him—and then the beam of a flashlight blinded her. A voice she didn't recognize said, "Oh good, you're home. Now we can get started."

CHAPTER 10

Denton, Pennsylvania

PRESENT DAY

Chief Bob Chitwood had been in his position for roughly six months, and yet his office still had a temporary air about it; there were no personal touches, and the banker's box with which he'd shown up on his first week as chief remained unpacked on the edge of the large desk. While Josie stood with Noah, waiting for Chitwood to get off the phone, she looked around, noticing the now-blank corkboard where she had had photos tacked and the empty walls where her degrees, certifications, and commendations had hung. She hadn't loved being chief—it was a lot of bureaucratic work and political maneuvering that Josie wasn't well suited to—but it did feel odd to be back at the other side of the desk.

Chitwood hung up the phone and leaned back in his chair, hands steepled, regarding Josie and Noah with eyebrows raised. He was a tall, thin man in his sixties with thinning white hair; wisps seemed to perpetually float over the top of his head as though they weren't firmly attached to his scalp. His cheeks were pitted with old acne scars, and gray stubble dotted his chin. Josie was never sure if he was trying to grow a goatee or if he just kept missing a spot when he shaved.

"I want to issue an arrest warrant for Detective Palmer," he said. "First-degree murder."

"What?" Josie blurted.

Noah, always the more measured of the two of them, said, "Chief, I'm not certain we have enough evidence to arrest Detective Palmer for first-degree murder."

"I've already spoken with the DA's office," Chitwood said. "We've got a twenty-three-year-old kid shot in the back on her driveway. There's evidence that she was at, or near, the scene when the shooting went down. She's AWOL and the MDT was removed from her vehicle. What more do you think I need to issue an arrest warrant? It's only a matter of time before the press gets wind of this whole situation. We don't want it to look like we're sitting on our hands."

"Chief," Josie interrupted, trying to moderate her voice. She knew she was reacting emotionally, and she tried to push her personal feelings aside. "I can take care of the press. I've got contacts. Listen, Detective Palmer is one of us. We've already got a BOLO issued for both her and the vehicle. We've faxed a warrant to her cell phone provider so we can try to locate her phone. I know Detective Palmer. I'm the one who hired her. I've worked with her for over two years. I don't believe she would do something like this. I think someone else is involved."

Chitwood's upper body levered forward, his chair creaking. He put his hands on the arms of the chair. "I'm not interested in what you think, Quinn. You think Tara didn't warn me about you and all your hot-shotting in this town?"

"Chief," Noah said, "Tara—Mayor Charleston—has always been biased where Detective Quinn is concerned."

Chitwood smiled, but it was an ugly thing. "Oh, and you're not? If I'm not mistaken, the two of you became an item when Quinn came back on duty. So don't talk to me about bias, Fraley, or I'll have your ass in a sling by the weekend."

Josie held up her hands. "Please," she said. "We're getting off track. We need to keep the focus on Gretchen—Detective Palmer. I was simply saying perhaps we should give Detective Palmer the benefit of the doubt. Maybe treat her as a missing person rather than a criminal on the run. I can see that it looks bad, but this is not open and shut. There's the photo of the young boy from 2004. Why would Gretchen shoot this guy in the back and then pin an old photo to his body? There is something more going on here, and I'd like the chance to figure out what it is before we start pointing fingers."

Chitwood considered this. Josie could practically feel the heat coming off Noah's body in waves. She chanced a look at him and noticed a flush in his cheeks she knew to be anger. Noah wasn't the hotheaded type. Chitwood had really gotten under his skin. Josie understood that. Their new chief was implying that their personal relationship kept them from doing their jobs effectively, when the opposite was true. They hadn't even had a relationship until Josie went out on medical leave—and could it really be called a relationship when they'd never even consummated it? Regardless, for the past two years they'd always put their work before anything else.

She caught Noah's eye and mouthed, *Let it go.*

He looked away from her. "At least give us some time," Noah implored. "Seventy-two hours. We work Detective Palmer's case as a missing person's. If we don't find her by then, you can issue the arrest warrant. Either way, the entire department and the state police are looking for her."

Chitwood stared at them for a moment longer, his flinty gaze moving back and forth between the two of them. Finally, he said, "You've got forty-eight hours."

CHAPTER 11

"We're not going to crack this case in forty-eight hours," Noah mumbled as they left Chitwood's office and made their way to the bullpen—a collection of desks in the center of the large room on the second floor where officers did paperwork, made calls, and conducted research. Josie, Noah, and Gretchen had permanent desks, whereas the other desks were shared by the rest of the officers. Noah had been the one to clean Josie's personal effects out of the chief's office while she was on leave. He had been the one to choose her new, permanent detective's desk, which faced his own. Gretchen's desk sat to the side of both of theirs, the three desks forming a T.

As Noah threw his notebook down angrily, Josie's eyes were drawn toward Gretchen's desk. As usual, everything was neat and orderly. All the files she was working on were stacked tidily in one corner. Pens rested in an old Denton PD coffee mug. She bypassed her own paper-strewn desk and started pulling out the drawers of Gretchen's desk. "We won't solve it in forty-eight hours," Josie agreed. "But we might be able to find Gretchen."

Noah took off his suit jacket and draped it over the back of his chair. Folding his arms over his chest, he watched her riffle through the contents of Gretchen's desk. "'Cause it's that easy," he said.

Josie looked up long enough to shoot him a nasty glare. "We work the clues, Fraley," she said.

He laughed as he took a seat behind his desk. "What clues are you referring to? Because from where I'm sitting, we've got a whole lot of nothing."

Gretchen's desk contained nothing but office supplies, some random personal hygiene items—floss, a bottle of ibuprofen, and some Alka-Seltzer—and work files. "I need her personnel file," Josie said.

She returned to Chitwood's office and waited several minutes while he located Gretchen's file. He hadn't bothered to unpack his personal belongings, but he had taken the time to change the filing system that Josie had had in place when she was interim chief. Finally, she returned to her desk with Gretchen's file in hand. Noah wheeled his chair around and sidled up next to her. "You're looking for her emergency contact, aren't you?"

"Yeah," Josie said. "When she started, she would have had to put someone down."

On the various forms that Gretchen had had to fill out upon being hired, she had written: CAROLINE WEBER, and under relationship: COUSIN. From the area code in the woman's phone number, Josie guessed she lived in or near Pittsburgh, which was about four hours west of Denton.

Josie pulled out her phone and dialed. A woman answered on the third ring. Josie said, "Ms. Weber? Caroline Weber?"

"Yes?" the woman said. Her voice sounded younger than Josie expected.

"This is Detective Josie Quinn with the Denton Police Department. I'm calling about your cousin, Gretchen Palmer."

"Gretchen?" the woman echoed, sounding surprised. "Is everything okay?"

"To be honest, we're not entirely sure. There was a shooting at Gretchen's home earlier this evening, and we haven't been able to locate Gretchen since then. She listed you as her emergency contact. We were wondering if you or anyone else in your family has heard from her."

There was a silence so long, Josie thought the call had dropped. "Ms. Weber?"

She cleared her throat. "Dr. Weber."

"I'm sorry?"

"It's Dr. Weber. I'm completing my residency at University of Pittsburgh Medical Center."

Josie wasn't sure what that had to do with Gretchen being missing, but she didn't push. Instead she said, "I'm sorry. Dr. Weber, have you heard from Gretchen recently?"

A sigh. "Listen, Detective…"

"Quinn," Josie supplied.

"Detective Quinn, I know why Gretchen put me as her emergency contact. I'm only a few hours away. I'm a doctor, so making medical decisions for her in the event she was incapacitated wouldn't be an issue—but Gretchen and I aren't close. I haven't heard from her in years. She sends me holiday cards. That's about it."

"So she hasn't been in contact with you today," Josie pressed.

"No. I mean, I can take down your number, and if I do hear from her, I'll call you, but I can't help you."

Josie could understand why Gretchen wasn't close to the woman. She was as cold as a winter day. She hadn't expressed even a small degree of concern for Gretchen's safety or well-being, hadn't asked a single question about the shooting. Briefly, Josie wondered if that was because she already knew what she needed to know from Gretchen, and she was simply lying about not hearing from her.

"Is there anyone else in your family that Gretchen might contact if she was in trouble or needed help?" Josie asked.

"No, not since our grandparents died a few years ago. I mean, I was probably the closest to her, and that's not saying much. My mom and Gretchen's dad were siblings. Gretchen's dad passed on. I have an older sister, but she lives in Ohio. Gretchen had some aunts and uncles on her mother's side, but I'm pretty sure she doesn't keep in touch with them. Especially because of—" She broke off suddenly, and the line went silent.

"It's okay, Dr. Weber. I know about her mother," Josie said. "Gretchen told me. You wouldn't happen to have any of their contact information, would you?"

"I wouldn't, but my mom would. I can get it from her and text it to you if you give me your number," she offered.

"That would be a big help. Thank you. One last thing—would it be okay with you if I texted you a photograph of a young boy? We found it on Gretchen's property. We're trying to figure out who the boy is."

"Sure, send it over. I'll let you know if I recognize him."

CHAPTER 12

Seattle, Washington

JULY 1993

Mary lay in bed, body tense as she listened. There it was again. A noise. Almost like glasses clinking, except not exactly. It sounded more musical. She nudged her husband with an elbow and was rewarded with a grunt. She clamped a hand on his shoulder.

"Tim," she whispered. "Wake up. I hear something."

It took several tries to rouse him. He had always slept like someone had drugged him. Finally, a hearty slap against his upper back woke him, and his head shot up from the pillow. Beneath a spike of brown hair, two angry eyes glared at her.

"Chrissake, Mare. What is it now?"

She put a finger to her lips to shush him. He rolled his eyes but listened anyway. The tinkling sound came again.

"It's the neighbors throwing bottles in their recycling bin," he dismissed, burying his face back in the pillow.

Mary gave his arm a hard pinch.

"Owww, dammit, Mare." But he was up out of bed, mumbling under his breath. Something about bullshit.

"I heard that," Mary hissed as Tim fumbled on his nightstand for his glasses and disappeared into the dark hallway.

Clutching the comforter to her chest, she listened to the sounds of him moving through the house. The telltale squeal of the front door sounded, and then a moment later, she heard it again. Then more of his footsteps. She heard him struggle with the back door. The humid weather had made it swell in its frame. She had been after him to shave it down so they could get it open and closed more easily. Then came a loud clanking, like he was fighting whatever it was that was making the noise. It didn't sound like a recycling bin full of beer bottles. There was a racket that made her wince, something landing on what she guessed was the kitchen table, then the back door slamming.

Even in the low moonlight streaming through the bedroom window, Mary could see that her husband was furious.

"Goddamn wind chimes," he said, climbing back into bed. He tossed his glasses onto his bedside table. "What were you thinking? If someone farts three blocks away, it wakes you up. You, of all people, do not need wind chimes."

Mary felt a slice of fear cut through her chest. "Wind chimes? I didn't buy wind chimes."

He rested his cheek on his pillow and closed his eyes. "Then who the hell hung them up out back, Mare? The tooth fairy?"

He was already drifting back to sleep when she threw the covers off and jumped out of bed. Muscle memory carried her feet to the kitchen in the dark, where outdoor streetlights revealed a set of wind chimes lying crumpled on her kitchen table. Drawing closer, she saw they were in the shape of a hot-air balloon.

She scurried back to the bedroom. "Tim," she said as she crossed the threshold, "I did not buy those. Someone else—" Her words lodged in her throat as the beam of a flashlight caught her eyes. She threw a hand up to shield herself from the glare. Beyond the circle of light, she thought she saw Tim's eyes, large and afraid. He was sitting up in bed, the barrel of a gun pressed into his temple.

"Run!" he said.

Then another voice came. Male. Unfamiliar. "Oh, Mary isn't going anywhere. We were just about to begin."

CHAPTER 13

Denton, Pennsylvania

PRESENT DAY

Caroline Weber didn't recognize the young boy in the photo from 2004 that had been pinned to James Omar's body. Josie asked her to forward it to her mother and sister to see if they recognized the boy, but neither of them did. They did, however, get the names and phone numbers of Gretchen's other family members to Josie fairly quickly. She and Noah split up the list and started making calls. None of the family members had heard from Gretchen; all agreed to accept a text message with the photo of the boy from 2004, but none recognized him.

It was nearly eleven at night, and they had hit a dead end.

Noah leaned back in his chair, stretching his arms up in the air and then lacing his fingers behind his head. "We should call it a night."

"Her mother is still alive," Josie said, ignoring his suggestion as she made notes in the file on her desk.

Without missing a beat, Noah said, "Her mother is in prison."

"I can call the warden," Josie said. "Ask that she be shown the photo. I don't have to go there."

"Yeah," Noah said. "I don't think going there would be the best idea."

Gretchen's mother was an inmate in the same prison that currently held Josie's mother—or the woman who had kidnapped

Josie from her real family and posed as her mother for her entire life. Lila Jensen was as evil and toxic as they came. Even advanced ovarian cancer couldn't kill her. When she had been incarcerated after taking a plea deal on the multiple charges facing her, the doctors had given her three months to live. That was six months ago, and the bitch lived on. Josie wouldn't have to see Lila Jensen if she went to visit Gretchen's mother at the Muncy prison, but still, she didn't want to be anywhere near her.

"Besides," Noah added, "wouldn't Gretchen's mother have been incarcerated in 2004?"

Josie said, "There's always the possibility that other members of her family kept in touch with her. The correctional facility would have a log of visitors and know how much correspondence she was getting and from whom. I know it's a long shot, but I don't think we should discount her so easily."

She pulled up the warden's number on her desktop computer and then picked up the phone. Noah stood, came around the desk, and placed a hand gently over hers. "I think you're forgetting that it's eleven o'clock at night."

Josie looked up at him and opened her mouth to protest, but Noah spoke first. "I know. I already know that you don't want to stop, but there's nothing more we can do right this second. There's already a BOLO out for Gretchen and her vehicle. If either one is located during the night, we'll get a call. The warrants are out to the cell phone providers for both Gretchen's and Omar's phones. I did one for Gretchen's bank account and credit cards too, so we can see if there's been any activity. We'll likely hear from them tomorrow, but not sooner than that. We can't talk to the warden at Muncy or to James Omar's family until tomorrow. We'll start first thing in the morning. Now, let's go get some disgusting minimarket sandwiches and go home."

Noah, always the practical one.

Josie stood, a small smile playing on her lips.

Noah lowered his voice. "Why don't you come home with me?"

His touch felt electric. Josie would love nothing more than to spend a couple of hours distracting them both from whatever was going on with Gretchen. She would love nothing more than to finish what they had started so many times in the last few months. As she opened her mouth to accept his invitation, her cell phone chirped on the desk with a text message from Trinity.

We brought home some cake from the restaurant. Are you coming home?

Then came a photo of all four Paynes in Josie's kitchen crowding around a birthday cake. They were all smiling. Her family. The family she'd always wished for growing up. The family she would have died to have during all those dark hours locked in the closet of Lila Jensen's trailer. A pang in her chest set off a feeling of longing that vibrated like a tuning fork within her. She turned the phone to Noah so he could see the photo.

"I can't tonight," she murmured.

He looked only mildly disappointed, and the sentiment only registered for a split second. Then he smiled down at her. "You should be with them. We'll have plenty of nights, you and I."

Josie resisted the urge to kiss him. Not here, not in front of everyone. Instead, she simply said, "Thank you."

CHAPTER 14

In spite of having celebrated with the Paynes well past 2 a.m., Josie was up at six, showered and padding around her kitchen, waiting for her coffee to brew. Her phone chirped. A text from Noah. He was on his way to the station. *Be there in ten*, she responded.

Hurriedly, she fished her travel mug out of the cabinet, dislodging a tower of Tupperware containers. She tried to stop them from clattering to the floor, but only managed to catch two of them. She gathered them all up and tossed them into her sink, then listened to see if the ruckus had wakened any of her guests. When she didn't hear anyone stirring, she fixed her coffee and snapped the lid down on her mug.

Her thoughts turned to Gretchen—her empty home, her list of relatives who barely had contact with her, and the photos of her beloved grandparents who now only existed in Gretchen's life as a collection of boxed-up possessions. She wondered if Gretchen had ever had a house guest while she'd lived in Denton. What would that be like for someone who booby-trapped her own windows? Josie wondered.

At first, Josie thought she would go mad with so many people around all the time; it was quite an adjustment after living alone for so long, but eventually she came to enjoy it. When her house was empty and silent, she had too much time to think about all that had happened in the last few months and all that Lila Jensen had taken from her. Then the dark thoughts and cloying anxiety set in. She used to numb her pain with sex and booze. Now she tried to do it with the company of the people she cherished most—the Paynes, her grandmother, Misty, baby Harris, and Noah.

If she didn't know any better, she might think she was growing as a person.

Josie grabbed a piece of day-old birthday cake and ate it in two bites as she left the house, her mind moving back to James Omar. Had he been Gretchen's house guest? How did they know one another? *Did* they know each other?

Noah was already seated at his desk when she arrived at the station, the landline receiver pressed to his ear. She settled into her chair as he finished up the call. "The warden will be in at eight, and he'll see to it that Gretchen's mother looks at our photo. He told me that Gretchen has never visited her in all the years that she's been incarcerated, so I doubt that she has any idea where Gretchen might have gone. But evidently she has two cousins of her own who have visited and written over the years, so you were right. It's worth at least having her look at the photo."

"Great," Josie said. "I'm not surprised Gretchen was never in touch with her. I think we're going about this all wrong. Think about it. Where did Gretchen spend most of the last fifteen years of her life before she came here?"

"She was Philly PD," Noah answered. "Homicide. We should be talking to her colleagues."

"Exactly," Josie said. She opened the center drawer of her desk, pulled out the personnel file she'd secured the evening before, and flipped through it, looking for Gretchen's resume and references. The first reference listed was a homicide lieutenant, Steven Boyd.

Josie used her cell phone to dial Philadelphia's Homicide Department and ask for Lieutenant Boyd, only to be told he wouldn't be in until four that afternoon. She would have to call back. With a sigh, she used her desktop computer to log in to Facebook and search for James Omar. She found his account almost immediately. His profile picture was a close-up of his face, curly hair blowing in the wind. Behind him, Josie could make out a beach. She clicked through to the rest of his photos. There weren't many. It didn't appear that he spent much time on social media. There were a few of him and a group of guys, and several of him and his parents and someone that Josie guessed was a younger sister, given her resemblance to both James and the older couple in the photos. There they were at an outdoor concert, a college campus tour, sitting down to Thanksgiving dinner, and cutting down their own giant Christmas tree. They looked happy. Josie felt a tug at her heartstrings. Today they would wake up to a world where they were never happy again. At least, never in the way they'd been before.

She skipped the rest of the photographs and studied his friend list instead. It was lengthy. With a sigh, Josie started working down the list, looking for any connections to Gretchen or Denton.

Three hours later she had a major crick in her neck and no clues. Most of his friends lived in Idaho. There were a few dozen who lived in or around Philadelphia. The rest were scattered throughout the country. There were no connections to either Gretchen or the city of Denton that Josie could find.

Why the hell had Omar rented a car and driven to Denton? What was he doing at Gretchen's house?

She clicked on his ABOUT ME tab. It was no surprise to find that his hometown was Boise, Idaho. He was also listed as single and had attended Purdue for his undergraduate degree. Presently, he was a graduate student at Drexel University in Philadelphia. She had gone right for his photos and friend list when the ABOUT ME tab had been there all along. That solved the mystery of why he was in Philadelphia.

"I was right," Josie said, looking across at Noah.

He came around and studied the computer screen. "Well, that's two connections to Philadelphia—Gretchen's old homicide lieutenant and Drexel University."

Josie stood up and headed to Chief Chitwood's office. Over her shoulder, she said, "We're going to Philadelphia."

CHAPTER 15

"You two are *not* going to Philadelphia," Bob Chitwood said. Standing behind his desk, hands on his hips, he stared at Josie and Noah.

"Chief," Josie said, "all the clues lead to Philadelphia. Someone has to go there."

"Sure," Chitwood said. "Someone. Not both of you. You think this department is paying for the two of you to take a romantic getaway? You're out of your damn minds."

Again, Josie saw the muscle in Noah's jaw tick as his posture stiffened. He opened his mouth to snap back at Chitwood, but Josie spoke first. "Chief, Gretchen lived and worked in Philadelphia for at least fifteen years before she came here. The odds of her having traveled there are good, and we're pretty short on clues right now. Plus, I need to look into Omar's life in Philadelphia and see if I can find out why he rented that car and came to Denton. It would only be a day, maybe two."

Chitwood sighed. "Fine. One of you goes. I need one of you here. Especially with Palmer AWOL. Quinn, you're the lead investigator, you go. But your ass better be back here by Wednesday, or I'm writing you up. Now, get the hell out of my office."

Noah spun on his heel and stalked out of the room. Josie followed him, but their paths diverged when they reached the bullpen. Noah kept walking—to get some air, Josie imagined, before he blew his top—but Josie went to her desk where the phone was ringing. "Detective Quinn," she answered.

A man's voice gave a reedy hello, and a small ache started in Josie's chest. She didn't even need to ask who it was. There was no sound in the world like the sound of grief in a parent's voice. "Mr. Omar?" she said.

He cleared his throat. "Randall Omar, yes," he said. "I'm...I'm James's father."

"I'm glad you called," Josie said. "First, let me say how sorry I am for your loss."

"Thank you," he said, and the strain in his voice deepened. "The, uh, medical examiner here in Boise contacted us. Told us about...about James. He said you were the detective in charge of finding his...his..."

"His killer," Josie supplied. "Yes, I'm going to do everything I can to find the person who killed your son and make sure that person is brought to justice. I promise you that."

"Thank you," Randall repeated, voice thick and husky. "Do you have any leads?"

Josie went over what they knew, sparing the more gruesome details as much as possible. There was no sense upsetting the grieving father more when he had only yesterday found out his son was killed in such a cold-blooded fashion. "Mr. Omar, your son was found in the driveway of a woman named Gretchen Palmer. Does that name sound familiar to you?"

"No, I'm sorry. I can ask my wife, but it doesn't sound familiar at all. What about the picture you mentioned? Of a young boy, you said? Would it be possible for us to see it?"

"That would be very helpful," Josie said. "I can text it to you now, if you'd like."

"Yes, please." He rattled off a number, and Josie used her cell phone to forward the photo to him. She waited, listening as he and his wife discussed it, their voices distant and muffled. Then Randall came back on the line. "I don't understand. We've never seen this boy. We don't know who he is. Do you know who the boy in the photo is, or why it was pinned to my son's...my son's body?"

His voice cracked on the word *body*. Josie's voice was gentle. "I'm very sorry, Mr. Omar. We don't know who the boy is—not yet. I'm trying to find out. When was the last time you spoke to your son?"

"Three days ago. It was my wife's birthday. He called to wish her a happy birthday."

"Did he mention anything to either of you about going on any trips?"

"No," Randall said.

"Did he seem like himself? Did he seem stressed at all or distracted?"

"No more than usual. He was always under a bit of stress with school."

"I understand your son was a graduate student at Drexel University in Philadelphia. Is that correct?"

She heard him swallow. His voice sounded stronger with a subject that put him on firmer emotional ground. "Yes, that's right. He was studying…"

In the background, Josie heard a woman's voice interject. "Genetics. He was studying genetics."

Nervous laughter filtered through the line. Randall said, "My wife said genetics. Sorry, I can't really think straight right now." He sucked in a breath. "I did know that. James is always going on about all this scientific stuff—oh God—he was…he *was* always going on about it. Jesus."

"It's okay, Mr. Omar," Josie said softly. "I know this is an extremely difficult time. Again, I appreciate your speaking with me. Can you tell me where James lived? Was it on campus?"

"Well, I don't think it was campus housing. He was a grad student. But there's a small apartment complex a few blocks from the sciences building. It's not much, but it's cheap."

"Did he live alone?" Josie asked. "Or with a roommate?"

"Uh, yeah, a roommate. Ethan."

"I'll need to interview Ethan," Josie said. "Do you have his number, by any chance?"

"Of course," Randall said. "Are you going to Philadelphia?"

"I'll be leaving in a few hours," Josie said. "If you could text me the names and contact information for anyone there you think I should talk with, that would be great."

"Of course," Randall repeated. "He had an adviser—Dr. Larson. I'll send you his phone number. He was a real mentor to James. He's also James's landlord. Maybe he can help you."

Josie thanked him again before following up with one last question. "Mr. Omar, can you think of any reason why your son would have rented a car and driven to Denton?"

A long silence followed, punctuated by the man's shallow breaths. Finally, he said, "No, Detective. I'm sorry. I can't."

CHAPTER 16

Three hours later, Josie had a reservation at the Hilton a few blocks away from Philadelphia's police headquarters. She'd made appointments to meet with both Lieutenant Steve Boyd and Professor Perry Larson the next day. She had tried contacting James Omar's roommate, Ethan, but his phone went straight to voicemail. She stopped at home to have a quick dinner with the Paynes before they all returned to their homes. She drove to Philadelphia in the dark, grateful that it was late enough that she didn't have to deal with city traffic.

Her hotel room was on one of the higher floors, with an expansive view of the twinkling lights of the surrounding city. She sat on the bed, bag still packed next to her, and stared out into the night. She was truly alone for the first time in months. Not just for a few minutes or a couple of hours, but for an entire night. As the night sky grew darker, her reflection in the window became sharper. Now every time she looked at herself, she couldn't help but see the face of her sister, Trinity. Her thoughts drifted from the family she had gained to all that had been taken from her. In these rare moments alone, she couldn't help but feel bitterness and anger for the turn her life had taken. She supposed all had turned out well. She had survived, hadn't she? She was alive while many others she had crossed paths with were not. Her family had been reunified. Still, the demons swirled at the corners of her mind.

The soft hum of the minibar's motor seemed to call to her. She stood and walked over to it, resting one palm on its handle. It would be so easy. Just a little something to take the edge off. To see her through the night.

"No," she whispered to herself. This kind of coping was not sustainable. She had watched Lila Jensen drown her pain and rage in every substance imaginable. It hadn't helped anyone. Empty-handed, she returned to the window, taking in the city Gretchen had called home for fifteen years. Josie wondered if the home Gretchen had lived in here had been booby-trapped like her house in Denton. Just what kinds of demons was Gretchen battling? What had she kept hidden? Josie had always known there were things in Gretchen's memory that she told no one. She recognized the walls Gretchen erected around herself, because she had hidden behind the very same ones.

The ring of her cell phone interrupted her thoughts. Noah. A smile slid across her face as she answered. "What's up?"

"You get in okay? How's the room?"

Again, Josie's gaze was drawn to the minibar. Quickly, she looked away. With one hand, she started unpacking items from her overnight bag. "It's fine," she said. "What do you have?"

"First, Gretchen's mother doesn't recognize the boy in the photo."

"No surprise there," Josie said. "What else?"

"No activity on Gretchen's credit cards or bank account in the last twenty-four hours. The bank and credit card companies will let us know if they see anything. Also, we got the triangulation from both Gretchen's and Omar's phones," Noah said.

Excitement prickled at Josie's scalp. "Tell me."

"Well, Omar still had the GPS on his turned on. Looks like it's somewhere in the Susquehanna River."

Josie sighed. "Let me guess—near the bridge where the MDT signal was lost."

"About a half mile downriver. The GPS puts it in the river at its last location, but I've got a team headed there first thing in the morning to search the banks."

"Gretchen's?"

"Her GPS was turned off. We had to triangulate. We got it down to an area of about two miles, but it's the same basic location."

"So the phones and the MDT are in the river." She tried to imagine Gretchen throwing everything that could track her into the river and then leaving Denton behind. She couldn't. "There's someone else involved, Noah. I know it."

His long sigh told her he wasn't sold on her theory but that he didn't want to argue with her again. "Well," he said, "you've got less than forty-eight hours to prove it."

CHAPTER 17

Josie waited outside the small gray stone apartment building near Thirty-Third and Ludlow Street. She leaned against the short stone wall surrounding it and sipped a cup of coffee she'd picked up at a nearby minimarket. She had taken a taxi the twenty-two blocks from the hotel to James Omar's apartment building, watching as the city passed her by, bustling indifferently to its own rhythm. She spotted Dr. Perry Larson sauntering down the street a few minutes later. Josie had checked out his faculty profile before contacting him to make an appointment. He appeared a bit older than his faculty photo—closer to sixty, she estimated. His silver hair blew in the breeze, and a pair of aviator sunglasses rested on his nose. He was dressed casually in a polo shirt and khakis, hands in his pockets as he strolled toward her.

He stopped a few steps away. "Detective Quinn?"

"Dr. Larson?" Josie responded.

He lifted the sunglasses onto the top of his head. Blue eyes smiled at her as he offered a hand. "Great to meet you," he said. "I wish it were under better circumstances. It's still so hard to believe."

"Were you close to James?" she asked.

"James and I worked closely together on some research papers. He was a very promising scientist. Very driven. Focused. I don't generally take on students who aren't completely committed."

"When's the last time you spoke to James?" Josie asked.

Larson touched his chin. "A few days ago in the lab."

"How did he seem to you? Was he stressed? Distracted?"

Larson shook his head. "No. He was the same as ever."

"Did he mention taking a trip?"

"No. I'm just as baffled as you are about his trip to Denton. I have no idea what was there that would have drawn him. Like I said, James was very focused. He wasn't interested in dating or partying. I'm not aware of any friends he had in Denton."

"Have you ever heard of a woman named Gretchen Palmer?"

The blank look in his eyes told Josie everything she needed to know. "I'm sorry," he said. "It doesn't sound familiar."

She took out her phone and pulled up the photo of the boy that had been pinned to James's collar. "We have reason to believe this boy has some kind of connection to James. Do you recognize him?"

Larson spent a long minute studying the photo before shaking his head. "I'm sorry, no. But listen, I didn't know James that intimately. You might have better luck with Ethan, his roommate."

Josie put her phone back into her pocket. "I've tried contacting Ethan a few times now on the cell phone number the Omars gave me. It goes right to voicemail."

Larson gave a short laugh. "That sounds about right. Ethan's always been a bit hard to pin down. I was thrilled when James moved in with him, because James always got the rent to me on time."

"Is Ethan your student as well?"

"Oh no, he's studying criminology. He was a tenant of mine for a year before James joined my program. After a semester, James was looking for inexpensive housing. I introduced the two, and the rest, as they say, is history."

"When's the last time you spoke to Ethan?" Josie asked.

"Oh, a few weeks. Like I said, Ethan is a little . . . flaky. He tends to get wrapped up in his own research projects and goes off the radar. James once told me he spent a whole weekend in front of his computer—didn't sleep for seventy-two hours. Evidently, he is quite obsessed with cold cases and serial murderers. Pleasant stuff."

His joke fell flat. Josie moved on. "Was he a close friend of James?"

Larson motioned for them to walk up the front steps, and she followed. At the front door, Larson keyed in a code that let them into a large, tiled foyer, one wall covered in gray cubes that Josie quickly realized were mailboxes. On the other side was a community corkboard with flyers tacked to it for guitar lessons, art shows, and people seeking work as dog walkers and house cleaners.

"Ethan and James did grow quite close," Larson answered as he took a set of keys from his pocket. He shuffled through them before finding one and sliding it into the lock of a heavy wooden door on the other side of the foyer. It creaked open before them.

Josie waved a hand around the foyer. "Do you have cameras in here?" she asked. "Inside this vestibule?"

"Why, yes," he said. "We were having some issues with packages being stolen. I had security cameras installed last year."

"It's always a good idea," Josie said. "Is there any chance you would be able to review the footage—how far back does it go?"

"Six months," Larson said. "It's very high-quality."

"I've been looking for a system for my own home. What kind do you have here?"

"I'm not sure what it's called, but it's made by Rowland Industries."

"Oh," Josie said, flashing back to her own run-ins with the security giant. "I'm familiar with Rowland Industries—their systems *are* very high-quality. In that case, could you review it for at least the last two weeks and see if you can find footage of the last time either James or Ethan entered and exited the building?"

"Of course. I'm not sure exactly how to access it, but I can certainly make some calls and find out. You should know that the Omars gave me permission to let you into their apartment, particularly since we can't get in touch with Ethan. Whatever you need, they told me, to help you solve James's case."

Josie was growing more and more concerned with the fact that Ethan Robinson was nowhere to be found. As Larson led her down a narrow hallway to a red door marked 19, she asked, "Dr. Larson, do you happen to have any contact information for Ethan's family?"

Larson fingered his key ring again until he came up with the correct one. "Oh yes, of course. I can text that to you when I get back to my office if you'd like. I think it's just him and his dad, but I've got his dad's number. Like I said, a few times he was late with the rent, and his dad called me to ask me not to kick him out while they came up with the money."

"Is Ethan from Philadelphia?"

"Oh no," Larson said. "Portland, I think. Oregon. At least that's where his dad lives now, as far as I know."

Inside, the apartment was dark and smelled of stale cigarette smoke, bacon grease, and sweat. Larson flipped on the lights as they moved through the small rooms. There wasn't much to the place. A living room, a narrow kitchen with a small alcove where a folding card table and two folding chairs sat, and then a hallway leading to a bathroom and two bedrooms. Textbooks and computer equipment littered the place. The furniture was spare and looked as though all of it had been bought at thrift shops. There was a plate and fork in the kitchen sink, a clean pan and mug in the dish rack. One end of the saggy red couch was cluttered with a balled-up blanket, a couple of dog-eared true-crime novels, and a half-finished bottle of Gatorade. The other half was pristine. The card table in the kitchen looked the same—one side clean and empty, the other beset with dirty dishes and fast-food wrappers.

"Which one of them was the neat freak?" Josie asked.

Larson laughed. "James. Here—this one is his bedroom."

James's bed was neatly made. No clothes on the floor. All items on his nightstand and dresser were arranged with precision. Hanging over the dresser was a framed photo of his family similar to the ones Josie had seen on his Facebook page. In the corner of the room was a small desk with a slim blue laptop on top of it. Josie gestured to it. "Do you mind?"

"Not at all," Larson said.

Josie sat in the desk chair, opened the laptop, and booted it up. As she anticipated, it asked for a password. Behind her, Larson said, "I think I can help with that."

She switched positions with him, and after two tries, he accessed the laptop. As he ushered Josie back into the chair, she said, "I thought you said you and James weren't close. He told you the password to his laptop?"

Larson chuckled. "I took a chance. He has a dedicated computer in my lab, and as administrator, I know the password. James likes to keep things efficient, so I figured maybe he'd use the same password for his personal laptop. I was right."

"Well," Josie said, turning toward the computer. "I'm glad you were able to figure it out."

He watched over her shoulder as she searched the files and internet browser. Everything she found was obviously to do with whatever he was studying. The scientific jargon was well beyond her capabilities. She'd only taken enough science courses in college to supplement her major and enable her to graduate. "James's mother said he was studying genetics," Josie said.

"Actually, James was studying epigenetics," Larson said. Josie swiveled in the chair just enough to see him.

"Is that a different field from genetics?"

Larson perched on the edge of James's bed. "Epigenetics is more specialized. The most simplistic explanation is that epigenetics is the study of heritable alterations in gene function that don't involve changes in the DNA sequence."

"Meaning changes in genes?" She waved toward the laptop. "These papers he's written and the journals he's logged into—it's all a little over my head."

"Not changes to the genes themselves, but in the way they're expressed," Larson explained. "The mechanisms that turn the genes on and off. External factors."

"Like lifestyle?" Josie asked.

"Yes. Again, this is all very simplistic—"

Josie smiled. "Simplistic works for me."

"Okay, well, lifestyle choices can have a large effect on activating certain genes. So can environment. If you don't mind me getting personal, I have to admit that I saw the *Dateline* last month about you and that news anchor, Trinity Payne."

Josie suppressed a groan. Trinity had caught her at a particularly weak moment when she agreed to go on television and talk about the two of them being reunited after thirty years. But she had also known that Trinity would never let it go. It was best to get it over with. So she had done some limited press for Trinity's sake, and Trinity had gone on to get the coveted anchor position on her network's morning show.

"I really prefer not to discuss that," Josie told him. "If you don't mind."

He waved a hand. "Oh no. I didn't mean to be intrusive. I'm simply pointing out that you have an identical twin. You probably know that identical twins share one hundred percent of their genes."

"Yes," Josie said.

"And yet, there are marked differences between you and Ms. Payne, aren't there?"

Josie considered this. Early on, when they'd first met, she and Trinity had been archenemies. They approached things differently, but they also had very different jobs. Josie's job was to solve crimes. Trinity's job was to tell the world about things they might not otherwise be privy to. They'd often butt heads over Trinity's insistence on reporting everything. To Josie, justice was more important than exposure. Also, Trinity had long been obsessed with being famous, whereas Josie was content to put criminals away as quietly as possible. And yet, they both had the same cutthroat approach to their goals. Josie had stopped at nothing to solve a missing girls case a few years earlier, just the way Trinity stopped at nothing to get to the heart of a good story.

"I would say there are definitely differences," Josie agreed. "But similarities as well."

"You won't get away from similarities. That's not my point. My point is that you can take identical twins whose genes are the same and put them in different environments where they experience different things and make different lifestyle choices, and their genes will express themselves differently. For example, in the research I've been conducting—which James was helping me with—we look at why identical twins with the same exact genes develop different health conditions. Did you know that identical twins rarely die of the same cause?"

"Uh, no," Josie said. "I didn't."

He stood up and started to pace the room, hands waving excitedly. "There's a chemical called methyl that floats around inside our cells. It attaches to the DNA in our bodies—that process, it's called methylation. When methylation happens, it can essentially turn down or hamper the activity of certain genes or even block some genes from producing certain types of proteins in our bodies. Almost anything can affect our methylation levels—sickness, diet, smoking, alcohol or drug use, medication, external things in the environment. You and your sister have the same genes, but your DNA methylation levels are different, and that will cause changes to your gene expression that can actually be passed on to subsequent generations."

"So you're saying that even though our genes start out the same, if I drink more, it can affect the methylation levels in my DNA and change the way my genes behave?" Josie asked.

"More or less," Dr. Larson said with a smile. "Imagine that every cell in your body, each one containing your DNA, is just there, waiting to be told what to do. The methyl groups in your body bind to your genes and basically tell them what to do. The methyl group tells the cell what it is—for example, 'You're a heart-muscle cell; here's what you do.' Then there are histones. They're protein molecules that your DNA wraps itself around, and they tell the cells how much to do—in other words, they regulate the genes."

"So between the methyl and the histones, your cells will know what they're supposed to be doing and how much of it they're supposed to do?"

"Again, an extremely simplistic explanation, but yes."

"If you don't mind me asking," Josie said, "is there a practical use for studying this stuff?"

His eyes lit up. He clapped his hands together. "Detective Quinn, our study of epigenetics could potentially have a profound effect on our ability to prevent and treat certain diseases—even cancer. What if we can develop drugs that will manipulate the methyl groups or the histones? We could cure so many diseases."

He looked as though he was going to launch into another lecture. Josie closed the laptop and stood up. "That is very fascinating. It sounds promising." She pulled out her phone and checked the time. "I'm sorry, Dr. Larson, but I have to get to a meeting with a detective on the Philadelphia PD soon."

Larson lowered his gaze sheepishly. "I'm sorry, Detective Quinn. I have a great passion for my work."

"And I do admire that," Josie told him, moving past him and into the hallway. "I really do appreciate your time, but I can't be late for my next meeting."

He followed her into the kitchen. "James had great passion for the work as well. It's a tremendous loss. I hope you find the person who killed him."

A photo affixed to the fridge caught Josie's eye, nearly buried among takeout menus and class schedules. "I'll do my best," she mumbled. Pointing to the photo, she said, "Who is this with James?"

The photo showed James from the waist up with one arm slung around another young man with dark, shaggy hair and brown eyes. Both were smiling and sweaty. Behind them, Josie could see a partially blurred sign that read BROAD STREET RUN.

"Oh, that's Ethan," Larson said. "They ran a local marathon last year."

Josie took her phone out and snapped a picture of the two young men. Larson walked her out, and she thanked him for his time. He tried to recruit her and Trinity for his research, citing that identical twins separated at birth were particularly useful to his project, but Josie politely declined. As she watched the professor walk away, she took her phone out and studied the photo of Ethan Robinson again, wondering where the hell he had gone.

CHAPTER 18

Seattle, Washington

SEPTEMBER 1993

Travis's lips trailed along Janine's neck, tickling her ear and making her giggle. The martinis had gone to her head. Or maybe it was him. It had been eight months, two weeks, three days, and seven hours between the time he was deployed and the time he arrived back at Fort Lewis. Things had been unexpectedly awkward once they got their first long embrace out of the way. It was Travis's idea to go out for drinks—and it had worked. Within two hours, things felt back to normal between them. They couldn't keep their hands off one another. Travis tipped the bartender generously, and they headed back to Janine's house, falling through the front door in a tangle of limbs.

They didn't bother turning on any lights as they collapsed onto the couch. Janine ran her hands up and down Travis's back. It had been so long, she was ready to explode. She pushed his chest, guiding him until he rolled onto his back. Straddling him, a smile curved her lips. As she lowered herself down to kiss him once more, he grimaced.

"Hold on, babe," he said.

They disentangled, and he began emptying his pockets, tossing his wallet, spare change, and car keys onto the coffee table. Janine walked her fingers up his thigh as she waited. When he spoke next, his voice was different—tense and suspicious rather than breathy and teasing. "What the hell is this?"

Janine looked up at him, searching his face. "What?"

He leaned down and scooped something off the coffee table, holding the object in front of her face. She strained to make it out in the dim haze of the streetlight that seeped through her windows.

"These are men's glasses," Travis said.

Janine smiled nervously. "So? They're not mine."

"How did they get here? Who's been here? Are you seeing someone?"

She blinked, trying to clear the fog in her head, suddenly wishing she hadn't had that last martini. "I don't... babe, those aren't mine. I don't know where they came from."

He stepped away from her, his dark-brown eyes glittering angrily down at her. "There are men's glasses on your coffee table, and you don't know how they got here? Do you think I'm stupid?"

She reached for his hand, but he pulled away. "No," she pleaded. "I swear. I don't know where they came from. They weren't here earlier. Someone must have been here. Maybe you should check—"

"Don't lie to me, Janine." He turned away from her and stalked off. A moment later she heard a thump, and Travis shouted, "Dammit!"

Janine stood, swaying slightly. "Wait, Travis—"

Then a new voice, male, one Janine had never heard before, sounded from the darkness. "Yeah, Travis, why don't you wait a minute?"

She saw Travis's form spin around. From behind her, a flashlight shone in Travis's face. He put a hand up. "Who the hell is that?"

"Travis, I'm scared—" Janine screeched as she felt a hand tangle in her hair, tugging her head back.

The stranger's breath was hot on her ear. "Oh, you should be, Janine."

CHAPTER 19

Philadelphia, Pennsylvania

PRESENT DAY

Josie made her way to Market Street and started walking in the direction of police headquarters. She made a quick call to Noah, but he had nothing new to report. At Thirtieth Street she hailed a cab that took her to Eighth and Race Street and dropped her in front of police headquarters. When she'd spoken to Steve Boyd on the phone, he had called it the Roundhouse, and now she saw why. The building was shaped like the double barrels of a shotgun. As Josie approached the entrance, a tall, thin man with a crisp gray suit and salt-and-pepper hair pushed himself away from the wall next to the front doors and walked toward her. "You're Josie Quinn," he said, extending a hand.

Josie took it. "Lieutenant Boyd?"

He smiled, brown eyes twinkling beneath a pair of bushy eyebrows. "That's me."

Josie looked beyond him to the entrance, but he shook his head. "You don't want to go in there," he told her. "You'll be twenty minutes getting through security, even as my guest. You hungry?"

Her stomach had growled loudly the entire cab ride. "Starving," she said.

"Let's go."

He pulled out a key fob and led her to an unmarked SUV in the parking lot across from the entrance to the Roundhouse. They drove in silence, Josie taking in the crowded streets as he weaved in and out of traffic. She lost track of where they were in relation to the Roundhouse and her hotel.

"You been to Philadelphia before?" Boyd asked.

"Only for a couple of concerts," Josie answered.

Finally, he parked in front of a place so small, it hardly looked like it could support a food establishment, but once inside, the smells of cheesesteaks and french fries made her stomach clench. Boyd pointed to a set of orange booths lining one wall. "Have a seat. You like onions, right?"

"Uh, sure," Josie said.

She sat in one of the empty booths and waited for Boyd to return. Ten minutes later he slid in across from her with a tray heaped with food and two sodas. Josie seized the cheesesteak nearest to her and began to devour it. The two of them ate in silence for several minutes while Boyd shot her knowing, appreciative smiles. Finally, he wiped his chin with a napkin and said, "I can see why Gretchen likes you."

A fry froze halfway to Josie's mouth. "What? You've talked to her?"

"Not recently. When she took the job in Denton, you were the one who interviewed her. She liked you. A lot. And Gretchen doesn't like many people. Well, if she does, she doesn't show it."

"She doesn't show much," Josie agreed. She abandoned the fry and took a sip of her soda. "When's the last time you did talk to her?"

"Christmas. She called to wish me a happy holiday. We chatted for a bit. Talked shop, that sort of thing. I only hear from her about once or twice a year."

That had been nine months ago. Josie said, "Does the name James Omar mean anything to you?"

"Nope."

Josie took out her phone and showed him the photo of the young boy they'd found pinned to Omar's body, but he didn't recognize the child. Next, she showed him the picture she'd snapped of Omar and Ethan Robinson from the fridge in their apartment.

"Sorry, don't recognize either of them."

With a sigh, Josie put her phone away. "Lieutenant—"

"Steve."

"Steve, I think Gretchen's in trouble."

He nodded. "From what you told me yesterday, I'd say you're right."

"How long were you partners?"

"Oh, about eight or nine years."

That was a significant amount of time to be partners in their line of work. Josie knew that the people you worked with in law enforcement could become closer to you than your own family. The things you saw and experienced on the job could bond you like nothing else. "Do you think she did this?" Josie asked him.

Boyd's eyes dropped to the table. His fingers folded a napkin into tiny squares. "I don't know," he said. "My gut says no, but Gretchen was a tough nut to crack. All that time we worked together, and I still don't feel like I ever got to know her. Not in a real way."

Josie thought of her own affection for Gretchen in spite of the fact that she knew virtually nothing about the woman. Then she thought about the spiked wood pieces lining Gretchen's first-floor windows. What the hell had she been hiding? Or running from?

"So you don't know where she would go if she was on the run? Who she would go to for help?"

"I'm sorry, I don't."

"Do you think she's capable of something like this?"

"I really don't know."

It was then that Josie thought of the more important question. "Do you think she'd throw her career away like this? Shoot a boy in the back and then go on the run?"

Boyd met her eyes. "Gretchen didn't strike me as a runner, and her job was everything to her. That I know. That I can say with one hundred percent certainty. I don't know what she did in her spare time. I know she wasn't married, didn't have any kids, but I don't know if she had hobbies or friends or even a pet. Hell, I don't even know if she's straight or not. I just know with one hundred percent certainty that she loves the job, and she's good at it."

That Josie couldn't argue with. She stuffed a few more fries into her mouth. This was looking more and more like a dead end. Gretchen was a locked door, and it seemed that no one had a key. As an image of Gretchen flashed across Josie's mind, her spine suddenly shot up straight. "Her jacket!" she said. "Do you know the story behind her jacket?"

Boyd laughed. "That nasty old leather jacket she never takes off? Yeah, I know the story."

CHAPTER 20

"A few years before she left for Denton, she caught a double homicide. Couple of bikers. You guys deal with a lot of outlaw biker gangs around your way?"

"Some," Josie said. "But it's mostly when they're passing through."

"You know anything about them?" Boyd asked.

"I know they're basically organized crime factions and have a hand in the usual stuff—drugs, prostitution, gambling. I know they feud with one another. A lot of them are violent as hell. Is that it? Gretchen's a biker?"

Boyd held up a hand. "Slow down, there. Gretchen's not a biker. Like I was saying, she caught a case where a couple of bikers had been murdered here in the city. It was over a turf war. A guy named Linc Shore was out here. Name ring any bells?"

Josie shook her head.

"Shore was a higher-up in the Devil's Blade gang. He was in charge of the Blade chapter out in Seattle for decades. We're still not sure what he was doing out here. Maybe lending support to the Northeast chapter. Like I said, they were wrapped up in a pretty dirty turf war with another gang called the Dirty Aces. Anyway, you know what a prospect is?"

"Someone who wants to be in the gang?" Josie guessed.

Boyd unfolded the napkin he'd managed to fold into a square the size of a nickel as he spoke. "A hang-around is someone who wants to be in the gang. Most of the time, a prospect is a step up, because they've gotten a full member of the gang to sponsor them."

"So the prospect is a little more 'in' than a hang-around," Josie said.

"Basically, yeah. Well, Shore had a prospect with him. Name was Seth Cole. Young kid. About twenty, twenty-one. Now we know that full members torture prospects. Make them do all kinds of nasty shit while they're waiting to be patched in."

"Patched in?" Josie asked.

"It's when a prospect becomes a full member. The club votes on them, they usually have to do something to prove their loyalty—like kill somebody or commit some type of crime—and then they're given a gang logo patch for their jackets."

"I see," Josie replied. "Was Linc Shore sponsoring this prospect?"

"We don't know," Boyd said. "We'll probably never know. The kid came with him from Seattle. Chances are Linc just brought him along to do shit for him—like a personal slave. Anyway, the Dirty Aces got them alone, shot them, and sliced both their throats."

"How do you know the Dirty Aces did it?" Josie asked.

Boyd said, "They left their calling card. A partially burned ace of spades. Apparently, they do that at a lot of their murder scenes. This way the other gang knows they've been put on notice."

"Jesus."

"Yeah. So right off we knew it was a turf war thing. For some reason, Gretchen really took that one to heart."

"In what way?"

Boyd leaned back in his seat and looked around the small sandwich shop. "Look, we work the case, right? Whatever it is, we work it. A murder's a murder. But when you get a seventeen-year-old student raped and murdered waiting for the bus, or a toddler hit by a stray bullet, or an elderly person beaten to death in a home invasion, it hits you harder. Maybe you work a little faster, spend a little more time on it, want to solve it more than, say, the murder of two people who chose a lifestyle of violence and killing."

"Linc Shore and Seth Cole were high-risk victims," Josie said.

"It was only a matter of time for guys like that. You join an outlaw biker gang, chances are you're going to end up murdered in a pretty unpleasant way. Most of us don't get invested when it comes to vics like that. We still do the job, but we're not as tied to the outcome 'cause as soon as you put away the killers, two more prospects will get patched in and take their places. But Gretchen—man was she emotional about that one. I never saw her like that before. I caught her crying a few times. It was just strange. It should have been just another case. Plus, none of the rest of us really wanted to touch it. You get involved in something like that—really double down—and you put yourself in the crosshairs of the gang whose members you're trying to put away. Gretchen didn't give a damn. She worked that case harder than any one she ever caught before that."

"Did she know either of them?" Josie asked, perplexed.

"No, that was the weird thing. There was no connection. I'm still not sure why the case meant so much to her. But anyway, she got the arrest and handed it off to the DA. They got the convictions—both Dirty Aces members got life in prison—and then Shore's crew gave her this jacket."

"Was it *his* jacket?"

Boyd shrugged. "Don't know. She never told me. Could have been Linc Shore's jacket or maybe the prospect's. Or maybe just a jacket they bought for her. But it was old. Looked like it had been stripped down of its patches. Anyway, I saw her after sentencing. A lot of times, if we're down at the criminal justice center for testimony, we'll shoot over to the Reading Terminal and get some lunch. Lots of different food places in there. Anyway, I was there for a hearing and stopped over for some lunch, and there was Gretchen in the burger joint with a Devil's Blade guy and Linc Shore's old lady."

"His wife?"

"Oh hell, I don't know. Wife? Girlfriend? I just know she was involved with Linc. She was at the trial the whole time. So was the guy she was with. Anyway, they were there with Gretchen. They gave her the jacket, and Gretchen never took it off after that."

"Did you ever ask Gretchen about why she took the jacket?"

"Course I did," Boyd said. "She told me it was none of my damn business. So I kept asking. She told me it was between her and Linc's friends, that I wouldn't understand, and that was all I needed to know. I badgered her some more, but it became pretty clear she wasn't ever going to tell me anything else, so I stopped asking."

Silence fell between them for a few moments. Josie listened to the sounds of the kitchen behind them—shouted orders, the clang of a metal spatula over a grill, the sizzle of meat cooking, the beep of the deep fryer announcing a batch of fries was finished. Gretchen was more of a mystery to her now than ever. She sighed. "Were there any other cases she got emotional about?" Josie asked.

Boyd took a moment to think about it before answering, "No, none that I can think of. None that stand out like that one did."

"Is it possible for me to have a look at that file? The Shore/Cole murders?"

Boyd frowned. "It's an old file. Closed. I'll see what I can do. For now, you could google it, go on philly.com and look it up. It got some press coverage at the time. If I can get my hands on it, I'll send you whatever I get—how's that?"

"Sounds good."

CHAPTER 21

Josie didn't go directly home. She checked out of her hotel in Philadelphia, fought the afternoon traffic, and drove instead to Gretchen's house while she still had a bit of waning daylight left. She parked on the street and walked up to the house, ducking under the crime-scene tape still pulled tight across the driveway and porch. Failing rays of sunlight bounced off the windows at the side of the house. Josie stood on her tiptoes and gently touched the spikes along one of the windowsills. Knowing what she did from Steven Boyd, Josie understood Gretchen's fierce paranoia about making sure no one got into her house—at least not without injuring themselves first. Had she been worried that the Dirty Aces would come after her for putting away two of their members? Had the gang tracked her down in Denton and taken their revenge after all? But if so, where did James Omar fit in? He couldn't be a random passerby in the wrong place at the wrong time. Not if he'd rented a car and driven from Philadelphia.

Josie circled the house and came back to the front door. She couldn't shake the feeling that she was missing something. But no new detail announced itself. At least not outside. She slipped under the yellow tape across the porch and tested the front door. It was unlocked and creaked as she pushed it open and went inside. Dust motes floated lazily through the shafts of sunlight peeking through Gretchen's gauzy curtains. The only thing different this time around was that Josie could see traces of fine dark powder where her evidence response team had dusted for prints. Again, she studied the dust-free circular imprint on Gretchen's living room end table. She knew that Noah had found it significant, but she wasn't certain that it meant anything. That was the problem with crime scenes. It was hard to know what was meaningful, so you had to treat all the clues as if they were—at least at first blush.

She moved through the house again, slowly, eyes searching for something that she had missed the first time around. But the only thing she noticed this time that she hadn't on her first pass was that all of Gretchen's dinnerware was made from plastic. Josie stood in front of the open kitchen cabinets, cataloging each item. Four bowls, four dinner plates, four large cups—all plastic. Her coffee mugs were all plastic travel mugs. Eccentric for sure, but did it really mean anything? Josie could practically hear Noah's voice in her head: "Maybe she's clumsy." But she didn't drop things at work and had no issue using ceramic mugs at the station house.

Josie's cell phone chirped in her jacket pocket, startling her. She fished it out and glanced at the screen. Dr. Larson had texted her Doug Robinson's name and phone number. She texted him back a thank you, turned off all the lights in Gretchen's house, and walked back to her car. She didn't start it right away, instead dialing Doug Robinson's cell phone number. It rang four times before a man answered.

"Mr. Robinson?" Josie said. "Doug Robinson? My name is Detective Josie Quinn. I'm with the Denton Police Department. We're in Pennsylvania—"

"Oh, hey," he said, interrupting her speech. "Yeah, uh, that professor Larson called me. Hey, I'm real sorry to hear about James. What a shocker. That's . . . that's real terrible."

Josie was glad that Dr. Larson had saved her the trouble of breaking the news. "Did you know James?"

"Oh, I met him a couple times. Ethan had him out here last year on spring break, took him on a tour of Portland. Good kid. Real serious."

"Mr. Robinson, when is the last time you heard from your son?"

There was a mumbling like he was calculating. Then he said, "Oh, maybe three weeks?"

"No calls? No texts? Is that unusual?"

Robinson laughed. "For Ethan? No, not at all. He's funny that way. Not real social. Never was, really. Didn't have a ton of friends at school. Always had his head in a book or glued to a computer. Great student, but hard to draw out, you know? My wife—his mom—she was real good at getting him out of his shell, but she passed away when he was in high school."

"I'm so sorry to hear that," Josie said.

"Thanks. Yeah, he took it hard. He's been doing good since he went to college though."

"I understand he's a graduate student. Where did he do his undergrad work?" she asked.

"Oh, right there at University of Pennsylvania." He laughed. "Right down the street from Drexel, and just as expensive. But I'm not complaining. He'll get a good start."

Josie brought the conversation back to his contact with Ethan. "So your son often goes long stretches without contacting you? What's the longest he's ever gone?"

"Maybe six weeks? Look, Detective, Ethan's a big boy, you know? Got his own life out there. I'm here for him—he knows that—but I don't bug him. Except when he's late on his rent and Larson gets on me."

Josie didn't know how to feel about how unconcerned the man seemed. Did he not worry about his son, or was Ethan that unpredictable and prone to going off the radar? She wondered if there was something he wasn't telling her, if there had been some kind of falling out between Ethan and his father. She knew not every family maintained close bonds, but she found Doug Robinson's cavalier attitude toward his son strange, especially given the fact that his roommate had just been murdered. "Well, if I could just ask you a favor," Josie said. "Could you try to get in touch with

Ethan for me? In light of James's death, I'd really like to know he is safe and accounted for. Also, if I could have his phone number as well, that would be great. Although, if he's as private as you say, he probably won't answer a number he doesn't know."

"Sure thing," Doug said.

"Also, I didn't see his name on James's list of Facebook friends. Does he have social media accounts?"

"Nah," Doug replied. "Not that I know of—thinks he's being rebellious that way."

"One more thing," Josie said. She told him that a photo of a boy had been found at the crime scene; they weren't sure if it was important or not, but they were trying to identify the boy. Robinson readily agreed to have a look, but only seconds after receiving it, he told her he'd never seen the kid before.

Now she had more dead ends and missing persons than she knew what to do with.

CHAPTER 22

Before she pulled away from Gretchen's, Josie texted Noah. *Did the search teams find the phone or the MDT?*

He tapped back almost instantaneously. *Nope. Nothing. A dead end.*

With a sigh, she moved on to something more personal, typing in: *I'm home. Want to come over tonight?*

His reply was rapid. *Would love to. Believe me. But my mom's hot water heater crapped out, and I'm helping her put a new one in. Will be a late night.*

Josie sighed again as she fired up her Escape. Noah's parents had divorced when he turned eighteen. He was the youngest of three, and the only one of his siblings who had stayed in Denton. Josie couldn't help but adore the way he looked after his mother. She almost typed back, *Tell her I said hi*, before remembering that the one time she'd met Noah's mother, the woman had looked Josie up and down and said, "This is the woman who shot you, huh?" Noah had explained *ad nauseam* about how Josie had been trying to rescue a teenage girl when she shot him, how she'd thought she was doing the right thing, how he hadn't pressed charges and had forgiven her instantly, but Mrs. Fraley still didn't warm up. Josie really couldn't blame her. She still grappled with her own guilt over the incident. She texted back, *No problem. See you tomorrow*, and pulled out of her parking spot, heading home.

The lights were still on at her house, and from the driveway she could see the flicker of the television through the living room window. Trinity's sporty red Fiat was parked in her driveway. Josie was surprised by the feeling of relief that washed over her.

After a night alone in Philadelphia, she was glad to still have company. Inside, Trinity sprawled across Josie's blue couch, wearing sweatpants and a T-shirt bearing the logo of her network news show, the remote clutched firmly in her hand. On the coffee table in front of her sat a large bowl of popcorn. Trinity pressed a button on the remote, freezing the action on the TV when Josie entered.

"You're still here," Josie said.

Trinity laughed, sitting up and patting the couch cushion beside her. "I'm happy to see you too."

Josie dropped her bag and her jacket on the foyer floor and plopped down next to her twin. She grabbed a handful of popcorn and ate it, talking around it. "I didn't mean it like that. I just thought you had to be back at work."

"I go back to New York tomorrow. I hope you don't mind me crashing here." She waved the remote around the room. "It still fascinates me to be in your space."

Now it was Josie's turn to laugh. "You should invite me to New York so I can see *your* space."

Trinity swatted her thigh lightly with the remote. "Please. You'd actually have to give work a rest to do that. Unless I could come up with some clue to whatever case you're working in the heart of Manhattan. That would get you there."

They were both equally as career-driven, so Josie made no apologies. Instead, she said, "Speaking of which, have you ever heard of the Devil's Blade or the Dirty Aces?"

"Outlaw motorcycle gangs," Trinity said. "OMGs. You're not working a case involving either of them, are you? They're bad news."

Josie had to stifle her groan. The last time Trinity had told her someone was bad news, the bodies piled up faster than Josie could count them. "I'm not sure. I mean, not directly. I don't think."

"That clears that up," Trinity joked.

"Do you know a lot about them?"

"I know a little. We did a big story on them last year. One of my producers had a deep contact within the Dirty Aces organization. They weren't the only OMG we covered, but they were the one we learned the most about. The Aces deal heavily in drug and illegal arms trafficking. They've staked their claim on the East Coast, and they don't take kindly to the other gangs encroaching on their areas. Anyone who gets in their way is either killed or mysteriously disappears."

"I heard that," Josie said. "My source said they leave a calling card."

"A half-burnt ace of spades," Trinity supplied. "That's not a calling card, it's a warning."

"What do you mean?"

Trinity placed the remote on the coffee table. "The Dirty Aces are responsible for a lot of murders, but they only leave the burnt ace of spades when they want to send a message to rival gangs."

"Okay, what about witnesses?" Josie asked. "Say someone saw one or two of their members commit a murder, and that someone was going to testify against them in court."

Trinity shook her head. "They make witnesses disappear. Those bodies aren't found."

"Do they ever target prosecutors or police officers who work on the cases?"

"Sure, but it's more effective to target witnesses, because cops and prosecutors need witnesses to prove their cases."

"But they wouldn't leave an ace of spades if they killed a police officer or made one disappear?"

"No. I don't think so. Is this about Gretchen? You think the Aces did something to her? You didn't find an ace of spades at the crime scene, did you?"

"No, and I don't know. She worked a case a few years back where she put away a couple of Aces for killing some Devil's Blade guys. I'm grasping at straws. Especially with our grad student murder victim, and the—"

Josie stopped short at telling Trinity about the photo of the mystery boy.

"It's okay," Trinity said. "I know you can't tell me certain things. Not that I care now. I'm not covering the local news anymore." She picked the remote back up and turned her show back on. "But you're not grasping at straws if you can find a connection between Gretchen, your victim, and the Aces."

Josie barked a laugh. "Easier said than done."

"Don't worry," Trinity told her with a wink. "You've accomplished a lot more with a lot less."

Josie stood and started walking out of the room.

Trinity said, "Just where do you think you're going?"

Josie turned and stared at her. "Upstairs. I need to do some research."

Trinity arched a perfectly plucked brow and motioned toward the couch again. "Laptops are made to be mobile, dear sister, so bring it down here and do your research while I binge-watch this show. I'll make you coffee if you think it's going to be a late night."

Josie raised her own brow to match Trinity's. "Are you buttering me up for something?"

Trinity laughed. "No. I'm still just trying this whole twin sister thing out."

CHAPTER 23

Two hours later, Trinity snored beside her as Josie combed the Philadelphia news websites for news of the Linc Shore/Seth Cole murders and the conviction of the two Dirty Aces members responsible for the slayings. The mug shots of the two Aces killers showed two nearly identical men in their late forties with round, bearded faces and graying hair tied back in ponytails. Both too old to be the boy in the photo. There were photos of both Linc and his prospect as well—mug shots or driver's license photos, Josie couldn't tell—but neither of them looked familiar to her. Linc was too old to be the boy in the photo pinned to James Omar's body. In his fifties, Linc Shore had greasy shoulder-length black hair and a long black beard threaded with gray. His brown eyes stared defiantly at the camera, and the smallest hint of a smile turned his mouth upward. He looked like a man who was keeping a secret. Or waiting for the punch line to a joke.

Seth Cole was young enough, but because the boy in the photo was only shown in profile, it was difficult to tell if they were one and the same. She paused her search for articles about the murder to punch Seth Cole's name into Google as well as a few police databases. He had almost no online footprint. A Facebook account showed a profile picture of him on a Harley Davidson, smiling with a beer in his hand. His hair was long and blond, past his shoulders. A long, crooked nose sat off-center on his ruddy, stubbled face. He looked much older than his twenty-one years. Either his Facebook page was little-used, or he'd switched his privacy settings to the strictest available, because there was nothing else on his page besides his photo and that he lived in Seattle. Her police databases offered little more. Only that he'd been convicted of a couple of misdemeanor drug offenses before taking up with Linc Shore and the Seattle chapter of the Devil's Blade.

With a sigh, Josie returned to her search for details about the double homicide in Philadelphia. There were several articles, but none told Josie much more than what Boyd had told her. The two men had been brutally slain, and Gretchen had worked tirelessly to bring their killers to justice in spite of the witnesses being repeatedly threatened. The Aces members were both sentenced to life in prison without the possibility of parole. Case closed. Two years later, Gretchen had sat across from Josie in the office now occupied by Chief Chitwood to interview for a detective position.

Josie spent the better part of the night searching every source available to her, trying to make a connection between James Omar and the Dirty Aces—or any outlaw motorcycle gang. She searched Gretchen Palmer and Dirty Aces; Gretchen Palmer and Devil's Blade; Gretchen Palmer and James Omar; even Gretchen Palmer and Ethan Robinson. Nothing. There were plenty of news reports quoting Gretchen as a Philadelphia homicide detective on the cases she'd handled, and Josie found the obituary for each one of Gretchen's grandparents, but nothing else of use.

Again, Josie's head swirled with unanswered questions, not the least of which was: Where the hell was Gretchen? If she had fled her home as Noah suggested, why hadn't she taken the $2,000 in her sock drawer? No, Josie was certain she'd been taken. Had the Aces kidnapped her? Made her disappear as revenge for helping put their club members away for life? Was James Omar caught in the crosshairs? Maybe his visit to Gretchen's house was completely unrelated to Gretchen's disappearance. Perhaps he had gone to see Gretchen for reasons that had nothing to do with the Dirty Aces, and he'd simply been in the wrong place at the wrong time. Maybe the Aces were trying to frame Gretchen for his murder. In which case, they'd done a damn good job. In the morning, Chief Chitwood would issue an arrest warrant, and once the press got wind of it, Gretchen's trial by publicity would begin.

But what about the photo? Who had pinned the photo to Omar's body, and why?

Beside her, Trinity stirred, sitting up groggily. She blinked sleepily at the cable box, which showed it was after three in the morning, and then turned to Josie. "Good lord, you're still at it?"

Josie snapped her laptop closed and threw herself back into the couch cushion with a loud sigh. "And I'm getting nowhere," she complained.

Trinity shook her head, stood, and took Josie's arm, dragging her up off the couch and toward the stairs. "'Cause you need to sleep. You'll have a clearer head if you get some rest."

Josie let Trinity pull her up the steps. She didn't protest when Trinity climbed into her king-sized bed, instead of going to the guest room, and promptly started snoring again. Exhausted, Josie got into bed next to her. A little ache yawned open in her heart as she wondered how many nights like this she had missed in the last thirty years—sleeping side by side with her sister. Pushing the thought away and the pain that came with it, her mind turned back to Gretchen, searching for some other angle, some new approach to the case. Again, she thought of the first time she'd met Gretchen. The first interview. Then she thought of what had made Gretchen's application stand out to her in the first place. All those years of experience, the stellar references. The references. Something sparked in the back of her mind, but as quickly as it came, it was gone. She tried to get it back, but sleep came too quickly.

CHAPTER 24

Noah was already at his desk when Josie arrived for work. He pushed a cup of coffee and a cheese Danish across her desk as she filled him in on all she'd learned in the last twenty-four hours.

"You think the Aces had something to do with this?" he asked.

Josie took a sip of her coffee and opened her desk drawer, searching for Gretchen's personnel file. "I don't know. I can't find anything connecting the Aces, Gretchen, and Omar. Omar is the wild card. He doesn't fit."

"And the photo," Noah pointed out. "That's pretty odd as well. How is it no one who knows either Omar or Gretchen can identify the boy in the photo?"

"It's baffling," Josie agreed. "I know this is a long shot, but do you think you could track down someone in Seth Cole's family and ask them to have a look at the photo? He was young enough, and he had blond hair."

"Of course," Noah said. His computer dinged, and he clicked the mouse a few times. "Remember I told you that I took the liberty of getting a warrant for both Gretchen's and Omar's cell phone records for the last two weeks."

Josie found Gretchen's file and put it in the center of her desk. "And you got them already?"

"I got Gretchen's," he said. "Still waiting on Omar's." Across the room, the department printer hacked and whirred to life. Noah went over to retrieve the pages it spit out. He spread them across his desk, and Josie came around, standing by his side as they studied the list of incoming and outgoing calls.

"There," Josie said. She pointed to an incoming call from two weeks earlier. "That's James Omar's phone number."

Noah ran his finger down the list and used his other hand to draw a star next to the other times that Omar's number appeared on the list. "He called her last week and the day of the shooting," he said. "Looks like they're all incoming. She never called him."

"Why?" Josie asked. "What could he possibly have been calling her for? Where would he have gotten her number?"

Noah didn't bother to answer her questions. He knew she was just voicing frustration. He sat down in his chair. "I'll identify the rest of these numbers."

As he went to work, Josie opened Gretchen's personnel file and sifted through it until she found the references. Two of them were from the Philadelphia Police Department—including Steven Boyd. It was the last reference that had set off a spark in her brain the night before as she fell asleep. Gretchen had listed the name, business address, and phone number for Jack Starkey, an agent with the Bureau of Alcohol, Tobacco, and Firearms in Seattle, Washington. Josie looked again at Gretchen's resume. Nothing in her work history put her in Seattle. She'd gone to high school in Allentown, Pennsylvania. Then there was a four-year gap from when Gretchen graduated from high school to when she started college. She'd gone on to graduate from Penn State with a degree in criminal justice, then gone directly to the police academy in Philadelphia. She'd worked patrol before moving to homicide, where she had stayed until her move to Denton.

So what was the Seattle connection?

Josie thought back to the interview. Back then, she'd only been interested in Gretchen's wealth of experience with the Philadelphia Police Department. She remembered asking Gretchen about the four-year gap between high school and college. Gretchen had given a generic answer about taking time off to travel. Josie had asked her how she knew someone in the ATF, and Gretchen had given another generic answer, saying she'd met him at a couple of conferences, but now Josie wondered if that was true. How did she really know Jack Starkey? Had her connection to him been more significant than meeting at a couple of conferences? Had she worked with him during her tenure with Philadelphia PD? How was that possible if he was based in Seattle? Had he worked on the East Coast before he went to Seattle? Linc Shore and Seth Cole had come from Seattle. Josie knew that the ATF worked outlaw motorcycle gangs. There was a very good chance that Starkey had been involved in investigations into the Devil's Blade gang. Had Gretchen been in touch with Starkey because of the murder of Shore and Cole? Perhaps Gretchen had contacted the Seattle ATF to get more information about the two men.

Josie picked up the phone on her desk and dialed his number, only to get his voicemail, which said he was away at a conference with limited access to his email and voicemail. Suppressing a sigh, Josie left him a message, giving both her cell and work numbers and urging him to call her as soon as possible.

Across from her, Noah finished up a conversation on his cell phone and stared at her with a defeated look. "Seth Cole is not the boy in the photo."

"Are you sure?"

"I talked to his mother just now. Well, he was adopted at the age of three, but she says it definitely wasn't him. Also, the rest of the numbers in Gretchen's records are all local and, from what I can tell, have to do with cases she worked on. Nothing out of the ordinary."

More dead ends.

Josie leaned her elbows on her desk and put her face in her hands. "Where is she, Noah? What the hell is going on? Chitwood's going to be out here by the end of the day wanting to issue an arrest warrant."

"He already did," said Sergeant Dan Lamay as he ambled up to their desks. A remote control sat in his hand, and he used it to turn on the television affixed to the wall across the room from them. They watched a minute of commercials before the local news came on. Gretchen's face appeared just above the shoulder of the news anchor, over the words ARREST WARRANT ISSUED FOR DENTON OFFICER. Josie only heard snatches of the story: "... college student, James Omar...her home...it is unclear how they knew one another or what led to this deadly confrontation...if you have any information..."

"Jesus," Josie said.

Lamay turned the television off and placed the remote on her desk. "Sorry, Boss," he said. "I just thought you should know."

Josie managed a wan smile for him. "Thanks, Dan."

He shuffled off, and Josie put her face in her hands again. "This is not good," she muttered.

The sound of Noah's chair scraping across tile drew her gaze. He lowered his voice as he leaned into his own desk, talking softly across their two desktops. "Hey, we're going to find her, okay?"

Alive? Josie wondered. Was Gretchen even still alive?

As if he'd read her mind, Noah added, "She's going to be fine. So Chitwood issued his arrest warrant? Even if we have to arrest her when we find her, she'll explain what happened and things will turn out fine."

Josie's desk phone jangled, and she snatched it up, hoping it was Jack Starkey calling her back. Instead it was Lamay again, this time calling from the lobby. "Boss," he said, "dispatch says they've got a murder scene over by the city park."

CHAPTER 25

Seattle, Washington

JANUARY 1994

The pottery wheel lay in pieces on the table in front of Kristen. It wasn't fixable. She didn't know that much about pottery, but she knew she'd broken the wheel beyond repair. With a sigh, she shuffled the detritus around. Darryl was going to be pissed. He'd bought her the wheel and turned their mudroom into a full-blown pottery studio to keep her from getting bored. All because once, when they first started dating, she'd told him she always wanted to try pottery. She didn't even want to know how much he'd spent on all the equipment and clay and the kiln.

"Oh my God," she muttered under her breath. "The kiln."

It must have cost over $1,000. So, she'd come clean about the wheel, get him to buy her another, and try again. Or maybe she could just get pregnant and be done with the whole thing. That had been the original plan after the restaurant she'd waitressed at closed down. "Stay home," Darryl had told her. He was making a fortune as a salesman for BMW. They didn't need her paltry waitressing income. Never mind that she had made a killing in tips. A family was the next step in the evolution of Kristen and Darryl Spokes. But then they'd needed a new roof and the transmission in her car had crapped out. Then Darryl's mom got sick, and the plan to start their family receded. But Kristen was still stuck at home. When she'd started looking for a job, Darryl had come up with the idea of the pottery studio.

Except she sucked at pottery. Badly.

"Babe, you okay?"

His words startled her. A glance at the clock on the wall showed it was after eleven. He was late coming home from work again. Well, not work, but the after-work drinks he insisted were absolutely necessary to keep him on the good side of his boss.

"Don't come in here," she called, but it was too late. There he stood in his shirtsleeves, tie undone and loose around his neck, a five o'clock shadow stubbling his jaw. One eyebrow cocked.

"What happened?"

Kristen sighed and wiped her clay-covered hands on her jeans. "What happened is I'm not very good at this pottery thing, Darryl."

He smiled. "You'll get there."

She was too tired to argue. He took a step farther into the room and pointed to the table next to her broken pottery wheel. "Is that—?"

"It's my attempt at a mug."

He walked over to the table and picked it up. "This is great, Hon." Kristen laughed weakly. "Please, don't."

It was gray, unglazed, and one side of it slumped as though it had melted. The handle of it hung limply as though it had started to dissolve.

"I'm going to take this to work," Darryl said, the corners of his mouth twitching.

Kristen slapped his arm. "Stop," she said, but laughed anyway.

He caught her in his arms and kissed her. "Come to bed," he told her. "Tomorrow you can make me coffee for my new mug."

Giggling, she slapped at him again but let him lead her into their bedroom. Clothes dropped to the floor as they moved toward the bed.

Darryl stumbled, falling away from her and catching himself on the bed.

"Are you drunk?" Kristen asked.

"Turn on the light," he said.

She snapped on her bedside lamp as he came up from the floor with a brown wallet in his hand. He opened it, and his eyebrows kinked upward. "Kristen, who the hell is Travis Green, and why is his wallet on our bedroom floor?"

She was about to tell him that she had no idea, that she'd never heard of Travis Green and had no idea why his wallet was on their bedroom floor. But the light blinked off and there was the sound of a loud hum dying—all the power in the house was out.

"Kristen," Darryl said.

"What the hell is going on?" Kristen said.

Then a bright light arced across the room, shining first in Darryl's face and then blinding Kristen. A male voice said, "Yeah, Darryl, what the hell is going on?"

CHAPTER 26

Denton, Pennsylvania

PRESENT DAY

Denton City Park was a green space between the college campus and Denton's main street where residents walked their dogs, jogged, and held community events. Margie and Joel Wilkins's single-story ranch-style home was one block away from the park, separated from the sidewalk by a white picket fence. Inside the fence, a large maple tree shaded the front porch. A wooden swing hung from one of its branches. On the porch, colorful potted flowers bracketed white wicker furniture. Josie and Noah stood just outside the gate, speaking with Mettner.

"They're newlyweds," he explained. "They were supposed to be in Philadelphia this morning. Apparently, they had planned to go on a cruise with a group of friends and Joel's sister. When they didn't show to board the ship, his sister called both their cell phones. Both went straight to voicemail, so she got freaked out. Called the department for a welfare check."

Josie could tell by the pallor of Mettner's face that he had been the one to do the check. "Both deceased?" she asked.

Mettner nodded and wiped sweat from his brow, even though it was a crisp fall day. "Yeah. The wife's in the living room. The husband is in the back of the house, in the master bedroom."

"You were the only one inside?" Noah asked.

Mettner nodded. "Just me, yeah. Then Hummel came by and helped me set up the perimeter." He gestured over his shoulder to where Hummel stood at the Wilkinses' front door with his clipboard. "I didn't disturb anything. I checked them both for pulses even though—" He broke off and swallowed, his Adam's apple bobbing.

"It's okay," Josie told him. "It's not something you get used to."

Mettner shook his head like he was trying to shake off his distress. "I never saw a female victim. Not like that, you know? Her eyes...I just..."

Noah put a hand on his shoulder. "It's all right. Call the EMTs and the medical examiner, would you?"

"Sure thing." With that, Mettner walked off to his patrol car.

Hummel was the unofficial head of their evidence response team, and his vehicle was equipped with everything they'd need to secure and process a scene. He'd left it unlocked so that Josie and Noah could don Tyvek suits and gloves before making their way to the front porch.

"Three homicides in one week," Hummel commented as he signed them into the crime scene log.

The fact hadn't escaped Josie's notice. Her stomach did a somersault as she and Noah entered the house. The interior was just as homey as the outside. The front door opened right into the living room. Shiny hardwood floors creaked beneath their feet. The room was bright and welcoming, with cream walls and two overstuffed blue couches circling a low, glass-topped coffee table. A colorful faux floral arrangement reached from its vase atop the table. Beneath the table a lush periwinkle area carpet cushioned Margie Wilkins's naked body. The young woman was faceup, mouth yawning open, eyes bulging from her head. The last terrifying moments of her life were frozen on her face. Josie could see why Mettner had gotten so flustered. She was young—probably early to midtwenties, Josie guessed. They'd find out soon enough when they finished processing the scene and talked to family members.

With a sigh, Josie knelt beside the woman, careful not to disturb anything before her ERT could photograph the scene. "She was strangled." She pointed to the finger-shaped purple and pink bruising on Margie Wilkins's delicate neck. "Look, you can see where the killer wrapped his hands around her neck. And here—" She gestured to her throat. "Those are thumb prints."

Noah had his notebook out, sketching out the scene and writing things down as Josie spoke. "Bruising on her inner thighs as well. It's likely she was sexually assaulted." She stood and took a moment of silence for Margie Wilkins. *No one should have to die like this*, she thought. To Noah, she said, "Get her photographed right away and cover her up, please."

"Of course," he replied.

Josie took a slow pan of the room. For the violence that had been visited on Margie, the room itself was curiously devoid of detritus. "There wasn't a struggle," Josie said.

"You think the husband killed her?" Noah asked. "Domestic dispute? Murder-suicide?"

"I don't know. Let's take a look at his body."

They made their way down a cheerily decorated hall dotted with various framed photos of the couple—half appeared to be vacation photos from different exotic locations where they'd gone camping, rock climbing, and white water rafting, and the other half were obviously from their wedding. Interspersed among the photos were small, painted wooden signs that said things like, THIS IS OUR HAPPILY EVER AFTER and ALL BECAUSE TWO PEOPLE FELL IN LOVE. Josie stopped to study one photo of the two of them on their wedding day, standing at the edge of a lake at sunset, gazing lovingly at one another. In life, Margie had been pretty, but most of her attractiveness seemed to come from an inner glow of happiness.

Josie tore herself away and followed Noah into a bedroom at the end of the hallway. It was considerably darker, the room-darkening miniblinds shut tight against the sunlight. A large queen-sized bed dominated the room, its teal and green floral-print comforter pushed to one side of the bed. Two open suitcases filled with clothes lay on the floor near an open closet door. They'd been in the process of packing for their cruise. Or maybe they'd packed most of their things and left their suitcases open to throw in the last of their things in the morning.

"We need to know the last time anyone heard from them," Josie said.

Noah scribbled on his notepad.

"Here he is," she said, moving toward one side of the bed. On the floor between the bed and the wall lay Joel Wilkins. "And this was not a murder-suicide."

CHAPTER 27

Joel Wilkins's hands and feet had been tied with what looked like climbing rope. He was bare-chested and only wearing cutoff sweatpants. He lay on his side, his curly blond hair matted with blood. A pool of red fluid congealed on the hardwood beneath his battered skull. His eyes were half-closed, as though he had just started to doze off.

"Jesus," Noah said.

Josie squatted and took a closer look at him, noting the thick silver wedding band around his finger. She stood and studied the room once more, her gaze falling on a small glittering crystal bowl, no larger than the palm of a hand, on the opposite nightstand. In it rested a diamond ring. It was a princess cut, Josie recognized, its band laden with tiny diamonds. Next to it was a smaller ring, a band with a half dozen small diamonds. Margie Wilkins's engagement ring and wedding band. On the large dresser opposite the bed was a black wallet. Josie didn't want to touch it before the scene had been photographed, but a cursory glance showed some bills peeking from the top of it.

"He didn't take anything," she said. "The killer. This wasn't a robbery." She moved to Margie's side of the bed and pointed to the rings. "This engagement ring alone is worth thousands."

Noah nodded. "Just from a quick walk-through, it doesn't look like anything was taken from any of the other rooms either."

Josie went back to the doorway. "Let's see if we can figure out how the killer got in."

Across the hall was the bathroom. The window was small. Too small for a grown man to fit through. The room looked undisturbed except for two cell phones that rested in the bottom of the toilet. "Noah," she called.

He came into the bathroom and stared at the toilet bowl. "So this guy breaks in, tosses their cell phones in the toilet so they can't call for help, ties the husband up, beats him to death, and then assaults and murders the wife."

It had grown hot in the house. Beads of sweat formed on Josie's brow. She moved out of the tiny room back toward the hallway and wall of happy photos. "Something like that," she said. Walking back to the front of the house, she went into the kitchen. It was large, with faux stone tiles and, at its center, a big island table with tall stools surrounding it. It was clean and neat. On the kitchen counter, chrome appliances gleamed. Two phone chargers poked from an outlet above the counter, their cords dangling like loose threads. "They must charge their phones in here at night," Josie said.

Noah said, "The killer must have grabbed them up on his way through here."

"Everything else looks undisturbed," Josie replied.

Plates, glasses, flatware, and two stainless-steel travel mugs—one that said Mr. and one that said Mrs.—dried in the dish rack. The sink was empty. A brown plastic travel mug with the words Wawa Coffee beneath the creamy outline of a flying goose sat next to the coffee maker. Josie used a gloved hand to lift its lid and peek inside. It was clean and dry. They'd obviously tidied up before they went to bed—or at least after they'd finished dinner—and then readied things for the morning. They had cleaned up, packed most of their things, and charged their phones, ready to go on a cruise. They'd probably been excited. Maybe they'd made love, or maybe they'd been too exhausted from preparing for a long trip and simply fallen into bed. No one would ever know. Sometime during the night, someone had come into their home and taken them from the world, destroying the love and light that filled up every inch of their cozy little home. A wave of sadness fell over Josie. She loved her job, but she hated this part of it. She thought of Gretchen's characteristic stoicism at scenes like these. Philadelphia often had more homicides in a year than some countries. How many scenes like this had Gretchen seen there? Josie knew she was inured to the aftermath of murder. What had it been about the Shore/Cole slaying that penetrated her walls?

Noah's voice drew her gaze from the mug beside the coffee maker. "Over here," he called. He stood a few feet away near one of the kitchen windows. As Josie drew closer, she saw it was open and screenless. Without touching the frame, Noah poked his head outside. "He got in here."

Josie waited for him to move out of her way, and then she did the same. On the grass outside beneath the window lay the screen. On the outer sill of the window were pry marks. Her eyes were drawn to the grass toward the back of the house where a long, thin, black object lay. "What's that?" she asked, even though she knew Noah couldn't see it any better than she could.

The two of them went outside, where Hummel's team was photographing the outside of the house. Josie and Noah rounded the side of the house, walking slowly, eyes sweeping the ground for anything unusual as they made their way toward the object.

"A crowbar," Noah said.

Josie knelt and looked at it. Short blond hairs, bits of bone and flesh stuck to the flat end of it. "Well, we found our murder weapon. Make sure the team marks it." She stood up. "I've seen enough for now. Let's get out of the way. Let the ERT do their job. Photos. Print the house. Bag this stuff. The whole nine yards. We can canvass the neighbors. See if anyone saw or heard anything. You get the husband's sister's number and give her a call. See what you can find out about this couple."

CHAPTER 28

Two hours later, Josie stood outside the picket fence, jotting down the last of her notes from her interview with the Wilkinses' next-door neighbor. The evidence response team was finishing up. Dr. Feist had come and gone. Josie knew she would be back at the morgue by now, awaiting the arrival of the bodies. Mettner came to the fence and waved to the ambulance sitting curbside. "We're ready for you guys," he called. The paramedics had been on scene for some time, waiting to go in and get the bodies so they could be transported to the morgue. Owen stood with his back against the side of the ambulance, scrolling on his phone. He looked up and nodded at Mettner.

"Who're we taking first?" he asked.

"Take the wife," Mettner answered. "She's in the living room."

"You got it."

Owen saluted Josie as he and his partner navigated their gurney past her. She was glad he had been on duty when the double homicide call went out. He was one of the few EMS workers who didn't flinch or turn green at the more gruesome bodies. She knew he would treat the couple respectfully. Josie couldn't get the image of Margie Wilkins's glassy, vacant eyes out of her mind.

Noah emerged from the passenger seat of Josie's Escape, where he'd been talking on the phone. "What'd you get?" he asked her.

Josie flipped a page in her notebook, reading over her notes. "The neighbor to the east didn't hear or see anything. The neighbor to the west said he saw them come home last night around six—dinnertime—first Joel and then about a half hour later, Margie. He said she's a part-time fitness instructor at the college, and Joel teaches at the high school. He said he chatted with Joel when he came home, and Joel told him they were leaving on a cruise this morning. He did notice both their cars were still here when he woke up but just figured that their plans changed."

Noah held up a hand to interject. "I just got off the phone with Joel's sister, and she said that she got a text from him around eleven thirty last night. It was a normal exchange. Him asking her questions about exactly where they'd meet and what time, that sort of thing."

"So, it was definitely him," Josie said.

"Yeah. She said there's no doubt in her mind. Then Joel texted that they were going to bed, and that was that."

Josie gestured toward the house. "Neighbor in the back said their dogs started going crazy around two a.m., barking and growling. The owner went outside, looked around the yard, didn't see anything unusual. By that time, the dogs had stopped barking, so he went back to bed."

"So, they were alive at eleven thirty, and the killer most likely came through the back around two, used a crowbar to pop the kitchen screen out and pry open the window. Climbed in and went to the bedroom."

"He took the phones on his way through the kitchen and dumped them in the toilet before he went to the bedroom."

"Unless the wife was sleeping on the couch, he had to have woken them both and then separated them. But how did he tie the husband up without the wife running or going after him?"

Josie chewed her bottom lip for a moment. It was ballsy as hell to go after a couple. Especially alone. "I think we should assume he had a gun. A scene becomes much easier to control when you have a gun. He could have had help. Another person with him. Or he bashed the husband's skull in before he even woke the wife."

"No blood on the bed," Noah pointed out.

"Maybe he dragged the guy out of the bed, tossed him onto the floor, and then hit him before either one of them knew what was going on. They were probably both completely asleep. Waking up to an intruder in your bedroom would have been very disorienting. The other scenario is that the killer woke them and then made the wife tie the husband up. What did the sister say about the climbing rope?"

"It's probably theirs. They did a lot of rock climbing. She said they were very outdoorsy."

"So, the killer didn't bring the rope. He either found it in the house or made them get it out," Josie said. "He could have seen the photos and had them get the rope out. My guess is he would have made the wife do it."

"Do you think the husband was dead before the killer even took the wife into the living room?" Noah asked.

Josie said, "If he wasn't, he was close to it. If the killer was alone, he wouldn't want to run the risk of the husband getting loose while he was committing his other crimes. He would have seen the husband as the biggest threat. Anyone with half a brain would neutralize the biggest threat right off the bat. He was smart enough to dump the phones before he even got started and find and use the climbing rope. Also, there were no lights on in there, and none of the neighbors—especially the guy in the back—remember their lights being on during the night. So, this guy was also smart enough to use a flashlight—I'm guessing—and to keep the lights off so he didn't draw any attention from nosy neighbors. This killer isn't an idiot."

"Well," Noah said, "let's hope he left us some evidence somewhere in that house."

"What've we got in the way of background on these two?" Josie asked.

"Joel Wilkins is from here. Went to college out west. Came back to Denton to settle down. Margie Wilkins is from Erie. Also went to school out west, which is where the two met. They're both into teaching and fitness. They were married roughly a year ago. They'd been dating for about three years before that."

"So no exes looking for revenge," Josie said.

"'Fraid not," Noah said. "I asked the sister if she could think of anyone who might have it out for them, but she couldn't. She says they were good people and well liked."

Josie sighed. "Yeah, that's what the neighbors said. All of them were pretty devastated to hear what happened. This is a pretty tight-knit block. No one can remember seeing anything out of the ordinary in the days before this, so I'm not sure if the killer randomly chose the house or if he did some reconnaissance before he struck."

They both lowered their heads as Owen and his partner brought out a gurney with a body bag on it. They watched as Margie Wilkins was loaded into the back of the ambulance. "We'll be back in twenty," Owen told them.

Josie and Noah nodded their acknowledgment. Once the ambulance drove off, Noah said, "The sister will be back in town in a few hours. I told her to wait until tomorrow, once we've got the scene cleaned up, and she can do a walk-through and tell us if anything is missing that we wouldn't recognize."

"Perfect," Josie said.

"What are we looking at here, Boss?"

She knew what he was asking. It wasn't whether or not the murders were particularly savage, because they were, or if they were calculated, because they were. Noah was asking if this was a one-off or if they would need to put the city on high alert. There was never any way to tell, of course, until you had another slaying. But from everything Josie knew, killers who exhibited this level of sophistication were neither first-time offenders nor likely to stop. Josie gave a long sigh. "We're going to need the press," she said. "Maybe this was personal—someone who knew the Wilkins and had some kind of beef with them—but I have a feeling it wasn't."

"The crime scene certainly has a cold and impersonal feel to it," Noah said.

"If it wasn't personal, and we're dealing with someone who enjoys killing for the sake of it, then we need to put the community on high alert."

Noah pushed a hand through his thick brown hair. "All right. Let's get back to the station and talk with the chief, and then we'll sound the alarm."

CHAPTER 29

Planning a news conference with Chief Bob Chitwood was about as pleasurable as getting a root canal, but after an hour, the three of them had a pretty good idea of which details the chief should disclose to the public. He asked them rapid-fire questions about the murders, the scene, the timeline, the family—almost as if he were testing their aptitude for police work and not just their patience. Leaving his office, Josie buoyed herself with the thought that for once, she wouldn't be the one in front of the cameras. Also, the news of the double homicide of a young, beloved Denton couple would keep Gretchen's name out of the press for at least another day or two. Josie sat back down at her desk and made a few phone calls to her press contacts. As she finished up her last call, her cell phone rang. A Philadelphia number.

"Josie Quinn," she answered.

"Detective Quinn," said a familiar male voice, "it's Dr. Larson."

"What can I do for you, professor?"

There was a beat of hesitation. "Well, it's about Ethan. Ethan Robinson? James's roommate?"

"Yes," Josie said. "I remember. I spoke with Ethan's dad just after you sent me his information. Have you gotten in touch with Ethan?"

"Well, no. That's the thing. His dad called me because Ethan hasn't answered any calls or text messages."

"Ethan's dad told me that wasn't unusual behavior for him," Josie pointed out.

"No, it's not. Ethan goes, how shall I put it? Off the grid some-times. But Mr. Robinson was concerned that when he turned up, he would have no idea about James's murder, so he really wanted to get in touch with him. He called me and asked if I could access Ethan's class schedule—there was a copy in the apartment, actually—and talk with his professors, see if he'd been in class. I'm afraid Ethan hasn't attended any of his classes for a week."

Josie felt a small kernel of anxiety in the pit of her stomach. "Dr. Larson, this is very concerning, but you have to understand that Philadelphia is well out of my jurisdiction. I think you or Ethan's father should report him missing to the Philadelphia Police Department immediately. Then try to help them establish when was the last time anyone has heard from Ethan."

"Okay, I can do that. I suppose I can make the report. We have campus police as well."

"Have you had any luck finding the footage we discussed? Of the apartment entrance?"

"I should have it within the next day or so," Larson answered. "I spoke with my contact at Rowland Industries, and they'll be emailing it over. The last two weeks. I will try to isolate any footage with Ethan and James on it."

"Perfect," Josie said. "When you get it, turn that over to the Philadelphia police. They'll likely ask for it right away anyway. Again, if you could let me know what you find on the footage, it would be very helpful. Also, perhaps the last time you can find the two of them together—that would help as well."

"Of course. Thank you, Detective. I'll keep you posted. Have you given any thought to my proposal that you and your twin participate in my study?"

"No," Josie said before he could launch into a spiel on the benefits of epigenetics. "I'm sorry, but we're not interested."

They hung up, and Josie again ruminated on the bizarre relation-ship—or lack thereof—between Ethan and Doug Robinson. It should have been his father showing this kind of concern, not his landlord. Unless the entire thing was just an excuse for Larson to call and try to get her and Trinity involved in his research.

Noah plopped into the chair behind his desk and tossed a sheaf of papers over to her. They fanned as they landed on her desk.

"This is from Gretchen's house?" she asked as she sifted through the pages.

"Yeah, her prints are all over the house, obviously. They found Omar's prints on the porch but not in the house. There are a number of other prints in the house, all unidentified, but those could be from former residents, or anyone who came in to repair something."

"What about the photo?"

"No prints on the photo," Noah said. "I mean, there were a few partials on the back, but they were so old, the techs couldn't get anything."

"But Gretchen's prints weren't on it," Josie noted.

Noah stared at her. "Somehow, I don't think the DA is going to put much stock in that. Not when she went to the house just before Omar was shot, the bullet they dug out of the kid was the same caliber as her gun, and she went MIA and removed the MDT from her car."

Josie bristled but said nothing.

Noah booted up his desktop computer. "We should order food," he said. "'Cause we're gonna be here all night doing paperwork." He lowered his voice. "When we're finished, I think you should come home with me. We'll get a couple hours of sleep..." He trailed off.

Josie's desk phone rang before her mind could fill in the rest. Hoping it was ATF agent Jack Starkey returning her call, she snatched up the receiver. "Quinn."

Sergeant Lamay's voice sounded strange, his words seeming to flutter in and out. "Uh, Boss? Can you... can you come down here?"

"What's going on, Sergeant?"

There was a long pause. Then Lamay said, "Uh, Detective Palmer's here, and she wants me to arrest her."

CHAPTER 30

Josie practically leapt the short flight of stairs to the first floor. Noah's feet pounded down the steps behind her. She burst into the lobby, pulling up short when she saw Gretchen standing in the center of the room, looking pale and wan. She wore the same pair of black slacks and the same white Denton PD polo shirt she'd been wearing on the day she disappeared. Except unlike in the video from the CCTV footage, now her white shirt was smudged with dirt and what Josie thought looked like drops of blood. A tear in the left knee of her pants exposed a shock of white skin. Dried blood caked around a two-inch gash over her left eyebrow.

"Gretchen," Josie said.

Her brown eyes darted all around the room, as if she could hear Josie's voice but not see her standing right in front of her.

Josie heard Noah tell Lamay to call an ambulance, which seemed to snap Gretchen into focus. Briefly she met Josie's eyes and then looked behind her to Noah and Lamay. "No, no," she said, extending her wrists toward the three of them. "I don't need medical attention. I'm turning myself in for the murder of James Omar."

Noah stepped forward, moving in front of Josie. "Gretchen," he said softly, "you've got quite the cut over your eye there. You probably need stitches."

Her arms shook. For just a moment, a look of desperation passed over her face. Then it was gone, and the blankness was back. "No," she insisted. "I don't need stitches. Just take me into custody. I want to turn myself in."

Noah looked back at Josie, as if to ask what to do. Josie reached for Gretchen's shoulder, but she shrugged her away. "Okay," Josie said softly. "How about this? We'll go into the conference room, just down the hall."

Fury flashed across Gretchen's face. Ignoring Josie, she thrust her arms at Noah, palms upward. "Take me into custody. I'm turning myself in."

"Gretchen," Josie interjected, "let's just sit down and talk, okay?"

"I don't want to talk," she snarled. "I want you to do your fucking job."

Josie kept her voice calm. "I'll do my job. But you have to let me."

"Arrest me," Gretchen said.

"We can arrest you. There's already a warrant out for you. But if you're going to make a confession," Josie replied, "then we'll need to call the state police."

She signaled to Lamay, and he said, "I'll call," but kept standing there, watching the exchange. It was protocol for them to call in the state police if one of their own officers was going to confess to a crime. This avoided any conflict.

Josie turned back to Gretchen. "Are you sure you don't want to have a seat and collect yourself first?"

Gretchen's voice was practically a growl. "Arrest me."

"Fine. Since you're turning yourself in, I don't think we need to cuff you. If you're going to be in custody, then we have a responsibility to see that your medical needs are taken care of. We need to get that cut looked at before we do anything else. Gretchen, you know this—"

Gretchen's punch came hard and fast—so fast that Josie had no time to react to it. She didn't even know the older detective could move that quickly. Or perhaps it hadn't been that fast. Maybe it was just that Josie was unprepared for the strike because it was coming from Gretchen. One moment Josie was watching anger and desperation flash across Gretchen's face, and the next she was on her ass on the tile floor, her cheek stinging with pain. Noah and Lamay pinned Gretchen to the floor beside her, yanking her hands behind her back. Josie's fingers touched her cheek and came away wet with blood. She stared across at Gretchen, whose cheek was now pressed firmly against the tiles as Lamay cuffed her. Her eyes were closed, but her face—relaxed now, its lines loose and slack—registered a single emotion: relief.

CHAPTER 31

Josie sat on the edge of the hospital bed, trying not to wince as a young doctor probed the raw skin of her cheek. Gretchen had managed to hit her right below the eye socket on the cheekbone, splitting the skin. Gloved fingers pressed along the edges of the cut, and pain throbbed through the entire side of her face. For a split second, she was taken back to her childhood—to being six years old with a large slash down the side of her face, the nurses holding her down to clean it. An involuntary shudder worked its way through her body. The doctor paused and moved his head back to meet her eyes. "I'm sorry," he said. "You okay?"

Josie's hand reached up to the cut, but the doctor gently stopped her, guiding her hand back into her lap. "Please," he said, "we want to keep the area clean."

She wanted to push past him and go home so she could numb the pain with a few slugs of Wild Turkey. But she couldn't. Instead, she silently reminded herself that she wasn't six anymore. That this wasn't her mother's work. Her friend and colleague was in trouble. The punch was a message to Josie, and Josie's job was to decipher it. "Just tell me if I need stitches," she told the doctor.

He smiled at her, his straight white teeth reminding her of the one photo she'd seen of James Omar smiling. The one of him and Ethan Robinson at the Broad Street Run. "No," he said. "I think just a butterfly closure should do the trick. Use some bacitracin and vitamin E on it, and you shouldn't have any scarring. Ice for the swelling. It will probably hurt a lot more tomorrow."

Josie stood up, ready to leave, but the doctor held up a hand and laughed softly. "I know you're in a hurry, Detective, but please. Just let me clean and bandage it."

Frustration made her face feel hot. It took everything in her not to take it out on this poor, well-meaning man who was only trying to help her. She did her best to flash him a smile, trying to make her tone pleasant instead of caustic. "Just hurry if you could, please? I have to get back to work."

He gestured for her to sit back down on the bed. "Of course."

As promised he was fast, and aside from the sting of the antiseptic he used, Josie felt no pain. In minutes, she was alone behind the walls of curtains, relieved to be finished with the entire thing. A pair of boots appeared beneath the curtain directly in front of her. "I'm in here, Fraley," she called.

Noah stepped through the opening and pulled the curtain closed behind him. He came closer, tipping her chin with a finger so he could get a better look at her cheek. Just his proximity, and his grimace that turned into a smile when their eyes met, eased some of her anxiety. She pushed out a long breath and leaned her forehead against his chest. For a moment, Noah took her into his arms and held her. The old memories receded. Then the moment was over. He released her and stepped back, leaving his scent lingering on her clothes. Aftershave, coffee, and something that was uniquely Noah.

"What did she say about the gash on her forehead?" Josie asked.

Noah didn't miss a beat. Their rhythm had been established years ago, and it was a great comfort to Josie, especially in times of stress. "She told the doctors she fell. She won't say how or where or when. The wound needs stitches, but since she won't tell them more, and it's been open longer than twenty-four hours, they'll have to leave it open for now. They don't want to seal in any infection by closing it now. The doctors are almost done dressing the wound. She says she doesn't have pain anywhere else. She looks pretty dirty, but from what we can tell, she's not otherwise injured."

"I won't press charges," Josie said.

"I think she knows that. I don't know what's going on with her, but she only calmed down when Lamay read her her rights."

"Has she said anything?"

Noah shook his head. "No, not to anyone from Denton. I called the state police. They're sending someone. Loughlin. I briefed her over the phone. She should be here any minute. Do you know her?"

Josie nodded. Heather Loughlin was an experienced investigator for the state police. Josie had only met her a handful of times, but she was professional and fair. "She's good," she told Noah.

"Actually, Gretchen did say she wanted a lawyer. But that was the only thing she said."

Of course Gretchen would want a lawyer. Countless times, she had been the person on the other side of the interrogation table, asking the questions, hoping that the suspect didn't clam up and request an attorney.

"I think she's going to confess, Josie," Noah added.

Now it was her turn to shake her head. "No, she's not. She said she was turning herself in. That's not the same thing as a confession. She's getting an attorney to cover her ass until this gets sorted."

"Josie, she punched you in the face so we would arrest her."

Josie sneered at him, and the motion made her face hurt. "I don't care what she says or does. She didn't kill James Omar."

"What if she did?"

Josie used both hands to push him out of her way. She yanked the curtain back, the rings making a loud, sharp noise as they shot across the rail affixed to the ceiling. Down the hall, in front of one of the treatment areas walled in by glass and hidden by more curtains, sat one of their patrol officers in a folding chair, scrolling on his phone. Josie walked up to him and stood before him, hands on her hips. He nearly dropped his phone, jumping to attention. "Boss," he mumbled.

"Detective," Josie corrected. "Is Gretch—is Detective Palmer in there?"

Noah appeared next to Josie. The officer gave him an apprehensive glance. "It's fine," Noah told him. "Has Detective Loughlin arrived yet?"

He nodded. "She's in there now."

Josie pushed past the guard and slid open the glass door just a fraction so she could listen. Noah stood behind her, crowding her so he could hear too. Through the crack in the door, Josie could see Gretchen in the bed in the same clothes she'd been wearing at the station. A thick wad of gauze covered the gash over her eye, kept in place by rolled gauze that had been tied around her head. Her arms were at her sides. She stared straight ahead, avoiding eye contact with Detective Loughlin, who stood beside the bed, tall and sturdy, with silky blond hair pulled back into a ponytail. Like Josie and Noah, she wore khaki pants and a polo shirt—except hers had the state police insignia on its right breast. "Detective Palmer," she said, "I understand your colleagues have been searching for you for a couple of days. Can you tell me where you've been?"

Gretchen didn't answer.

Loughlin pointed to Gretchen's forehead. "Who did that to you?"

"I fell."

"How? Where? When did you fall?"

Gretchen's head fell to the side, her gaze focused on a crash cart in the corner of the room.

"What was James Omar doing at your house? How do you know him?"

"I want a lawyer," Gretchen said in a low voice. She sounded almost defeated.

Loughlin softened her tone. "Gretchen, you know how this works. I can help you. Whatever happened in your driveway that day, I can help you. But you have to talk to me. I need to know what happened. The truth."

Gretchen swallowed. "Call Andrew Bowen. Please. Tell him I can pay him."

Josie turned her head and met Noah's eyes. *Andrew Bowen?* she mouthed. Bowen was a well-known criminal defense attorney in Denton. Everyone in the police department knew him, but the Denton police—namely, Josie—had arrested his mother on murder charges six months earlier. The whole business was quite ugly and had put a damper on the easy rapport that Denton PD investigators used to have with him.

Loughlin took out her cell phone and swiped a few times before turning the screen toward Gretchen. "Lieutenant Fraley shared this with me. Can you tell me who the boy is in this photo?"

Gretchen took a quick glance but didn't answer.

"This photo was pinned to James Omar's dead body. Who is this boy?"

Something passed over Gretchen's face—shock or fear, or maybe both—and it was gone as quickly as it came. She didn't answer. Loughlin held the phone out in front of Gretchen for several more seconds, but when Gretchen refused to look at it, she put the phone back in her pocket. "I'm happy to call Mr. Bowen for you, Gretchen. But you know how this works. You've been on my side of these kinds of exchanges what? Hundreds of times? Thousands, maybe? Are you sure you don't want to talk to me about what happened before we get attorneys involved? Are you sure you don't want to tell me first who killed James Omar?"

More silence. Then Gretchen turned toward her, looked her in the eyes, and said, "I'm responsible for that boy's death."

"No," Josie murmured, wanting to burst into the room and shake Gretchen. But she knew she couldn't. Noah's hand settled onto her shoulder. Josie turned to him and whispered, "Someone else was there."

Josie turned back in time to see a single tear slide down Gretchen's cheek. "Please," she said to Loughlin. "Just call Andrew Bowen. I need a lawyer."

CHAPTER 32

Andrew Bowen looked like he had just gotten out of bed. Looking at the time on her cell phone, Josie thought maybe he had. It was after 11:00 p.m. when he trudged into the police department wearing a pair of suit pants and a wrinkled white button-down shirt. In one hand, he carried a briefcase. His thick blond hair looked hastily combed away from his face. He was in his late thirties, tall, with a handsome, angular face and piercing blue eyes. He glared at Josie as one of the uniformed officers led him down the hallway to where Josie and Noah stood outside the conference room with Detective Heather Loughlin.

"Thank you for coming," Noah said to Bowen after introducing him to Loughlin. "She's in there."

Bowen merely nodded and disappeared into the conference room.

"Well, that was a warm reception," Josie remarked.

"Guess he's taking her case," Noah said.

Loughlin asked, "You said she just showed up here; how did she get here? Did anyone ask her?"

Noah shook his head. "She wouldn't tell us, but Lamay checked the external footage. She drove up in her Cruze and parked in the municipal lot."

"So, we've got the car?" Josie asked.

"It's at the impound until the evidence techs can get over there and process it," Noah replied.

Josie felt something like relief mixed with hope wash over her. No matter what Gretchen said or implied, she didn't believe for one second that she had killed Omar. Something else was going on. Someone else was involved. Josie would find out who, starting with the car. Gretchen had left and returned in the vehicle. Whoever had been with her had surely been in the car. There had to be something there. Prints. DNA. Even if it was a single hair, Josie would find it.

"What about the gun?" Josie asked. "Her service weapon?"

"Not on her person or in the car," Noah answered.

Then another thought occurred to her. "Was her jacket in there?"

"What?"

"Her leather jacket," Josie said. "The one she got from the Devil's Blade gang. The one she never takes off."

"I'll find out." He walked off to make a phone call.

"You guys have coffee here?" Loughlin asked.

Josie led her across the hall to the small first-floor kitchenette and made them each a cup of coffee. Loughlin's cell phone rang, and she answered it, plopping into a seat at the table and speaking softly to whoever was on the line. Josie was stirring extra half-and-half into her own mug when Noah returned.

"No jacket," he told her.

Josie walked out into the hallway and gestured with her coffee mug to the camera mounted on the ceiling. "She was wearing it when she got the call from Omar. We saw her on the footage."

"So?" Noah said.

"It's not at her house. It's not in the car."

"It's probably in the river with the rest of the stuff she ditched."

Josie took a sip of coffee and shook her head. "No. She wouldn't toss that jacket into the river. Whoever took her has it."

"You still think there's another person?" Noah asked. "Josie, she turned herself in. She punched you in the face so we'd arrest her. She told Loughlin that she killed him."

"No," Josie said. "She said, 'I'm responsible for that boy's death.' That's not the same thing. That's not a confession."

Noah raised a brow. "I think a jury might feel differently. Listen, I know you feel a certain…loyalty toward Gretchen, but I think you need to consider that she did this. We don't know what went down—why Omar was there or what happened between the two of them—but we have no evidence that another person was involved. Gretchen turned herself in. She hasn't implicated anyone else."

"Because she's not talking. She's freaked out. Something is going on. There is more to this."

"Maybe there is," Noah said. "Maybe there isn't. Sometimes even people who are trained to do the right thing don't do it."

Josie put one hand on her hip. "What are you talking about?"

"Look what happened to Luke," he said. She shot him a wilting glare, and he put his hands up. "Just hear me out."

Luke had been a state trooper. When Josie's marriage to Ray Quinn disintegrated, she'd started dating Luke, and eventually they got engaged. After two and a half years together, he'd been involved in an off-duty shooting, and instead of reporting it, he'd covered it up, ruined his career, and faced criminal charges.

Noah said, "Luke was trained, just like us, on how to respond to a crime. That was his job as a police officer. It should have been a no-brainer for him. I'm sure it wasn't the first time he caught a homicide. Doing the right thing should have been easy for him. Second nature. But he didn't do it. He freaked out. He did everything wrong. Sometimes people get it wrong. Even when there is no good reason. Even when it's the very last thing you'd expect them to do. People get things wrong."

"Luke wasn't responding to a call," Josie argued. "He was going to visit a friend. He lost people close to him. It wasn't the same thing."

"No, it wasn't the same," Noah agreed. "But to this day don't you ask yourself why he didn't just call 911?"

She hesitated a moment. Then she conceded, "Of course I do."

"Because sometimes people get it wrong. No rhyme. No reason. It just happens."

As annoyed as she was, Josie knew there was truth to what he said. People thought they knew who they were until they were tested. They thought they knew exactly how they would respond to frightening situations. But the disturbing truth was that even decent, law-abiding people with strong moral compasses were thrown off course sometimes. Still, she couldn't keep her voice from rising an octave. "You're telling me that Gretchen, an experienced investigator with almost four times as much time on the job as Luke had, shot someone she didn't know and ran? That she deliberately destroyed evidence? That she just 'got it wrong'?"

If Noah was stung by the acerbic tone of her voice, he didn't show it. He merely shrugged. "I'm not saying that's what happened. We don't know what happened. I'm saying we should consider the possibility that yeah, Gretchen shot this kid and then ran."

Josie pointed a finger at him and said only one word, clearly and firmly. "No."

Before Noah could respond, the door to the conference room creaked open and Andrew Bowen stepped out, looking even more weary than he had when he'd gone inside.

"I'll get Detective Loughlin," Noah said.

Seconds later, she joined the three of them in the hallway. The officers stared at Bowen.

"You can process her," he said. "I'll enter my appearance on her behalf with the court in the morning."

Once Gretchen entered the system, she would be picked up by the county sheriff and taken to their facility forty miles away in Bellewood. She would remain there until trial, unless she got out on bail or was able to strike a plea bargain.

"Will she be giving a confession?" Detective Loughlin asked.

"Detective Palmer will not be answering any more questions this evening." He gave a long sigh and ran a hand over his blond locks. "But we will meet with you tomorrow so she can give you a confession. She's instructed me to enter a guilty plea on her behalf."

A small gasp escaped Josie's lips. "To . . . to first-degree murder?"

Noah said, "She could get life in prison. Even the death penalty."

Bowen gave a pained smile. "I'm not at liberty to discuss my client's legal strategy with you, detectives. But it's my job, as her attorney, to try to keep the death penalty *off* the table, as I would with any of my clients facing such serious charges."

Loughlin stepped forward and handed Bowen a business card. "Call me in the morning."

Bowen took it and tucked it into his briefcase. "Thank you. Tomorrow she'll be transferred to the county jail in Bellewood. I'll speak to the DA, and we'll make arrangements for you to take down her confession so that a plea can be entered."

Josie said, "Who's the boy in the photo? Did you ask her about the boy in the photo?"

"Really, Detective," Bowen said, sounding exhausted. "You know I can't discuss privileged conversations between my client and myself."

"What if the boy in the photo is in danger?"

"In danger from the woman you've got in your custody? I don't think so. But I'm sure Detective Loughlin will get all the relevant information from Detective Palmer tomorrow."

They wouldn't get anything out of Andrew Bowen. Josie knew this. If Gretchen didn't want to talk, she didn't have to. Bowen was her buffer against their barrage of questions. Besides, at this stage, Josie and Noah were largely out of the loop. Their job now was to do all the requisite paperwork, tie up the loose ends of the investigation, and hand the case over to the district attorney for prosecution. Even though Bowen had told them Gretchen would plead guilty, they were still required to prepare the case for the DA to take to trial in the event that Gretchen changed her mind and decided to plead not guilty. But the state police detective would be the only law enforcement agency to have access to Gretchen. If Gretchen confessed to Loughlin as promised, then from that point on, what happened to Gretchen would be largely up to the attorneys and the court system.

Gretchen seemed determined to send herself to prison for life. But why? Why not fight? Take it to trial and try for an acquittal? Or at least try to negotiate a lesser plea? Josie knew what Noah would say: because she felt guilty for having killed Omar, and she was holding herself accountable. But Josie was certain there was more to the story. And if there was, and Josie was right, there was a killer still out there on the loose.

"Good night, detectives," Bowen said, and helplessly, Josie watched him walk away.

CHAPTER 33

Josie went home with Noah, but less than five minutes after they walked through his front door, Josie's phone rang. It was work.

"Don't answer it," Noah said as he went into his living room and started flipping lights on.

"It's work," Josie said. "If I don't answer, they'll just call you." She pressed the phone to her ear. "Hello?"

Bob Chitwood's voice was almost a shout. "I need one of you on the street right now. You drew the short end of the stick, so I called you first. Tell me you're sleeping, and I'll call Fraley instead. Unless the two of you are together. Then you can flip a coin, and whoever wins can get their ass down to the strip mall over by Corinthian Place. There's been a couple of break-ins."

Josie sighed. "I'm on it."

Chitwood hung up without another word. She looked at Noah, who said, "I heard. I'll go. You get some sleep."

"You think I'm going to be able to sleep?"

The argument about Gretchen's guilt still lingered between them, tense and unfinished.

Noah handed her the remote to the television. "Eventually, yeah. I'll take this one. You can do the walk-through with Joel Wilkins's sister in the morning." He picked up his keys from where he'd tossed them onto the coffee table and walked past her. "Help yourself to whatever's in the fridge."

Josie stepped in front of him before he reached the door. "Do you really think Gretchen is guilty?"

"Do we have to talk about this right now?"

"I want to know."

He touched her cheek, slid a lock of hair behind her ear, and ever so gently moved in to plant the softest kiss on the butterfly stitch the doctor had put on her cheek. Then he said, "It doesn't matter what I think. It matters what the evidence shows and what Gretchen does. She wants to plead guilty. The case is closed. We've got the Wilkins double murder and everything else that goes on in this city to deal with."

She stepped back from him. "We're supposed to stick together, Noah."

"We who?"

"Me, you, Gretchen. The Denton PD. We're a team. We have to look out for each other."

He raised a brow. "There's a fine line between looking out for one another and police corruption."

Josie felt the color drain from her face. "You know that's not what I mean."

Noah folded his arms across his chest. "Then what do you mean? Because I did look out for Gretchen by doing my job. She's a grown woman. She made choices and now she's holding herself accountable for those choices. I know you don't want to hear that or believe it, but—"

"It's not that I don't want to, it's that it's just not true. Gretchen didn't do this. I know it in my gut, and my gut is rarely wrong."

His arms loosened and his annoyed expression softened. "Josie, I understand your impulse to want to somehow exonerate Gretchen. Hell, I even understand the need to answer all the questions. It's frustrating for the case to close on our end when we don't know why the hell things happened the way they did, but you need to face the fact that you barely know Gretchen. None of us really know her. Even that lieutenant in Philadelphia told you he wasn't close to her. She accepted a gift from the Devil's Blade. A gift she wore each day since they gave it to her. I know you've probably done your homework already, but the Devil's Blade is no joke. They're criminals—murderers, drug dealers—and the way they treat women…and I can see her accepting the jacket, fine, just to be polite, but why did she wear it? Why was that case so important to her? Has it ever occurred to you that the thing you think Gretchen is hiding is something criminal?"

A dozen replies flew through her head, but all of her arguments came down to one thing: she just knew. She also knew this wasn't the kind of reasoning that Noah would accept. His cell phone rang. He glanced at it, silenced it, and said, "I have to go. We'll talk about this when I get back."

"I won't be here," Josie said to his back. "I'm going home."

He turned back to her. "Josie, please. Don't make this personal."

But it was already personal. Gretchen knew—probably better than any person Josie had ever met—what it meant to have a toxic mother, what it was like to be raised by someone who hated you and hurt you at every turn. Gretchen knew how hard it was to talk about the abuse. When Josie was too weak and too gutted to put together the final pieces of the puzzle that exposed the woman who claimed to be her mother, Gretchen had done it for her. Gretchen understood Josie in a way that no one ever had, and possibly no one ever would.

And Josie understood that Gretchen was lying.

"If Gretchen broke the law, you know I wouldn't stand in the way of her being prosecuted," Josie told him. "But I don't think Omar's death is on her."

"Then we have to agree to disagree."

CHAPTER 34

Robyn Wilkins paced just outside the picket fence encircling her brother's home. Brown leather boots reached to her knees, covering a dark-blue pair of skintight jeans. Over a long-sleeved cream-colored T-shirt, she wore a wine-red pashmina. Her fingers fidgeted with the fringe on the end of it. Long, silky blond hair sat atop her head in a messy bun. Her blue eyes were rimmed red from crying, and her face was drawn. Josie parked her Escape curbside and got out, introducing herself and extending her condolences.

Robyn put one hand to her chest. "Oh my God, it's you. The chief of police, the one with the twin sister—"

Josie cut her off. "Detective now. I was only interim chief. If you're not comfortable doing the walk-through with me, I can get Lieutenant—"

Robyn touched Josie's forearm. "No, no. I'm glad you're here. It's a pleasure. I just wasn't expecting to ever meet you in person, that's all."

Not for the first time, Josie wished Trinity hadn't talked her into doing all those episodes of *Dateline*. She gestured toward the house. "Shall we?"

A balled-up tissue appeared in Robyn's other hand, and she swiped it under her nose. "I guess we have to, don't we?"

One hand on the gate, Josie stopped. "No, we don't have to do it today. If it's too difficult, we can reschedule. I certainly understand. But it would be helpful to our investigation if we knew whether or not anything was disturbed or taken."

Robyn stared straight ahead at the house. Her brow furrowed, as if she was making some kind of decision. Then she took a deep, shuddering breath and said, "I want to get it over with. I mean, I'm going to have to come back soon anyway to get clothes for the funeral, go through their things…oh God."

Josie gave her a moment to compose herself. Then she nodded, and Josie opened the gate. Side by side they walked up to the front door, and Josie let them in. "We found your brother's keys inside."

Robyn pointed to the key hanger mounted on the wall just inside the door. It was made from a piece of driftwood. "My brother made that. He got the driftwood from a beach on the Oregon coast." Tears welled in her eyes. "They loved to travel. You know, Margie's parents died when she was a teenager—car accident—they left her a nice little trust fund. Still, she was really good at stretching their travel money. 'Do more with less,' she always said. But that's how they managed to take so many trips."

"Your parents," Josie said. "Do they still live in Denton?"

Robyn nodded. "Yes. I told them yesterday. They're too…too devastated to deal with any of this."

"I understand," Josie replied. "It's good that they have you."

Aside from the fingerprint dust marring the various surfaces of the house, it was just as the evidence response team had found it the day before. Robyn walked through the rooms slowly, with Josie behind her. "You can touch things," Josie told her. "Our evidence response team has already processed the house."

At the door to the master bedroom, Robyn said, "They didn't take Margie's engagement ring?"

"No," Josie said. "It doesn't appear that anything was stolen. That's why we've asked you to take a walk-through. We just need to confirm that there was no robbery."

They went from room to room, Robyn touring the house three times without finding anything missing or out of place. She asked questions about the crime, about the way the bodies were found, about the timeline, and Josie answered as best she could without compromising their investigation. On Robyn's final pass, she lingered in the kitchen, standing at the island where Josie imagined she had stood many times while a guest at her brother's house. It was Josie's turn to ask questions. "How long did Margie and Joel live here?"

"Oh, about three years. They bought the house before they got married. They knew they would be together forever."

"I see they were quite adventurous. Did they have a routine at home, or was it different every day?"

Robyn reached to the center of the island, plucked a napkin from the napkin holder, and used it to wipe beneath her eyes. "They stuck to a routine at home. It made things easier. They were both very much into fitness and working out. They were both usually up at six to take a run together, three times around the park, then my brother left for work. Margie didn't have to be over at the college until later in the day. Margie got her workout in at her job, but Joel usually hit the gym after teaching all day. They were usually both home by six thirty, though, at the latest. They took turns cooking dinner. All healthy stuff."

So anyone who wanted to learn their routine would have had an easy time doing so, although it struck Josie that the killer had chosen to attack them when they were home together. Especially when there was a period of time each day that Margie was home alone. Either the killer hadn't done much reconnaissance at all, or sexual assault hadn't been the primary reason for the home invasion. Nor had robbery. A chill ran down Josie's arms. More and more this looked like it was simply murder for the sake of murder.

"I know Lieutenant Fraley probably asked you this already, but was there anyone that Joel and Margie were having trouble with? Possibly feuding with? Anyone giving them trouble? Anyone Margie might have been having a problem with independent of Joel?"

Robyn shook her head. "No, no one I can think of, and believe me, yesterday after I got off the phone with Lieutenant Fraley, I racked my brain. But I couldn't come up with anyone. My parents couldn't either. I called a couple of Margie's friends—women who were bridesmaids at the wedding—to see if they knew of anyone she was having trouble with, and they couldn't think of anyone either."

Josie said, "Actually, if you could get me a list of names of her close friends so we can contact them directly, that would be very helpful."

Robyn nodded. "Of course." She stood, taking one last pan of the kitchen—and froze. She pointed to the countertop where the coffee maker showed their reflections. "That," she said. "That's not theirs."

Josie followed her gaze to the plastic travel mug beside the coffee maker. The one that said WAWA COFFEE on it. "The mug? That was here yesterday when we arrived."

Robyn walked over to the countertop and went to pick it up, but Josie stopped her with a gentle hand. "Wait," she said. "Don't touch it. If you think it's important, I'll want to bag it as evidence."

Robyn snatched her hand back as though she'd been burned, and hugged herself.

Josie sent a quick text to Hummel, asking him to come and retrieve an additional piece of evidence from the Wilkins house. Josie didn't have any bags or labels with her, and besides that, they'd need to establish a chain of custody. That, and she wanted to double-check the photos taken at the scene the day before against the cup's current location to make sure no one on her team had disturbed it. "Why do you say it's not theirs?"

Robyn walked around the kitchen and opened each one of the upper cabinets. "Do you see anything plastic anywhere in this kitchen?"

Josie took a careful scan of the contents of the cabinets. "No," she said. She stepped over to a cabinet whose bottom shelf was crowded with additional travel mugs much like the MR. and MRS. mugs in the dish rack. "They're all stainless steel," Josie said.

"Right," Robyn said. "They thought they were being environmentally conscious and avoiding carcinogens by not using anything plastic. They were the people who brought their own cloth tote bags to the grocery store. They'd never have a plastic coffee mug in this house. Besides, we don't even have Wawas around here."

"Wawa is in southeastern Pennsylvania," Josie said. "New Jersey and Delaware too, I think. They could have picked it up if they were in any of those areas."

Robyn shook her head emphatically. "Yes, they could have. I'm sure they've been to a Wawa at some point in their travels. They did like to go to the Jersey shore in the summers. But they didn't buy this. Maybe someone on your team left it?"

Josie knew without a doubt that no one on the evidence response team would ever be wandering around an active crime scene with a coffee cup in their hands, much less leave it behind, but she didn't say this to Robyn. "Or maybe Joel and Margie had a guest who brought it with them?" she suggested.

Robyn's shoulders slumped. "Oh. Yes, I suppose. I mean, I don't remember them having any guests recently, but I don't know every detail of their lives."

Josie touched her shoulder and guided her toward the front door. "Regardless, we'll take it into evidence and I'll ask the lab if they can try to get some prints from it. We have to treat everything as potential evidence."

Robyn nodded. "Thank you."

CHAPTER 35

Seattle, Washington

MARCH 1994

Billy's snores woke Gretchen from a sound sleep. If dragons were real, she imagined they sounded like her husband when he was deep in the throes of slumber, his snoring reverberating through the entire house. She rolled toward his side of the bed and patted the space where Billy normally was—when he was home—but he wasn't there. She turned onto her back and stared at the ceiling, trying to decide if she could get back to sleep in spite of the racket he was making. A minute later she was padding through the darkened house to the living room, where the television cast a blue glow over the room. Billy sprawled across the sofa, his feet, still in boots, dangling over the end.

Slowly, Gretchen unlaced each boot and pulled them off. His white tube socks were gray with dirt and grime, and the big toe of his left foot poked through a hole. She wondered if wives were supposed to keep their husbands in clean, holeless socks. But Billy didn't seem to care about things like that. He only wanted her. Had only wanted her since the day they met back East.

She positioned herself between the couch and the coffee table, her eyes catching on the strange mug-like clay formation sitting between his wallet and keys. It was gray and looked half-melted and half-formed, like someone had been trying to fashion a coffee mug in a lava pit. It wasn't exactly the type of thing she would expect an

ATF agent working undercover in an outlaw motorcycle gang to bring home from work, but Billy had always been full of surprises.

His long beard was coarse beneath her fingers. She woke him with a kiss. Even before he pulled her down on top of him, she knew he was awake because the snoring had finally ceased. His body was warm beneath hers, his hands roving up and down her back, fingers finding their way beneath her nightgown, cupping her ass. They kissed long and slow, and Gretchen felt the stirring of desire. It was the feeling she had chased all the way across the country.

"You said you wouldn't fall asleep on the couch," she whispered as his lips traveled down her neck.

"I'm sorry. Rough night. But I'm almost patched in."

A thrill of fear ran down Gretchen's spine. Patched in meant becoming a full, official member of the Devil's Blade, the outlaw biker gang he'd been undercover with for nearly two years. She'd been worried about it from the day she'd first heard the expression. What if they found him out? The smallest slip in his cover could prove fatal.

"That's a good thing," he reminded her, sensing the tension in her body.

"I know," she said. "But I worry about you."

"I'm in tight with Linc, Gretch. He won't forget what I did for him."

She didn't point out to him that Lincoln Shore was a criminal, and regardless of the fact that Billy had saved his life, a cop was still a cop, and Linc would kill Billy without hesitation if he found out that Billy was working undercover for the ATF. It was an argument they'd had at least a dozen times, and it wasn't worth having now, not while his hands caressed her body and his lips probed behind her ear.

Changing the subject, she said, "Nice mug, by the way."

"What?"

"That... thing. It's a mug, right? Or it was. What'd you do? Drop it in a deep fryer?"

His hands and mouth stopped moving across her body. In the glow from the television screen, she saw his eyes, confused. She sat up and pointed at the unfinished ceramic piece on the coffee table. He practically threw her off his lap, bolting to his feet.

"Where's my knife?"

"What?" Gretchen said.

His eyes tracked across the coffee table. Wallet, mug-like thing, keys. He pointed. "My knife was here."

All Devil's Blade members—prospects or patches—carried a blade.

"Are you sure you—"

He cut her off. "It was right here." He turned and looked at her, lowering his voice. "Gretchen, remember when I showed you how to use the Ruger upstairs?"

She nodded, an unpleasant tingle filling her stomach, spreading to her chest.

"Go to the bedroom and get it. Meet me in the foyer. Go fast."

"Are you sure that's nece—"

His voice remained quiet but held a firmness that almost sounded panicked. "Just do it," he told her.

She raced back to their bedroom. The drawer of Billy's nightstand slid out with a groan. Her fingers scrambled along its undersurface until they found the tiny key. She put it between her teeth and climbed onto the bed. Over the headboard hung a painting they'd bought at a local arts festival. A small wooden boat, floating empty on the still surface of a lake at dusk. As quietly as she could, Gretchen lifted the painting off the wall, gaining access to the built-in wall safe behind it. It took three tries for her trembling fingers to get the tiny key into the lock and open the safe.

The Ruger wasn't there.

Panic rolled through her, a cold sweat filming her skin. She scrambled back to the living room, pulling up short in the foyer when she saw Billy standing stiffly in the doorway. It took her a moment to realize what was wrong. His hands. They were behind his back. The long barrel of a gun pressed against his temple. Before Gretchen had a chance to focus on the black form beside Billy, the beam of a flashlight blinded her.

A voice she didn't recognize said, "Hello, Gretchen."

Billy said, "Run!"

CHAPTER 36

Denton, Pennsylvania

PRESENT DAY

Josie waited for Hummel to arrive. She took a photo of the Wawa travel mug with her cell phone and let him bag it and take it into evidence. They went over the photos the team had taken the day before. The mug was in the same place—so it hadn't been moved or touched by anyone on their team. All the way back to the station, the mysterious mug nagged at her. It hadn't seemed important at all the day before, but that was the thing with crime scenes—you just never knew what might turn out to be of critical importance. It was exactly the reason they'd asked Robyn to do the walk-through. Once Josie got to her work station, she phoned a contact in the state police crime lab and called in a favor. Across from her, Noah's desk was empty. She hoped he was sleeping. As she sat down at her desk, she noticed a small pastry box from Komorrah's Koffee. Inside was a cheese Danish. Her favorite. Noah must have left it for her before he went home. It was his way of trying to smooth things over, but Josie wasn't sure it was enough. It bothered her that he was so quick to believe that Gretchen was a murderer.

Still, she was hungry, so she ate the Danish and then tried calling Jack Starkey, the ATF agent on Gretchen's list of references. His outgoing message still said he was out of town at a conference. Josie left another message. Then she looked up the number for the ATF office in Seattle and called. She got another agent who told her the same thing Starkey's voicemail had told her. He was away. She left her cell phone number and asked the agent if he could get in touch with Starkey and ask him to call her right away.

Josie called down to holding to see if Gretchen was still there, but she was gone. The sheriff's deputies had come to transport her to the county jail in Bellewood while Josie was meeting with Robyn Wilkins. Not that Josie could have spoken to her. Loughlin was due to take a confession later that day, and Gretchen was represented by counsel. With a sigh, Josie returned to her regular duties, spending a couple of hours writing up reports on the Wilkins case. Dr. Feist called to let her know that the autopsies didn't turn up any surprises. As they suspected from the scene, Margie Wilkins had been sexually assaulted and strangled, and Joel Wilkins had been bludgeoned to death; the fractures to his skull were consistent with having been struck with a crowbar. It would take a few days to get the prints back, and weeks for them to test the DNA found on Margie Wilkins's body. Real police work was not at all like what people saw on television.

She took a call for a domestic disturbance where the woman decided not to press charges. After she finished up more paperwork, she got lunch. Noah still wasn't back when she returned to her desk. She used her cell phone to call Dr. Perry Larson. He answered on the third ring.

"Dr. Larson," Josie said, "I was wondering if you had had a chance to talk to the police about Ethan Robinson and to review the footage of the apartment lobby."

There was the sound of traffic in the background, then what sounded like the whoosh of an electric door, and finally silence before he spoke again. "Oh yes. The detectives were out yesterday. They took down everything, had a look around the apartment. We reviewed the footage of the lobby, and it turns out that Ethan and James left together the day that James came to Denton."

"Really?" Josie said. "Do you think you could send me the footage?"

"Of course."

He took down her email address, and a few moments later, the surveillance was in Josie's inbox. She queued it up. It was only about ten seconds long. The view was from above the door leading outside. The two men walked out of the inner door, Omar first, dressed in the same T-shirt and pants he'd been wearing when they found him in Gretchen's driveway. Ethan Robinson was slightly taller than Omar, his brown hair straight. He too wore a T-shirt and a pair of jeans, and he carried a laptop bag over one shoulder.

With a sigh of frustration, Josie reset the footage and watched it again. They walked from one door to the next. Ethan talked to Omar's back as they moved. He had been in mid-sentence when they entered the tiny foyer and appeared to still be in mid-sentence as they left it. Josie reset the footage to the beginning and replayed it, trying to read Ethan Robinson's lips. Again and again, she watched it. She couldn't tell what he was saying, but she was pretty sure it was five words.

"He's saying, 'When you get there, don't,' and then he's out the door." Noah's voice over her shoulder made her jump so violently, she knocked her pen and pad off the desk.

She swiveled in her chair, shaking her head, and bent to pick up her things. "You scared the hell out of me."

Noah was dressed in his usual khakis and Denton PD polo shirt. His hair looked freshly washed, and the intoxicating scent of his aftershave made Josie's earlier anger toward him slip just a little. He smiled. "Sorry."

"Thanks for the Danish," she said. "How can you tell what this kid is saying? You never told me you can read lips."

He shrugged and walked around to his desk, plopping into his chair. "Only a little."

"You read Gretchen's lips on the CCTV footage of her."

"I had a girlfriend once who was partially deaf. She read lips. She taught me how to do it. We used to make a game of it."

It was the first time he'd told her anything about his former girlfriends besides their names and how many there had been. He was a couple of years younger than Josie, had never been married, and hadn't had a steady girlfriend since joining the force.

Noah said, "Is that James Omar?"

"Yes," Josie said. "It's from the morning of Omar's murder. Omar and his roommate, Ethan Robinson, left their apartment together."

"But it doesn't sound like they were going to the same place," Noah pointed out. "Robinson said, 'When you get there.'"

"So, Robinson knew what Omar was doing—where he was going and why—and according to Professor Larson, Ethan is still missing."

"The Philly PD are working on that, right?"

"Yes," Josie said. Changing the subject, she told him about the walk-through of the Wilkinses' home and the mug that Robyn insisted didn't belong to Joel and Margie Wilkins.

"You have a photo of it?" Noah asked.

Josie pulled it up on her phone to show him.

"No one from our team brought this to the scene," he said.

"Hummel and I double-checked. It was there when the ERT arrived."

"There were two travel mugs in the dish rack if I remember correctly," Noah said.

"Right. The Mr. and Mrs. mugs."

"But only one beside the coffee maker."

"Because it's not theirs and they didn't put it there," Josie confirmed. "There is the slight possibility that a friend or houseguest brought it to the house and that's why it's there."

"But why next to the coffee maker?"

"Right," Josie said. "Makes no sense. I think the killer brought it and left it there."

"On purpose?"

"It would be a strange thing to do intentionally, but I'm inclined to think so. This guy was seen by no one, had the foresight to toss their phones into the toilet, and managed to control two victims. There's some degree of sophistication there. It's hard to believe he would just accidentally leave his clean, empty coffee cup at the scene. At two a.m."

"Well, he did leave the murder weapon," Noah pointed out.

"Yes, but lots of killers leave their murder weapons at the scene. Besides, he left his DNA on Margie Wilkins, so it's not a matter of him not wanting to leave behind something that has the potential to identify him. The mug is something else entirely."

"Okay," Noah said. "Let's say he brought the mug with him and left it at the scene on purpose. Why?"

"It's a game," Josie said. "I mean look, if we hadn't had the walk-through with Robyn—if she hadn't noticed the mug—we would never even know it was important. This guy killed for the sake of killing. The mug is his way of taunting us, or at least enjoying how stupid he thinks we are."

Noah leaned back in his chair, using one of his feet to swivel his chair back and forth in a semicircle as he thought about what she said. "We don't have Wawas in Denton. Wawas are in Philadelphia."

Josie said, "Right. When I was in Philadelphia, there was a Wawa practically every few blocks."

"You think the killer came here from Philadelphia," he said.

"Not exactly."

Josie used one hand on her desktop computer's mouse to pull up the electronic file on James Omar's murder, specifically the photos the evidence response team had taken inside Gretchen's house. She found the photo of the end table with the shiny circle in the dust where some round object had been. She clicked to enlarge the photo and turned her monitor toward Noah. She expected skepticism, but instead he sat forward, took a long look at the photo, and asked, "Does the size match up?"

She grinned at him. With some finagling of the mouse and computer software, she was able to pull up a photo of the same dust-free circle with bright yellow rulers alongside it measuring its size. She then pulled up a photo of the bottom of the Wawa mug she and Hummel had taken into evidence that morning. Josie had held the same yellow rulers to measure its size for the shot. On screen, she brought both photos up side by side. "Yes," she told Noah. "They're a match."

"But we have no way of asking Gretchen whether or not it's her cup," Noah said. "No way is Bowen going to let us talk to her. I mean, I guess we could get Loughlin to ask her."

Josie said, "I already called Denise Poole—my contact in the state police lab."

"I remember her," Noah said. "She'll expedite getting the prints?"

Josie nodded. "Well, she said it could be hard to get prints from a curved surface, but she'll try her best. I had Hummel drive it out to her."

Noah's eyes bulged. "Are you kidding me? Isn't that a four-hour drive? Chitwood's going to flip when he finds out."

Josie smiled. "But Lieutenant Fraley, the mug was found at the scene of a double homicide that the press is now covering. In fact, Chitwood went on television last night and told the public that we're doing everything we possibly can to find the killer."

Noah returned her smile. "Good point. So let's say we find Gretchen's prints on this Wawa mug. Then what?"

"Then we know there was someone else at her house the day that Omar was killed."

Slowly, Noah shook his head. "No, we don't. All we can infer from finding Gretchen's prints on the cup is that she was at the Wilkins scene."

Josie's heart did a double-tap. Gretchen was unaccounted for on the night of the Wilkinses' murder. Still, Josie didn't believe for a second that Gretchen had been there. "Well, we know Gretchen didn't leave semen on Margie Wilkins's body," Josie shot back. "I don't think we can infer that from her mug being found at the scene."

Before Noah could respond, Chief Chitwood's voice boomed across the room from where he stood in the doorway to his office. "You two! Loughlin's here. She's got Palmer's confession. Get your asses down to the conference room."

CHAPTER 37

Gretchen had given Detective Heather Loughlin a handwritten confession. It was terse, the handwriting a scrawl. Josie knew Gretchen's handwriting—it was usually neat and precise. Josie could practically feel the tension and desperation oozing from the hastily written words. She and Noah read it over while Loughlin sipped coffee and Chitwood paced near the head of the table. When they were finished with it, Josie handed it to Chitwood, who barely glanced at it.

Josie asked Loughlin, "Do you believe her?"

Loughlin shrugged. "It doesn't matter what I believe. She confessed. She had an answer for everything."

Chitwood tossed the pages onto the table, and Noah picked them up once more. "She says she met Omar in Philadelphia a few years ago. That's pretty vague."

"A few years ago, Omar wasn't even in Philadelphia," Josie said. "He lived in Idaho and did his undergrad in Indiana. He started at Drexel after Gretchen had already left Philadelphia to come work here."

"So what?" Chitwood said. "She had friends in Philadelphia. Maybe she met him when she went back to visit. Maybe she's got her timeline mixed up, and she saw him last summer."

Josie was fairly certain Gretchen had not been back to Philadelphia since her move to Denton, even for a visit, but she had no way of proving that, so she kept quiet. Instead she asked Loughlin, "Where did Gretchen say they met?"

"Jogging along the Schuylkill—he was jogging, not her. She says he bumped into her and knocked her down. She hit her head. He helped her get up, find a bench, and sit. They talked, and when he found out she was a cop, he had all kinds of questions about the job. She had a headache and didn't feel like talking, so she gave him her number and said he could call her any time if he had questions about police work."

"That's pretty thin," Josie said.

Loughlin shrugged. "I have no reason to disbelieve her, although her story about him being interested in her position as a police officer seems like just that—a story. I don't know that she's telling the truth about how they knew one another. But she says he tracked her down here, and she felt threatened by him, especially by the fact that he had driven two hours to her home."

"What did she say the altercation was about?" Noah asked. "All this says is she asked him to leave multiple times, and he refused and became combative."

Josie looked over his shoulder at the confession again. It was written in the broadest and vaguest terms possible.

"She says for some reason he had become obsessed with her. She doesn't know why and said she doesn't believe it was a sexual thing, but that him showing up at her home without an invitation felt very intrusive and threatening. She says he'd been harassing her by phone for two weeks."

Josie remembered that the phone records from Gretchen's phone showed only two calls from Omar's number to hers. That hardly constituted harassment.

"If she thought he was harassing her," Josie asked, "why didn't she report it?"

"Like I said," Loughlin replied, "I don't think she was being truthful about whatever it was between them. I think maybe whatever was going on—she was embarrassed and thought she could make it all go away on her own, and when it went south, she ran."

"You think they were having a sexual relationship?" Noah asked, and Josie could tell by the skepticism in his voice that he was having an equally difficult time envisioning Gretchen carrying on some kind of affair with a college student in his early twenties.

Loughlin shrugged. "Stranger things have happened."

Noah pointed to the second page of the confession. "She disabled the MDT and threw it, as well as her and Omar's phones and her gun, into the river. Then she 'drove around' for a few days before she decided to turn herself in. She wouldn't say where she went?"

Loughlin shook her head. "She got agitated when I pressed her on it."

"Why did she park on the block behind her house when she went to meet Omar?" Josie asked. "Did she tell you? And what about the photo of the boy? Did she say who it was and why she pinned it to Omar's collar?" She snatched the pages away from Noah and riffled through them. "She doesn't mention the photo of the boy at all."

"I asked her about it," Loughlin said. "About both of those things, actually. She said she parked on the block behind her house and snuck onto the property from the back because she was afraid Omar might be dangerous, and she wanted to assess the situation before she made herself known."

"And the photo?" Josie asked.

"She said she found it on the ground near Omar after she shot him. She assumed that it was his and had fallen out of his pocket, so she pinned it to his shirt."

"Where did she get the safety pin?" Josie asked.

"Her grandmother's sewing kit, she said," Loughlin answered.

"You're telling me she snuck up on this kid, they argued about something, she felt 'threatened,' so she shot him in the back as he was leaving, and then she went back into her house to dig up a safety pin so she could fix the photo she says fell out of his pocket to his shirt?"

Loughlin frowned. "Yeah, that does sound thin. But why would she confess to killing this kid if she didn't do it?"

That was what Josie hadn't figured out yet. Without even thinking, Gretchen had confessed to cold-blooded murder. But why?

Chitwood said, "She shot this kid. Maybe she's not being honest about why or how they knew each other, but she had prior contact with Omar. They were both at her house at the time of the shooting. The bullet they dug out of his back was the same caliber as Gretchen's service weapon. Plus, she confessed. Wrap it up. You've got the Wilkins homicides to work."

Chitwood strode out of the room. The three detectives slowly ambled into the hallway.

"Heather," Josie said. "What about her jacket? Did you ask her where her jacket was?"

Heather nodded. "She said she lost it."

There was no way in hell Gretchen lost her jacket. But Josie was tired of being the only one in the room arguing for Gretchen's innocence. She needed proof that someone else was there the day Omar was killed—that there was something more going on.

Josie and Noah said goodbye to Loughlin and went back to their desks. Josie picked up the receiver of her desk phone.

"Who are you calling?" Noah asked.

"The only person besides Gretchen who would have any idea what Omar was really doing here on the day he was killed is Ethan Robinson."

"The roommate? He's missing."

"Yeah, but his dad's not."

CHAPTER 38

Doug Robinson answered on the fourth ring. He sounded rushed and a bit flustered as Josie introduced herself once again and asked him if he'd heard from his son yet. "Uh, no," he said. "I got the police in Philadelphia trying to find him. I told them I'd call them right away if he turned up, but I know he won't turn up at my house."

"Why is that, Mr. Robinson?" Josie asked, seizing the opportunity to ask the questions that had been nagging at her since they first spoke.

"What do you mean?"

"The last time we spoke, it seemed like you felt there was some kind of rift between the two of you."

He gave a long sigh. "I think I told you that his mom passed when he was in high school."

"Yes, I remember," Josie said.

"Well, they were real close. Always. After she died, he found out…"

He broke off, and Josie listened to his breathing for a long moment—not sounds of grief or sadness she realized, but frustration.

"Mr. Robinson?" she coaxed.

"I love my son, okay?"

"Of course."

"But after my wife passed, he found out that we had adopted him. As a baby. My wife never wanted to tell him. At least, not while he was still a kid. I thought that once he was old enough to know what being adopted meant, that we should tell him. He was always a real curious kid, you know? Real smart. Always asking questions. Always down at the library reading books way above his grade level. You know, when he was twelve, we found him reading books about serial killers? My wife went through the roof!"

"I can imagine," Josie said, keeping the conversation moving.

"Well, after she died, we had to go through a lot of stuff. Paperwork and things like that. He was snooping around and found some documents. He confronted me. I told him the truth."

"He was angry that you and your wife hadn't told him?" Josie guessed.

"Yeah. Really angry. I tried to tell him that it was his mom's idea to keep it from him, but that only made things worse. He said I was throwing her under the bus since she wasn't there to defend herself."

Josie could see how Ethan would think that but kept silent. "So that's what caused the tension between the two of you?"

"It hasn't been the same since. To be honest, Detective, I don't hear from Ethan unless he needs money. I call him once a week, but he never answers or calls me back. Even when he's here at home— which is not very often—he only talks to me if he absolutely has to, and most of the time he's not even home. That time he brought James with him, I thought we were making progress—James is, I mean was, a good kid—but once they went back to Philadelphia, Ethan started ignoring me again. I've tried over the years to patch things up, but he's so angry. There's no getting through to him."

"Have you contacted all your relatives to see if anyone else has heard from him? Your wife's relatives?" Josie asked.

"Yeah," Doug said. "The Philadelphia police asked me to do that straightaway. No one's heard from him."

Josie had a thought. "Do you know if he ever looked for his birth family?"

"No, not that I know of. I mean he was mad, you know, but I think it felt like a betrayal to his mom, you know? Adoption or not, she was his mother. She raised him. She loved him."

Then there was no chance that Ethan Robinson was off somewhere hiding with his biological family. Josie said, "I'm very sorry about your wife, Mr. Robinson. Thank you for speaking to me today. If you hear anything at all, you should call the Philadelphia police immediately. Then, if you wouldn't mind keeping me up to date, I'd certainly appreciate it."

"Of course," he agreed. "Hey, did you guys get James's killer yet?"

Josie hesitated. She looked across the desks at Noah, who was engrossed in something on his computer. "We're still working on it," she said.

CHAPTER 39

They grabbed a bite to eat, and when they returned to their desks, they were greeted with James Omar's phone records for the two weeks prior to his murder, and also a list of Margie Wilkins's closest friends and coworkers, which had been sent over by Robyn Wilkins. Josie made phone calls to Wilkins's friends, while Noah went down the list of incoming and outgoing phone numbers on Omar's call log and traced the owner of each number. An hour later, Josie hung up from her last call.

"No one was stalking Margie Wilkins," Josie told Noah. "At least, her friends don't know of anyone who was giving her trouble. It's a dead end."

"There's still the DNA," Noah said. "We've got the killer's DNA."

"Yes, and I might be retired by the time we get those results back from the lab. You're assuming they'll match someone already in the system. We still need leads to run down, and I've got nothing."

He beckoned her over to his desk. "Take a break then. Come see what I've got here."

Josie rolled the chair around to sit beside Noah. Before him was a list of phone numbers from Spur Mobile, all marked up in Noah's handwriting. Beside that was a stack of pages he had printed out with the names and other identifying information of various people. On top was a page with Ethan Robinson's name and phone number in the page header.

Noah pointed to what Josie knew to be Ethan's phone number, which Noah had highlighted dozens of times in pink highlighter.

"These are all incoming and outgoing texts and phone calls between Omar and Ethan Robinson."

Josie reached over and flipped through a few pages. "You couldn't get the content of the text messages?"

"You know Spur Mobile. They make you jump through a lot of hoops to get that stuff if you don't have the actual phone," Noah answered. "But I'm waiting for the content. It will just take longer."

Josie knew this was true. Different phone carriers offered varying levels of cooperation with law enforcement. Spur Mobile was the least cooperative and had the most red tape to go through. They could get the content of the text messages, but it would take a lot longer.

"What else have you got?" Josie said.

Noah went through the numbers. There were the three members of Omar's immediate family—mom, dad, and sister. There was Dr. Larson. Some of the numbers were to restaurants he'd obviously ordered takeout from. Several were from other students at Drexel University, and Noah had been able to find most of their Facebook accounts. He handed her the printouts of each person's profile page, and Josie went through them quickly. Then there were the calls to Gretchen.

"There's one call here to a volunteer ambulance company in Norristown—that's outside of Philadelphia."

Josie frowned. "That's odd." She ran her finger across the page until she found the date. "Omar called there two weeks before he was killed. It's a one-off."

"Wrong number?" Noah asked.

"Probably," Josie said. "What's this?"

There were three calls to the same number in the two weeks of records they had, including a call to the number on the morning that Omar was killed.

"It's a burner," Noah said.

"Did you try to call it?"

"Of course. It's out of service. Prepaid. Whoever was using it didn't keep up the payments."

"Can we try to triangulate its signal? Where it was last?"

Noah nodded. "Probably. I'll write up a warrant."

"What about this call to Ethan Robinson? Is this after Omar was murdered?"

Noah looked at the time and then checked his notebook. "Either it was made after his murder or right before it. We can pin down his death to within an hour window based on when Gretchen left here and when patrol first showed up, but not much more precise than that."

"But this call was made between the time that Gretchen left and patrol found Omar in her driveway."

"Yeah, but closer to the time patrol showed up. I would guess it wasn't Omar who made the call."

Josie's desk phone rang. She wheeled her chair back around and answered, "Detective Quinn."

"Hi, this is Jack Starkey returning your call."

CHAPTER 40

Josie's heart momentarily went into overdrive. Would she finally get some answers instead of more and more questions? "Hi, Agent Starkey," she said. "Thanks for calling me back."

"Well, someone on my team in Seattle called me. Said you sounded pretty bent."

"Bent" wasn't the way Josie would describe herself, but she let it go. "Well, it's important," she told him. "I'm calling about Gretchen Palmer."

"Lowther," he said.

"I'm sorry?"

"I knew her as Lowther, not Palmer."

It took Josie a moment to process what he was telling her. She knew that Palmer was Gretchen's family name, because her grandparents had been Agnes and Fred Palmer. She pulled her notebook over to her and flipped through the pages, looking for the list of contacts that Caroline Weber's mother had provided from Gretchen's mother's side. Lowther was not her mother's family name. Which only meant one thing.

"Wait a minute," Josie said. "Gretchen was *married*?"

Starkey laughed. "Yeah. She was just a kid. She was married to my buddy, Billy. William Benjamin Lowther. She must have changed her name when she moved back East."

Josie started making notes on a clean page of her pad. Across from her Noah stared, a look of curiosity mixed with disbelief lining his face. "They lived in Seattle, then?"

"Well, yeah, Billy was an agent."

"With the ATF?" Josie clarified, feeling like she couldn't quite keep up. Starkey must think she was a grade A idiot.

"Yeah. He was a damn good one too."

Josie hadn't missed his use of the past tense to describe Billy Lowther, but she put those questions aside for now. "How long were they married?"

Starkey made a low noise under his breath like he was calculating. Then he said, "I don't know. A couple of years. Not long."

"You said Gretchen was a kid. How old was she when they met?" Josie asked.

"Eighteen," Starkey said and laughed. "Believe me, we checked. Billy was on the East Coast for some training when they met. He brought her back to Seattle with him and said he was marrying her. They'd only known each other two weeks. She didn't look a day over sixteen. We wanted to make sure he wasn't getting himself into trouble."

Josie wondered why Caroline Weber hadn't told her about Gretchen's marriage. Was it possible that Gretchen hadn't told anyone? If the marriage hadn't lasted that long, perhaps she hadn't, or perhaps it had been so long ago that Caroline hadn't thought it was relevant.

Starkey went on, drawing Josie out of her thoughts. "But they were in love, boy. Big time. Billy was about twelve years older than her, but that didn't bother either one of them. They went to city hall and did the deed. Used a couple of secretaries there for witnesses."

Josie tried to imagine Gretchen as a young woman, deeply and madly in love with a man she'd only known a couple of weeks, getting married in a municipal building with no one she actually knew present except her new husband. The last part sounded like Gretchen, but the young and crazy-in-love part was simply too hard for Josie to imagine.

"It didn't work out?" Josie probed.

Starkey's voice was suddenly heavy. "Billy died."

"I'm sorry," Josie said. "What happ—"

Starkey interjected, "So what's going on there with Gretchen? I know she put me as a job reference, but since your messages sounded so urgent, I assume she's in some kind of trouble."

You don't know the half of it, Josie thought. She gave him the bare bones of an explanation: Omar was found shot in the back in Gretchen's driveway, and Gretchen had run off. She didn't yet tell him that Gretchen had returned or that she had confessed to his murder. She wanted to know what he knew first.

"No connection between Gretchen and the kid?" Starkey asked.

"None other than Gretchen worked in Philadelphia and Omar was from Philadelphia," Josie explained. "I went to Philadelphia and met with Gretchen's old partner there, Steve Boyd. We talked about a particular case Gretchen caught a couple of years before she came here. A couple of Dirty Aces had murdered two Devil's Blade members who were out here from the West Coast. Linc Shore and Seth Cole. Apparently, Gretchen really took the case to heart, worked her ass off to make sure the Aces members went to prison for life. I thought at first that maybe Gretchen was targeted by the Aces for having put their guys away, but I can't find any evidence of that. I also can't find any connection between Omar and either gang."

Starkey said, "Did you say Gretchen was the one who worked the Linc Shore case?"

"Yeah, that's what her partner told me."

"Gretchen Palmer?" he asked skeptically.

"Yeah," Josie replied. "You didn't know about Linc Shore?"

"Well, yeah, I knew he was killed on the East Coast. We work outlaw motorcycle gangs in Seattle. He was the chapter president. Something like that doesn't go down without us finding out. But I didn't follow what happened after that. We just knew the Aces took him out. That's all."

"So Gretchen never called you about the case? To get some intel on the Devil's Blade gang or find out more about Linc Shore or Seth Cole?"

Starkey erupted into a fit of laughter. He laughed so hard, he started to cough. Josie held the phone away from her ear as she and Noah exchanged a puzzled look. "Agent Starkey?" Josie said, trying to break through his laughing-coughing fit.

"The only way Gretchen Palmer would call me to get intel on Devil's Blade and Linc Shore would be if she fell and hit her head and got amnesia. Or if someone gave her a lobotomy."

Frustration bubbled up inside Josie's stomach, but she pushed it down. "What are you talking about?"

"Detective Quinn, Linc Shore and the Devil's Blade kidnapped Gretchen when she was just twenty. They held her for over a year. No one could find her. We thought she was dead. Then one day they dumped her off in front of a federal building, beaten, sliced up, and loaded with drugs."

CHAPTER 41

The air around her seemed to freeze, a bubble of perfect stillness descending over Josie. "I'm sorry," she said into the phone after clearing her throat. "What?"

Starkey said, "She didn't tell you? Well, I guess she didn't. She didn't much want to talk about it when she recovered. In fact, she wouldn't tell anyone anything."

That sounded familiar. "How do you know it was the Devil's Blade that took her?" Josie asked.

"They took her because of Billy. They found out he was an undercover agent. Gretchen was kidnapped not long after his death. We had a couple of informants who traveled in Devil's Blade circles. We worked them hard to try to find out where she was being held. No one saw her, but they knew Linc had her."

Josie couldn't even imagine what had happened to Gretchen during that year. It was interesting that even after her mother had tortured her by convincing doctors to perform unnecessary medical procedures on her, Gretchen had still been open to love—falling for an older ATF agent and running all the way across the country with him. But from what Josie could tell, once Gretchen returned to Pennsylvania after the death of her husband and her ordeal with Devil's Blade, she hadn't had any lasting relationships. Even her partner in Philadelphia's homicide department hadn't known her sexual orientation—because she had no relationships. Was it the year in the clutches of the Devil's Blade gang that had closed Gretchen off? Was that why she had booby-trapped her own windows? Were the Devil's Blade members what she feared?

But if that was true, why had she taken Linc Shore's murder so personally? Why had she helped get justice for Shore and Cole? Had she felt threatened by the gang in some way? But surely the type of justice the Devil's Blade's own members could have meted out would trump anything that Gretchen could do via the justice system. None of it was making sense.

"What did Gretchen say once she was found?" Josie asked.

"Nothing. Not a damn thing. She wouldn't talk. I told her we'd protect her, but she kept saying, 'No one can protect me.' She spent some time in the hospital, and after she got out, she decided to move back East. I always told her if there was anything I could do, all she had to do was call. I guess it was five or six years later she called me and said she wanted to go into law enforcement. She asked if she could throw my name around if she needed to, and I told her sure." He laughed. "I sure as shit didn't think that little gal would become a police officer, but I guess she did."

"She's a great officer," Josie said. "A fantastic detective."

"I guess she is if she could put aside her personal feelings and put Linc Shore's murderer away. That's some heavy shit right there."

"Do you have any idea why she would take the case?" Josie asked. "I'm trying to make sense of this. She could have passed it off to someone else easily."

"Don't know. I mean, what they did to her was horrible. A year. I don't know how she survived it. Especially after—"

He stopped. Josie waited for him to go on, but the line remained silent.

"After what?" Josie prompted.

There was a moment of hesitation. Then Starkey said, "Billy was murdered."

"I gathered that," Josie said. "You said the Devil's Blade found out he was an undercover ATF agent. I assume once they found that out, they weren't too happy about it."

"They didn't find out until after he was murdered."

"So the Devil's Blade didn't kill him?"

"No, wasn't them."

"Oh. Well, what happened?"

"Detective," Starkey said, "there are some things I'd rather discuss in person, if you don't mind."

"I don't think my chief will pay for a flight to Seattle, Agent Starkey. This is pretty pressing. If there's anything you can tell me about Gretchen's past, I need to know sooner rather than later."

"Well, Detective, I'm not in Seattle right now. I'm in New York City. If you can make your way up to me, I'll be happy to tell you everything I know. But I can't do it over the phone."

CHAPTER 42

Seattle, Washington

JANUARY 1995

The room smelled of sweat and stale cigarettes. Paint chipped away from the yellowed walls. A single lightbulb hung from a kinked wire in the center of the ceiling. A stained mattress covered half of the hardwood floor. Exhausted though she was, Gretchen couldn't bring herself to lie on it. She didn't even want to think about what it smelled like up close. The only other option was a scuffed wooden chair. A smattering of dried, rust-colored spots fell across the wooden slats in its back. She tried not to think about what—or who—had left them there. As she settled into it, she couldn't help but notice that the arms were worn right where her wrists rested. With a shudder, she placed her hands in her lap.

There was no way to tell how long she was there. No clocks adorned the ugly walls. The single window had been boarded up. No daylight seeped through. By the time Linc came for her, she had fallen asleep, her chin resting on her chest. He shook her shoulder to wake her, and she blinked up at him, eyes bleary.

"Hey," he said, leaning down into her face.

Up close, he smelled like the outdoors, like he had brought a crisp breeze with him. Under that was the faint smell of motor oil and something earthy that Gretchen had never quite put her finger on. His jeans were torn and muddy. His Devil's Blade knife hung from his left hip. A bandanna capped his scraggly black hair. She didn't need to see the top of his head to know what was on the bandanna: a white skull with bloody eyes over two crossed knives. Blade colors: black and red. His worn leather jacket made him seem much bigger than he really was.

"I'm awake," Gretchen said.

Linc stepped back, giving her some space. "You ready?"

She nodded even though every fiber of her being screamed against what she knew was to come. Linc must have seen it in her face. His eyes narrowed. "You sure about this?"

"Yes," she said weakly. Tears flowed from the corners of her eyes. She hated herself for crying, but she had learned in the last few months that she had very little control over her own body.

"You have choices," Linc said.

A strangled laugh bubbled up from her throat. "No good ones," she said.

"I could make things easier on you."

She shook her head. "I've made my decision."

He sighed and pulled his knife from its sheath. Gretchen's body shook, making one of the chair's uneven legs tap a ragged beat against the floor.

Linc said, "You gonna cry the whole time?"

Biting her bottom lip, she did her best to suck back the emotion crashing over her, to stem the tide of tears overwhelming her. *Breathe in, breathe out*, she told herself. She lifted her chin and met Linc's eyes. "Let's just get this over with."

CHAPTER 43

Denton, Pennsylvania

PRESENT DAY

As Josie jotted down Agent Starkey's hotel information, Noah came around to her side of the desk and stood behind her, looking over her shoulder. He had been paying attention to the entire call.

"You've got to be kidding me," he said when she hung up. "He wants a meeting?"

Josie sighed. "He wants me to come to New York. Says what he has to tell me he can't get into over the phone."

"That's a crock," Noah said. "What could he possibly have to tell you that he can't say over the phone?"

Josie shrugged. She pulled up the internet browser on her desktop computer and googled hotels in New York City.

"You cannot be serious," Noah said.

"Oh right," Josie mumbled. "Why am I looking for a hotel when my sister lives in New York City?"

She took out her cell phone and started tapping out a text until the heat of Noah's gaze stopped her movements. She looked up at him. His face was fixed in an expression of frustration and disbelief.

"What?" Josie said.

"You're going to drive to New York City to meet with this guy. A complete stranger."

Josie raised a brow at him. "Lieutenant Boyd, Gretchen's old partner in Philly's homicide unit was a complete stranger. So was Dr.

Larson, Omar's mentor. I managed." Her last words were sarcastic, but she couldn't help it. Noah had never patronized her or treated her like some helpless female. She wasn't about to let him start now.

Noah's face relaxed slightly. "You know I know you can handle yourself. That's not what I was implying. I just don't trust this guy. There's no reason to request a face-to-face meeting. There is literally nothing this guy could possibly have to tell you that he needs to do face-to-face."

Josie had to agree. Starkey seemed borderline paranoid to her. Either that, or he just liked the idea of inconveniencing her, or maybe he was a manipulative type. There was no way to tell from a single phone call. He had certainly been forthcoming about everything else.

"I agree," Josie said. "But I have to know what he knows. Even if it turns out to be nothing. Noah, Gretchen's life could depend on this."

"On what? You finding out what she did in Seattle when she was in her early twenties? How is anything you find out going to keep her out of prison? Josie, she confessed."

How could she explain it to him in a way that would get through? She knew Gretchen was lying. She didn't know why, but she knew there was much more to the story of James Omar's murder than the paltry confession Gretchen had offered. Josie wasn't the kind of person who could leave stones unturned. She had to gather all the information out there. She could decide later what was and wasn't useful. Maybe nothing she uncovered would be of use, but she didn't have it in her to close the book on Gretchen without exhausting every last avenue available. If there was even the slimmest chance of Josie exonerating Gretchen, she had to act.

"I'm going," she told Noah in a tone that left no room for argument.

He spun on his heel and walked out of the bullpen.

Josie looked at the time on her phone. She could be in New York City by dinnertime. She fired off a text to Trinity. *Hey, remember how you wanted me to visit you in NYC?*

CHAPTER 44

Josie stood in the center of bustling Penn Station, disoriented by the sheer number of people swarming the train station. Trinity had told her not to drive. Josie had only ever been to New York City on a class trip as a teenager. She vaguely remembered crowded sidewalks and congested streets. "If you drive, you'll spend hours stuck in traffic," Trinity told her. "Drive the two hours to Philadelphia's Thirtieth Street Station and take a train from there." Josie had followed her instructions, finding Philadelphia easy to navigate and the train ride short and uneventful. It wasn't until she got off the train in New York City and found herself swept up in the throngs of people that she began to feel a bit overwhelmed. Her late husband Ray had booked a trip for them to Disney World for their first wedding anniversary, and she'd thought that place was crowded. This made Disney World look like a ghost town.

She took out her cell phone long enough to text Trinity and let her know she had arrived. Then she wheeled her small suitcase along behind her, trying to maneuver through the swarms out to the sidewalk where she planned to catch a cab. Forty minutes later she was finally in the back of a taxi on her way to Trinity's midtown Manhattan apartment building. She checked her phone once more. Nothing from Noah. The cab pulled to an abrupt stop in front of a silvered glass building that stretched far into the sky. Just gazing up at its face made Josie a little dizzy. The driver was gone before she had even pulled her little bag onto the pavement. Trinity appeared before her as a pair of automatic doors flashed behind her.

"Hey, sis," she said, giving Josie a quick squeeze and taking control of her bag. A frown formed on her face. "What happened to your cheek?" she asked, pointing to the cut Gretchen had given Josie.

Gingerly, Josie touched the butterfly closure over it. "Long story that I don't care to discuss."

Trinity raised a brow but left it alone. "Fair enough," she said, spinning on her heel and striding toward the building.

Josie followed as Trinity wheeled the bag into the opulent lobby decorated in white and beige tones. Marble tiled floors dotted with straight-backed white leather chairs led to a set of glass elevators. They had to pass by a semicircular white security desk manned by two burly men in uniforms to reach the elevators. Trinity introduced Josie proudly, her megawatt television smile reaching ear to ear. As they stepped inside the elevator, Trinity gushed, "I can't wait for you to see my place. I just moved in a few months ago. My old place was a dump compared to this building."

Josie's phone buzzed as the elevator climbed and climbed, finally stopping on floor thirty-four. She looked at it to see a missed call from Noah. Clutching the phone in one hand, Josie tried to keep track of each turn she and Trinity made in the maze of hallways so she would be able to find her way back to the elevators when it was time to meet Jack Starkey. Josie was momentarily paralyzed by the breathtaking view that drew her gaze the moment she stepped over the threshold. An entire wall of Trinity's apartment was made of windows that gave an expansive view of the city.

"Pretty cool, huh?" Trinity asked, wheeling Josie's suitcase in and setting it next to the front door.

The view was fantastic, but to Josie, the apartment itself was small. "It's huge by New York City standards," Trinity assured her. The living room, dining room, and kitchen all seemed to be squeezed into a single space roughly the size of Josie's living room. A short hallway led to a bedroom and bathroom. The furniture was sleek and white, everything small and understated, with gold and silver accents—abstract metallic wall art, shiny satin throw pillows, and tall glass vases with willow branches reaching toward the ceiling. It was modern and elegant, and Josie could imagine it being the subject of a magazine article. One of those celebrity-shows-off-her-home pieces.

"Do you like it?" Trinity asked.

"It's beautiful," Josie said, although she preferred a more homey space where she wouldn't be so afraid to spill food on the furniture.

As if reading her mind, Trinity said, "Don't worry about getting stuff dirty. I've got wear care on the upholstery. You can pour red wine all over it and it will come out in minutes."

Josie wondered how much that cost. She moved into the living room space, where a large square of white shag area carpet held a couch, a glass-topped coffee table, and a large-screen television. "I have to call Noah back."

"Go ahead," Trinity said. "I made coffee. I'll get you some while you call him."

Josie nodded, taking a seat on the couch and dialing Noah's number as she watched Trinity busy herself in the kitchen space only a few feet away. She had rarely seen her sister so happy and carefree. It occurred to Josie that beyond their parents, who would be proud no matter what, Trinity really had no one to share her life or accomplishments with. Josie couldn't even imagine how high the rent must be for an apartment like this, but she knew Trinity had worked her butt off to be able to afford it. If they hadn't lost thirty years, they would have shared everything. Not for the first time, Josie wondered how their lives—even their personalities—might have been different if they'd been together. She thought of Dr. Perry Larson and his study of how genes expressed themselves differently, and wondered if that also applied to tastes and preferences.

On the eighth ring, Noah picked up. "Hey," he said. "I've got some news."

He didn't ask how her trip was or if she had arrived safely. It was their old rhythm. Right to the point. There was work to be done. Talking like this—like they always had—made her feel better about things between them. "Tell me," Josie said.

"The Wawa mug? It came back with Gretchen's prints on it."

A gasp lodged in Josie's throat. Part of her had been sure she was grasping at straws when she'd sent the mug to the lab for expedited processing. Even though she'd suspected the mug had been Gretchen's, she was still shocked at the hard evidence. "Anyone else's prints?" she asked.

"A partial, but the quality isn't good enough for them to run it through AFIS."

"Shit."

Trinity waved to her from the kitchen, and she stood and walked over, accepting the cup of coffee Trinity offered, prepared exactly the way she liked it. On the phone, Noah went on. "I already got Loughlin down here. We met with Bowen. Loughlin wanted to question Gretchen about the mug—at least try to confirm that Gretchen owned a Wawa travel mug—but Bowen put the brakes on everything."

"What?" Josie said.

"He's concerned that an item found with Gretchen's prints on it at a second crime scene will only do damage. He said if we want to charge her with the Wilkins murders, then we need to develop our own case. He's not going to help us by letting his client answer questions."

Josie sipped her coffee while Trinity opened a glossy magazine on the kitchen counter. Josie knew she was listening, though she pretended to be engrossed in the pages. "I guess I can see that, but there's no way we can make the leap from a mug with her prints on it to double murder. Margie Wilkins was sexually assaulted. Gretchen didn't do that."

"Bowen thinks we're going to nail her as an accomplice to the murders."

"I can see Chitwood trying to do that. What I've been saying all along is that there's someone else involved, but not as an accomplice."

"Or maybe she is protecting her accomplice," Noah suggested.

"No," Josie said instantly. Gretchen was so frightened that she would rather punch a colleague in the face and be in prison than be exonerated. Like the spikes lining the windows of her house, her actions were driven by a fear of something, not by a need to protect a murderer.

"Well," Noah said before she could start another argument between them about Gretchen's guilt or innocence, "Loughlin's going to give it another go with Bowen and see if she can't get a conversation with Gretchen."

"Keep me posted," Josie said tersely and pressed END CALL before she was tempted to have a longer conversation with him. They'd been over everything repeatedly. Nothing about either the Omar case or the Wilkins case fit—and now nothing made sense at all. Josie didn't think for one moment that Gretchen had been at the Wilkinses' house. She was certain that whoever shot Omar took Gretchen's travel mug from her home and left it at the Wilkinses' house after their murders. Why was a question she wasn't ready to tackle yet. She needed more information. She had no idea where she would get it, but she would keep kicking over stones until she found something useful. Starting with ATF agent Jack Starkey and whatever he knew about Gretchen's secret past.

"Well, that was tense," Trinity noted as Josie rinsed out her coffee mug in the tiny sink.

Josie gave a wry smile. "We're agreeing to disagree."

"Sounds fun." Trinity walked her the few feet to the door. "Oh, I should tell you. A professor from Drexel University contacted me. He's doing some kind of study. Genetics or something like that."

Josie groaned. "Epigenetics."

Trinity arched a perfectly plucked brow. "Yes, that's right. He's doing a study on twins separated at birth. The only reason I took the call is because he told my assistant he had already spoken with you."

"He did speak with me," Josie said, irritation edging her voice. "And I told him we weren't interested."

She hadn't pegged Perry Larson for the pushy type—not the kind of person who would go behind Josie's back after she had already told him no.

Trinity put one hand on her hip. "You told him 'we' weren't interested? Without even asking me?"

Josie raised a brow. "You can't possibly be interested in a twin study. No, let me rephrase. You can't possibly have time for one."

Trinity said, "Well, that is true, although he was quite compelling. Apparently, it's quite hard to find twins who were separated at birth."

"Not my problem," Josie muttered. "I've got murderers to track down."

Trinity smiled. "And I've got news to report. But in the future, maybe we could decide something like that together?"

It was hard for Josie to get used to having a sister. She touched Trinity's hand. "You got it."

"Now, go meet your mystery ATF agent and call me if you need rescuing."

CHAPTER 45

New York City was far easier to navigate on foot, even with the throngs of people filling every square inch of sidewalk and the men in polo shirts on every corner trying to sell tourist bus rides. As Trinity had instructed, Josie had asked Starkey to meet her at a restaurant not far from the apartment. It was a small pub on the ground floor of a narrow brick building sandwiched between two other tall structures. Josie found a small table in the back near the restrooms. Everything inside was shiny wood beneath hazy yellow lights. Josie checked her phone. Starkey was late. When the waitress asked if she would like a drink, she ordered a whisky sour and then immediately canceled it, ordering a Coke instead. If the waitress thought her indecisiveness was strange, she didn't show it.

Josie played with her straw wrapper and had downed nearly all of her first Coke by the time Jack Starkey finally showed up. The first thing she thought when he slid into the seat across from hers, his rotund stomach pressing against the table's edge, was that he was Santa Claus. His thick white hair was brushed back away from his face, flowing down to his shoulders. A robust white beard and mustache framed a jovial smile beneath a bulbous nose and twinkling blue eyes.

"You Quinn?" he asked.

Josie nodded, her eyes traveling down to the leather jacket he wore over a torn black T-shirt. The smell of tobacco and sweet-smelling alcohol drifted toward her. He didn't look like any kind of federal agent that Josie had ever met. But if his team routinely worked undercover with outlaw motorcycle gangs, then he looked just right.

"Agent Starkey," she said. "Thank you for coming."

He waved the waitress over and ordered a beer. "Just Starkey. Sorry to make you go through all this," he said. "A long time ago, Gretchen made me promise…"

He drifted off, his eyes glazing over just a bit, as if a sudden memory had taken him right out of the room. Josie cleared her throat to get his attention. "Gretchen made you promise what?"

"Maybe I should start at the beginning. You mind if I see your credentials?"

Josie raised a brow but replied, "I'll show you mine if you show me yours."

Starkey chuckled and took a worn wallet out of his back pocket. He tossed it over to her. The leather was warm in Josie's hands as she opened it to see his federal ID. He was considerably more kempt in his photo.

He studied hers a beat longer than she had studied his. "You were on TV," he said.

"Yes," Josie said. "Twins separated at birth. Trinity Payne is my sister. I'd really prefer not to discuss it, if you don't mind."

One of Starkey's bushy eyebrows kinked. "Twins? Nah. This was a couple years ago. All those missing girls found up there on that mountain."

The missing girls case had turned Josie's world upside down and nearly destroyed the city of Denton. "Yes," she answered. "That was me."

"Well," he said, "I can see why Gretchen would want to work with you. That's a nice gash you've got on your face there. What happened?"

Josie smiled tightly. Her fingers itched to touch the cut, but she kept them on Starkey's ID. "I fell," she lied, not wanting to get into the truth behind it. As they returned each other's credentials, Josie changed the subject. "Starkey, if you could tell me what you asked me here to tell me, I'd really appreciate it. Every moment I don't figure out what really happened with this shooting is another moment that Gretchen is in trouble."

The waitress arrived with Starkey's beer, and he gulped down half of it in one long swig. Golden droplets of liquid sparkled in his beard. He dropped the thick glass onto the table with a firm thud and said, "I'm gonna need more drinks and more information."

With a sigh, Josie replied, "What kind of information?"

He narrowed his eyes at her. "Who'd you work with in the FBI? When you caught that missing girls case."

"Why do you ask? What does this have to do with Gretchen?"

"I need someone to vouch for you," he told her.

Josie raised a brow at him. "Call my chief, then."

As the waitress brought another beer, Starkey said, "No. Someone not in your department."

"My chief is new," Josie said. "I only met him six months ago. He might as well be not in my department."

Starkey slugged down half his beer. "Nah, I'd feel better if I talked to a federal agent. That missing girls case—there was a big police-corruption scandal, wasn't there? Seems to me if the FBI got called in, they'd send someone from the Civil Rights Division. Those guys get paid to make sure everyone's aboveboard."

"You're questioning my integrity?" Josie asked, defensiveness making her skin prickle.

"I have to," he said. "It's for Gretchen's own good."

"Fine," Josie snapped. "Special Agent Marcus Holcomb. You want his number too?"

Starkey grinned. He took out his phone and stood up. "No need. I'll get in touch with him."

She watched him walk away from the table to the far end of the bar, punching numbers into the keypad on his phone. Josie clenched her fists beneath the table. She didn't know whether she should tell him off or just leave. She wanted to do both, but she couldn't shake the suspicion that this man had information that could help her sort out the mess Gretchen had gotten herself into.

After twenty minutes on his phone, Starkey sauntered back to the table, smiling. He plopped down in front of her and slurped down the rest of the beer he'd abandoned. "Talked to Holcomb," he said. "You checked out."

Through gritted teeth, Josie said, "I don't have time for games, Agent Starkey. Are you going to talk to me about Gretchen? Because if you're not, I'd just as soon get back to Denton and back to my investigation."

Starkey signaled the waitress for yet another beer. "Fair enough," he told her. "You ever heard of the Soul Mate Strangler?"

CHAPTER 46

Josie stared at him. "I'm sorry. The who?"

"The Soul Mate Strangler. He was a serial killer operating in Seattle in the early nineties."

She shook her head. "I haven't, I'm sorry. What's this have to do with Gretchen?"

He held up a hand as if to tell her to wait. Lifting the mug to his lips, he gulped down the rest of the beer and signaled the waitress for another. "Well, I guess he wasn't real famous outside of Seattle. He was never caught. In 1994, he broke into Gretchen and Billy's house, killed Billy, and raped Gretchen."

"My God," Josie said, unable to hide her shock. She hadn't been sure what to expect from Starkey, whose strange paranoia had seemed particularly bizarre, but it wasn't this.

"Yeah. She was the only one of his victims to survive."

Now, Josie thought more seriously about the drink she had declined. "Please," she said, using her straw to stir the ice cubes in the bottom of her glass, "tell me more."

Starkey looked around as though someone might overhear them, but the other patrons were engaged in conversation or in the soccer game playing on the flat screen televisions that peppered the place. "Like I said, he was active in Seattle in the early nineties. Actually, from March to March—1993 to 1994. Had the whole city in an uproar. People were freaked out. With good reason."

"Why was he called the Soul Mate Strangler?" Josie asked.

The waitress arrived with another beer, and Starkey slugged it down, nearly finishing it. He set the glass on the edge of the table and swiped a meaty hand over his beard. "Well, the strangled part you can guess—he choked all his victims. But the press dubbed him the Soul Mate Strangler because he only ever attacked couples."

A cold feeling crept up Josie's spine. "How many?"

"Seven couples."

Josie felt punch drunk even though all she had had was soda. "Jesus. Gretchen and Billy were the last?"

"No. There was one more couple in 2004."

"That's a big gap," Josie noted.

He nodded. "Ten years. It was a shock 'cause, honestly, everyone thought he was dead."

"No chance it was a copycat?"

"Nah, see, he liked to take things from one scene and leave it at the next one. He took Billy's knife when he left the scene at their house. Ten years later it turned up at the Neal crime scene—that was the name of the couple, Justin and Amy Neal—plus, everything else was the same. He disabled the power, got in through a window, tied up both victims with rope he brought with him, assaulted the female, and then strangled both."

Josie couldn't help but think of that damn Wawa cup making its way from Gretchen's living room to the Wilkinses' kitchen. And yet, Omar had been shot and Joel Wilkins had been bludgeoned—and during the walk-through with Robyn Wilkins, she hadn't noticed anything missing.

Then there was the photo of the boy running through tall grass—with the date 2004 printed on the back.

"What did he take from the Neal scene?" Josie asked abruptly, leaning into the table. A waitress shimmied past with a tray full of drinks, and Josie longed for the burn of Wild Turkey sliding down her throat. But she kept her focus on Starkey.

"Nothing. That's why we think he was done. Some people think he stopped. Gretchen said he was probably late thirties when he attacked her—although she never got a real good look at his face—so in 2004 he would have been in his late forties. A serial killer pushing fifty?"

"You think he aged out?" Josie said. "He knew he was getting older, less able to control a scene with two people, and so he somehow managed to stop himself?"

"That's a theory that's been kicked around, yeah. Some FBI shrinks say his testosterone levels would decrease as he got older, and his compulsion to assault and kill would lessen with time. Nobody knows. It's all theories. Obviously, he was able to stop for ten years. Some people think he's really dead this time. That, or he went to prison for something else. Although, if he had gone to prison, his DNA would be on file, right? He left DNA at every damn scene, and after twenty-five years, there's still no match."

Josie took out her phone and pulled up the photo from 2004 and showed it to Starkey. He took the phone out of her hands and held it at arm's length, looking down his nose and squinting. Then he said, "Hold on." A pair of reading glasses appeared from the inside of his jacket, and he perched them on the bridge of his nose so he could study the photo.

"That was found pinned to James Omar's body after he was shot in Gretchen's driveway."

He handed the phone back to her. "Never saw the kid before."

"Did the Neals have children?"

Starkey laughed so hard, his eyes watered. He put his glasses away and drank what was left of his beer. Seconds later, the waitress replaced the empty glass with a full one. He held it in one hand but didn't drink it yet. "Are you telling me that you think the Seattle Soul Mate Strangler was in your city?"

"I'm not telling you anything," Josie said. "I'm asking you if his last-known victims had children. There was something missing from Gretchen's house. A couple of days later, we caught a double homicide. A couple. The husband was bludgeoned but the wife was strangled—and raped. A travel mug with Gretchen's prints on it was found at the scene."

Starkey sipped his beer this time, regarding her over its rim with skeptical eyes. "The Neals didn't have children."

Maybe Josie was crazy thinking a serial killer from twenty-five years ago who had killed people in a city 3,000 miles away was now killing people in Denton—using methods he hadn't used before—but there were a lot of strange coincidences that she couldn't otherwise account for.

"How did Gretchen get away?" she asked. "You said she was the only person to ever survive him."

Starkey set his beer back down and nodded. His face sagged, and a bone-deep sadness shrouded him. "It was Billy. Initially, he told her to run, and she did. The killer shot Billy in the leg. Gretchen—she hesitated, and the killer caught up with her."

Josie's heart paused for two beats and then kicked back into overdrive, fluttering wildly. Her heart ached for her friend, who had been a young wife, a woman in love, trying to make a new life after her mother had spent years torturing her and her sister.

"The killer," Starkey continued, "he would have the women tie up the men and then he'd make the men lie down on the floor, facedown, and he'd put plates and glasses on their backs."

"Plates and glasses?" Josie asked.

"Yeah, like dinner plates, drinkware. Anything glass that would make a shitload of noise if you tried to roll over and knock it onto the floor. They actually didn't know what the hell the stuff was for at the earlier scenes. It wasn't until Gretchen survived and told them what went down that they figured out that's what he'd done at the earlier scenes."

"So he tells the husband if they move and try to get help and make noise—"

"That he'll kill their wives."

"Jesus."

She thought of the plastic plates, cups, and bowls in Gretchen's kitchen, and the soda burned her stomach. How horrific had the experience been that twenty-five years later, Gretchen couldn't have glass dinnerware in her own home?

"We think Billy was going to bleed out, and that he knew it, because he didn't stay put. Gretchen said eventually she heard the plates crash to the floor. The killer was done with her by then. As soon as she heard the racket, she knew he was going to kill her. She knew he was going to kill them both anyway. He hesitated for only a second, got off her long enough to go to the bedroom doorway, and she hit him over the head with a lamp. She kicked him into the hallway, closed and locked the door, and climbed out the window. By the time she got help, the killer was gone, and Billy was dead. From the condition of the living room, the police think they had some kind of confrontation, a struggle, and Billy lost. The killer shot him again in the chest at close range. It was the only time he ever used a gun. They thought he had one—that he was using it to control the scenes—but they didn't know until he got Gretchen and Billy. Gretchen gave the police a lot of good information, but it never led anywhere."

It wasn't lost on Josie that Starkey kept saying "they" and "them" and "the police." She said, "You're ATF. How do you know so much about the case?"

"Well, we kept a close eye on it. It was personal, you know?"

"Of course."

"But the main reason is I did a lot of my own digging. You see, Gretchen was always convinced that the killer was someone in law enforcement."

"ATF or Seattle PD?"

"We didn't know."

"What made her think that?"

"I told you Billy was undercover. His undercover identity was Benji Stone. He was in deep with the Devil's Blade for nearly two years when he was killed. Almost patched in. You know what that is?"

Josie nodded.

"Everyone called him Benji Stone. His driver's license said Benjamin Stone. The lease to his house was in the name Benjamin Stone. Utilities, vehicle, everything. Even Gretchen had a driver's license for Gretchen Stone. The only people who ever called him Billy were us guys."

"In the ATF," Josie clarified.

Starkey nodded. "Yeah, and in the Seattle PD. We coordinated with them on an illegal arms bust not long before Billy went undercover. Wasn't related to any biker gang. Anyway, he got hurt, had to go to the hospital. Was there a few days. So some of the Seattle guys knew him from that bust." He picked up his beer again. Josie wondered if she should have ordered an appetizer or something. Then again, this conversation was killing her appetite.

"So everyone called him Benji," Josie said. "Go on."

"When the killer heard Billy knock the plates off his back, Gretchen said he muttered under his breath. He said, 'Goddammit, Billy.'"

"So the killer knew his real name," Josie said. "Is there any chance he heard Gretchen call him that?"

"That's what I thought. Truth is we'll never know for sure, but then what happened afterward really convinced me."

CHAPTER 47

"What happened after Billy was killed?" Josie asked.

Starkey sipped on his fourth beer. "She didn't have anywhere to go, and she couldn't go back home. There was a female officer on Seattle PD, a uniform, who took pity on Gretchen. Gave her a couch to sleep on for a week or two. Then someone tried to break into the officer's house."

"Let me guess," Josie offered. "By prying open a window?"

"Bingo. That was the Strangler's MO. Anyway, Gretchen found people to stay with, but every time she moved, something would happen. Someone would try to break in, or she would get... phone calls."

"What kind of phone calls?"

"It was him. He always found out where she was, and he'd call for her—they eventually figured out he was calling from pay phones." He chuckled. "Remember those?"

"Vaguely," Josie joked.

"Well, he would call and taunt her. For a while, the police tried to use her as bait. They stayed wherever she was, waited for him to call, tried to track him. It never worked out. She came to me and told me how she thought the killer was in law enforcement. We checked out every guy we could on the Seattle PD, but none of them looked good for the Strangler. So we tried hiding her."

"The ATF?"

"Nah, not officially. It was just a bunch of us guys who knew Billy. We knew he would want us to help her. We kept moving her around, letting her stay at our houses, but the windows kept turning up disturbed and the phone calls went on. Originally, since she was such an important witness, the Seattle PD had to know where she was at all times. Then we decided we wouldn't tell them anything. That if they needed her for anything, they could call me, and I'd bring her to them. It stopped after that. That's what made us think it was Seattle PD. I mean, I guess it could have been ATF, but there were only about four of us handling her safety, and when we stopped reporting her whereabouts to the Seattle PD, the killer stopped his antics."

"But the Devil's Blade found her?" Josie asked.

Starkey signaled the waitress and asked for shots of tequila. They waited until she brought them over. Josie declined with a shake of her head. Starkey just shrugged and slugged hers down as well. "When Billy got killed," he said, "the local police responded. Things moved pretty fast, and somehow it leaked to the press that he was an undercover ATF agent. Believe me, we were not happy, but we never thought that Devil's Blade would retaliate. I mean, Billy was dead, right? He never got patched in. There was no case. No harm, no foul."

"But Linc Shore didn't see it that way," Josie said.

"Apparently not."

"How did they get to her if you were protecting her?" Josie asked, keeping her tone as non-accusatory as possible.

Starkey ran a hand over his face. The skin of his cheeks glowed red, whether from memories or alcohol, Josie couldn't tell. Maybe both. "She had to go home to pack things up. She couldn't afford rent without Billy. For a couple of days, I dropped her off at the house before I went into the office. One of my colleagues met us there and stayed with her, helped her pack up. It was tough, but she said she wanted to do it. Having someone there with her made her feel better though. She couldn't stand being there."

"I don't know how she could have," Josie said.

"On the second day, I swung by there around lunchtime to see how they were making out, and she was gone. My buddy was unconscious near the front door, bleeding from his head. I thought he was dead. They cracked his skull. He had quite a long recovery. Didn't remember a damn thing about what happened. His gun was a few feet from his body, and his wrist was broken. He never got off a shot. House was all torn up like there'd been a struggle. There was a ripped piece of a Devil's Blade bandanna in the living room. We don't know if it was Billy's from before, or if it was from her trying to fight off the Devil's Blade guys."

Again, Josie had to think long and hard about having a real drink. She couldn't imagine being so young, having just lost your husband in a brutal home invasion, being taunted by his killer, and then being kidnapped by an outlaw biker gang. On one hand, Josie wondered if any one person could truly have such horrible luck. On the other hand, Billy's undercover assignment had put him and Gretchen at risk. Had she not been married to him, and had his true identity not been leaked, she would have been able to put her life back together without the added violence and trauma.

Starkey continued, "But we found out pretty fast they had her. Like I said, through informants. I pulled out all the stops. We kept it out of the press though. We didn't want the Strangler to know we had lost the star witness against him. As far as he knew, she was still in hiding."

"But you didn't find her," Josie said. "They let her go."

Starkey nodded. The waitress returned with the bottle of tequila, and Starkey touched her arm. "I'll pay for the bottle, sweetheart," he told her.

With a smile, she put it on the table. She shot Josie a subtle raised-brow look and pointedly asked her, "Anything I can get you, Sugar?"

Josie smiled. "I'm fine, thank you. I'll let you know."

With a nod, the waitress left them, and Starkey poured more shots, drinking them down as he continued his story. "A couple times we thought we had good leads, but they didn't pan out. Then one day they dumped her in front of the building. Early morning. 'Round five a.m. Tossed her like a sack of potatoes. We had CCTV of it, but it was grainy, and we couldn't make out the license plates of the bikes. But we knew it was the Devil's Blade."

"How long did you say she was gone?"

"Thirteen months."

"Why did they let her go?" Josie asked, although she knew Starkey wouldn't really have the answer to this. Only Gretchen and Linc Shore knew why Devil's Blade had let her go after thirteen months in captivity. Linc Shore was dead, and Gretchen wasn't talking. She wanted Starkey's theory.

He took two more shots. The amber liquid of the tequila sloshed over this time and dribbled down his chin. "Don't know," he said.

Josie waited for more, but Starkey offered nothing. She said, "I'm sure they kill plenty of people. Make them disappear. Why did they let her live?"

His eyes were glassy now. Josie had lost track of just how much he had had to drink, but the tequila bottle had only a finger left in it. "I can't figure," he said. "It's always bothered me. Gretchen would never talk about that time."

She wondered if he really had no theory after twenty-five years, or if he was just too drunk now to comment. With a sigh, she said, "Why did you ask me to come here? You could have told me these things over the phone."

He reached across the table as if to grasp her hand, but Josie put both her hands in her lap. "The Strangler is still out there," Starkey said. "I mean, he could be dead, but we thought he was dead before, and he came back. With the law-enforcement connection...Gretchen was really paranoid. She made me promise if I ever talked with anyone in law enforcement about the case, that I would check them out first. No matter how much time had passed. I had to meet you. Make sure you were really who you said you were."

This sounded dubious, and he must have seen the skepticism on Josie's face, because he said, "You don't understand what it was like for her. He always found her. Always."

"What about when she moved back East?" Josie asked. "Did he ever make contact?"

"I don't know. If he did, she never told me. We lost touch..." He trailed off, his eyes tracking the waitress across the room, his tongue flicking along his lips. Josie wondered if they'd lost touch or if Gretchen had cut off contact. She also wondered if the Soul Mate Strangler had in fact followed Gretchen to Pennsylvania. If not all those years ago, perhaps more recently.

She needed more information about the killer and his victims, but clearly Starkey had reached the limits of his own usefulness.

Good thing for Josie she knew just who to ask.

CHAPTER 48

Josie watched Trinity pace the short length from one end of her apartment to the other, her cell phone pressed to one ear. Behind her, the lights of New York City dazzled, making it hard for Josie to focus on her sister. She'd been on the phone for twenty minutes, working a source she claimed knew everything there was to know about the Seattle Soul Mate Strangler. She stopped at the kitchen counter and tore a paper towel from the roll by the sink. Grabbing a pen, she scribbled something down on the towel. Finally, she said into the receiver, "I really appreciate this. Yes. You're a lifesaver. Of course. I promise."

Josie suppressed a groan. She didn't know what Trinity had promised this guy, but she was quite certain it had something to do with exclusive interviews, since that was the currency Trinity most often dealt in. Trinity ended the call and brought the paper towel over to Josie.

"What did you promise this guy?" Josie asked.

"If this helps Gretchen and solves a few cases, does it really matter?"

This time, Josie didn't bother to withhold her groan.

"Oh, it's not that bad," teased Trinity.

"Please. You're not the one who has to do these interviews. You know I hate press."

"Not press. Just information this time. He'll want to know whatever you know, before things break, if possible. He can be trusted."

Josie looked at what Trinity had scribbled onto the paper towel. A website with a username and password. "Who is this guy?"

"A very good and very useful source who has proven to be extremely discreet over the years. He also happens to be an expert on serial killers—well, the ones who haven't been caught yet. That web address will take you to a set of online forums where bloggers, journalists, and other people basically try to solve these cases by sharing information."

Josie gave her a skeptical look. "Internet trolls and loons are not what I need right now."

Trinity smiled and tapped the paper towel in Josie's palm. "No trolls. No crazies. These forums are all by invitation only, and the members are carefully vetted by my guy."

Josie thought about Starkey and Gretchen and their paranoia. "He's not law enforcement, is he?"

"No. No law enforcement allowed. He likes to maintain a 'fresh set of eyes' approach. People who come at these cases from different perspectives. Don't get me wrong—he has law-enforcement contacts, and many of the members are journalists outside of the anonymity of the forums, and they do have access to a lot of information from law enforcement. By the way, he asked that you not make any posts or comments. You may take a look around, but don't engage. He wants you to be as discreet as possible since you actually are law enforcement."

"Who is this guy?" Josie asked.

"I can't tell you that. He's a protected source. I told you, valuable. I can't compromise that. Also, when you sign in, there will be a set of rules on the home page: no public sharing, no violating the privacy of other forum members—that sort of thing. You must follow them. You understand, I hope?"

"Of course." Josie looked again at the information. "Is this some dark web stuff?"

Trinity laughed. "No, not the dark web. Although I do have a contact with dark web expertise if you need it."

"No, just a laptop will do for now."

Trinity set up her laptop at the kitchen table while Josie changed into sweats and a T-shirt. She had a feeling it was going to be a long night.

CHAPTER 49

The Cold Serial Case Forum was relatively easy to navigate, and within moments, Josie found a discussion board with several threads on the topic of the Seattle Soul Mate Strangler. There were maybe two dozen users who had contributed to the various conversations, and as she clicked through the more recent threads, there appeared to be about five or six people who regularly pitched in. The titles of the threads included everything from *Will SSMS's Brain Be Donated to Science When Caught?* to *SSMS—Dead or in Prison?*

She clicked on *Household Items Taken/Left at Scenes* and found that someone had done a very simple outline:

Victims 1 and 2, Alexandra and Martin Wrede, March 1993, taken: son's drawing.

Victims 3 and 4, Luisa and Josh Munroe, May 1993, found: Wrede drawing; taken: hot-air-balloon wind chime.

Victims 5 and 6, Mary and Tim Donegal, July 1993, found: hot-air-balloon wind chime; taken: a pair of men's glasses.

Victims 7 and 8, Travis Green and Janine Ives, September 1993, found: a pair of men's glasses; taken: Travis Green's wallet.

Victims 9 and 10, Kristen and Darryl Spokes, January 1994, found: Travis Green's wallet; taken: a mug.

Victims 11 and 12, Gretchen and Billy Lowther, March 1994, found: mug; taken: a knife.

Victims 13 and 14, Justin and Amy Neal, March 2004, found: Billy Lowther's knife; taken: nothing is said to have been taken from this scene. This is the last-known SSMS crime.

It was a strict pattern. Even after ten years, the killer had brought Billy Lowther's knife with him and left it at the scene. It was almost a compulsion. In a corner of her mind, a voice asked if she was going to be able to add James Omar and the Wilkinses to the victim list. But they didn't quite fit, did they? Not exactly.

She clicked back to the list of threads and searched again. She clicked on a thread called *Why Are There No Composites?*, which was a half dozen people complaining about why no sketches of the Soul Mate Strangler had ever been circulated by the press. Two other people replied, reminding their forum counterparts that no one except Gretchen Lowther had ever seen the killer, and when she saw him, it was dark, and she didn't get a good look at his face.

Josie moved on, clicking on a different thread called *FBI Profile*. It appeared to be the actual profile prepared by the Federal Bureau of Investigation based upon a review of materials submitted by the Seattle Police Department. A cursory glance at the lengthy report was enough to assure her that someone on the super-secret forum had indeed secured the actual FBI profile of the Seattle Soul Mate Strangler. It had been prepared over ten years earlier, after the final murders in 2004. Josie knew that sometimes when cases became old enough and cold enough, law enforcement became more inclined to release certain details about the case in the hopes that it would jumpstart the investigation. Of course, the profile, while detailed and thorough, hadn't led to an arrest.

She skimmed over the descriptions of the victims, their residences, and the analysis of the crime scenes. There was nothing that stood out to her as particularly helpful. Helpful to what end, she wasn't sure. She still wasn't sure what she was hoping to accomplish by researching the Seattle Soul Mate Strangler. Her theory that he had been at Gretchen's home, shot Omar, and kidnapped Gretchen wasn't supported by any physical evidence or even by

Gretchen herself. It also didn't explain why Gretchen would take the fall for Omar's murder rather than trying to catch the man who had killed her husband. For a moment, Josie felt doubt creep in. What if Noah was right? What if the most obvious thing was the correct thing? What if Gretchen had simply shot Omar and was now paying for it? Was she making too much of the situation? Was she trying to force something into the scenario that wasn't there because she wanted to save her friend? No, she thought. There were too many inconsistencies and unexplained coincidences. The Soul Mate Strangler was a viable lead, and if he was back on a killing spree twenty-five years after his initial crimes, and he had killed the Wilkins couple, then the DNA would prove it.

With a sigh, she moved on to the offender characteristics. Given his ability to plan and execute the crimes and control the scenes, he was believed to be intelligent. They knew from Gretchen's account that he was a tall white male between the ages of thirty-five and forty. Since no one ever saw anything suspicious, he obviously blended well in the middle-class communities from which he chose his victims. He likely drove a reliable vehicle that also would not stand out in those same neighborhoods. The report also noted that he had to have some means, since he never stole any valuables from the residences. Because of the sophistication shown from the very first crime, it was likely he had a criminal record for burglary and also probably some run-ins with law enforcement for domestic violence.

Friends, family members, and coworkers would describe him as neat and organized but also domineering, arrogant, prone to anger, and extremely manipulative. He likely had some experience either in law enforcement and/or the military and was probably a hunter. It was unlikely that he would just stop, said the analysis. He may be in jail, or was dead, or had moved to another part of the world where his crimes could not be linked to the ones in Seattle. The report went on for several pages about the probable nature of his relationships with women. The bottom line was not a surprise: the killer harbored an extreme hatred toward women.

"No shit," Josie muttered to the computer screen.

"What was that?" Trinity said as she breezed past in a silky pair of pajamas. She went to the refrigerator and took out several items that looked suspiciously like the makings of a turkey sandwich. As if in response, Josie's stomach growled.

Josie stood and stretched her arms over her head. "I was just talking to myself. Can I ask you a question?"

"About serial killers?" Trinity asked as she took two plates from her kitchen cabinet.

"No, about outlaw motorcycle gangs."

Trinity looked up from the two sandwiches she was cutting into slices, and Josie was struck by how much it was like looking into a mirror—especially at moments like these when Trinity's face was clean of all the television makeup. "We're back on biker gangs? I thought your big lead was the Soul Mate Strangler."

Josie took the sandwich offered but didn't eat it right away. "I'm pretty sure it is, but I need a break for a few minutes. Besides, there's something bothering me."

Trinity plopped into a chair at the kitchen table and bit into her sandwich, eyes on Josie as Josie mulled over the questions that had been nagging at her since she talked with Starkey.

Josie said, "If a gang like the Devil's Blade kidnapped the wife of an undercover cop in retaliation for said cop having tried to infiltrate their organization, what would they do with her?"

Trinity set her sandwich down on her plate and stared at Josie, her expression serious. "Josie," she said. "You've been in law enforcement long enough to know the answer to that. What do men like that always do to women?"

Josie knew they were both thinking of the case that had forged a tenuous friendship between them. The missing girls case. A shiver ran through Josie's body.

"Would they let her go? After holding her for a long time—a year even? Would they just dump her back off into the hands of law enforcement?"

"No," Trinity said. "They might keep her long enough to use her for whatever they wanted, but they'd kill her. Maybe there wouldn't be a body, but no one would ever see her again."

"Thought so," Josie said, biting into her own sandwich.

CHAPTER 50

Josie was still sifting through the threads on the discussion boards when the first hint of daylight drifted across Trinity's apartment. Fifteen minutes later, an alarm clock sounded from the recesses of the hallway. It was abruptly cut off a moment before Trinity emerged, her pajamas wrinkled and her hair in disarray. She squinted at Josie as if she wasn't sure what she was seeing. "Dear lord, Josie. You're still at it?"

For the first time, Josie noticed her eyes were burning and her back was achy and stiff. Blinking, she clicked on a new thread labeled *The Neal Family*. "This is the last one I'm reading," she said to Trinity. "Then I'm getting some sleep."

Trinity pointed to the digital clock on her microwave. "Better make it fast. You won't have much time to sleep before you catch your train."

"I'll sleep on the train," Josie said.

She had spent hours devouring information about the Seattle Soul Mate Strangler and all of his victims. She had abandoned the forum a few times, using her browser to search for any connections between the killer and James Omar or the victims and James Omar. There was nothing. It was easy enough to make a case for the killer having come out of retirement to murder the Wilkinses, leaving Gretchen's travel mug at the scene. She might have thought he had nothing at all to do with the Omar murder except for the photo that had been pinned to Omar's body. If she could find a connection between the Neals and that photo, she might be able to convince the chief to take her theory seriously and possibly take an important step toward freeing Gretchen.

Starkey had said the Neals hadn't had children, and from the reading Josie had done on the discussion boards so far, this was borne out. In fact, even though the murders of Amy and Justin Neal were the most recent, they were the one couple no one knew much about. The only threads she'd found to do with the Neal couple so far were centered around why the killer hadn't taken anything from their home. Some theorized that he had intended for the Neals to be his last murder, and that's why he hadn't taken any trophies. It was his signal to the world that he was finished. Other people theorized that he had, in fact, taken something, but that no one knew the Neals well enough to be able to identify the missing item.

Josie wondered if this discussion would be more of the same, but when she opened it, she saw that it appeared to be a collection of court documents. They were in PDF files. Josie clicked each one and read through it. Both Justin and Amy Neal had had criminal records. Almost all the charges were drug-related except for an assault charge, which it appeared Justin was on probation for when he was killed.

There were several more PDF files, and Josie fought fatigue as she clicked and read, clicked and read. She almost didn't bother with the last few, but she couldn't leave them. Not after she had wasted so much time already. The very last PDF was a petition for adoption. She knew at once this was a sealed, confidential court document. Whoever had gained access to it and posted it on the forum had done so illegally. No wonder the person in charge of the forum didn't allow law enforcement to peruse it.

"Coffee?" Trinity asked.

Josie had nearly forgotten she was there. "No," she said tersely. She didn't need coffee when adrenaline was shooting through her veins faster than lightning. Amy and Justin Neal had had a son, and they had given him up for adoption several months before their deaths.

Josie stood and went over to her purse, which she'd thrown onto the couch. She dug out her notepad and wrote down the names of the couple who had petitioned the court. The Neals' son's name and other information had been redacted since he was a minor, but Josie had what she needed to track his adoptive parents down. She checked the clock in the lower right-hand corner of the laptop. It was too early to start making calls. But once the sun came up and she'd had a few hours of sleep, she'd start with a call to Jack Starkey.

CHAPTER 51

Seattle, Washington

MARCH 2004

Amy Neal shrieked when her husband tore the bed covers from her body. The flashlight she'd clutched in one hand tumbled into the pillows behind her, its beam lost. Her other hand pressed a photo to her chest. "Dammit, Justin," she said. "What the hell are you doing?"

His six-foot frame loomed over the bed, a shadowy figure in the darkness of their bedroom. Her bedside clock said it was 2:13 a.m. As usual, Justin had fallen asleep on the couch. She had left him there after watching the evening news. As her eyes adjusted, she saw the hand he held out to her.

"Give me the picture, Amy."

She pushed it into the folds of her nightgown. "No."

He gave a heavy sigh. Frustration or defeat, she couldn't tell. The next thing she felt was his weight settling onto the edge of the bed. His voice was softer this time. "Amy, he's fine. We did the right thing."

Tears stung her eyes. "Did we, Justin? Is he fine with those... those strangers?"

His fingers found her bare knee and squeezed gently. "They're his parents now, Ame. You're the one who keeps obsessing over the photo. Does he look unhappy to you?"

A sob lodged in her throat. No. Their son didn't look unhappy. He looked free and healthier than he ever had under their care. "It makes me want to use again," she squeaked.

Justin's fingers squeezed again. "I know. Me too. That's why I think we should put the photo away. We need to move on."

Now the tears fell, streaking her cheeks. "How? How do you move on from your own son?"

"I don't know."

"Are you really ready to move on?" she asked.

"No, but we can't stay like this—in this constant state of…"

He trailed off. Grief. Loss. Doubt. Those were the words she knew he couldn't say. They'd only been clean a few months. They had criminal records, and Justin was still on probation. They'd given their son's foster family permission to adopt him. They knew it was best. What they hadn't known was how hard it would be.

"I saw the knife," Amy said, her voice thick and husky with tears. "What are you planning to do?"

Justin's head snapped up. "Knife?" he said. "What knife?"

"The bowie knife. You left it on the kitchen counter. Where did you get it? Who'd you steal it from?"

"Ame, I didn't bring a knife into this house. Are you crazy? What are you talking about?"

"You know what I'm talking about. Don't lie to me. We said we weren't going to lie to each other anymore."

The bed creaked as Justin stood. "This is bullshit," he said. "I don't know what you're talking about."

"Then go look!" Amy said.

Justin took one step, and then a blinding light swept suddenly across the room, cutting into both their lines of vision. The sound of a man's laughter followed it. "I have a better idea," said the strange voice. "You both stay here, and we play a game."

CHAPTER 52

New York, New York

PRESENT DAY

It was a call from Noah that woke her. Josie was facedown in Trinity's bed, drool spilling out of her mouth, when the incessant ringing of her cell phone yanked her from the warm clutches of sleep. Bleary-eyed, she fumbled for the phone on Trinity's nightstand. She saw Noah's name on the screen and pressed ANSWER, scratching out a hello.

"Are you still in New York?" Noah asked.

Josie turned her head and looked at Trinity's bedside clock. "Shit," she said. "I have to catch the train in an hour."

"Chitwood is asking questions," Noah said. "I told him you had a family issue and had to take a personal day."

"Instead of telling him I was in New York City as part of the Omar investigation?" Josie said.

"You know he wouldn't have approved it. The press are on him about the Wilkins homicide. He called in some favors to have the DNA analysis expedited."

Josie sat up and threw her legs over the side of the bed. "That's a good thing. We need to have it run through the federal database when it comes back. Listen, I'll be back in time for lunch, okay? I've got a lot to tell you, but I have to get ready to catch this train."

"Of course. Also, I got the warrant out to the phone provider to see what we can find out about the burner phone that Omar was calling in the last two weeks. They said it will take five to seven days, unfortunately. The good news is that we got Omar's text messages from the last two weeks."

A burst of energy shot through her. "What do they say?"

Noah sighed. "Nothing conclusive. You can look at them when you get back."

The energy gave way to disappointment. "Can you send them to me as a PDF? I can read them on the train."

"Sure. I'll get them over in a few minutes."

They hung up, and Josie readied herself for the day in record time, in spite of her exhaustion. She was on the curb in front of Trinity's building with her suitcase in tow a half hour later. She hailed a cab, and during the drive to Penn Station, she called Jack Starkey.

He answered sounding as though he had stayed up all night drinking. His hello was somewhat slurred. "Quinn?" he said as if he didn't believe it was her.

"Yeah," Josie said. "Listen, I'm sorry to bother you again, but I had a couple of questions."

There was silence. Then he said, "Sure, okay, but I have a question for you first."

"Okay," Josie said. "Go ahead."

Hostility filled his voice. "What are you playing at?"

"I'm sorry, what?"

"I did some internet research last night. You didn't tell me Gretchen was arrested for that kid's murder. Why the hell not? What's going on down there in central Pennsylvania?"

Josie sighed. "I didn't tell you because I didn't think it was relevant at the time."

"Not relevant?" he boomed.

"Is there something you're holding back that you want to tell me now that you know Gretchen is being charged with murder?"

"What? No. No, it's not like that. I told you what I know."

"Did you know that Amy and Justin Neal had a son?"

"A son? No, no. They didn't have kids."

"Except they did," Josie said. "A little boy. He was in foster care for years before they finally gave him up for adoption to the couple fostering him."

"How the hell do you know that?"

"I have my sources," Josie said. "Did you know the Neals had criminal records?"

"Yeah, yeah, I knew that," he replied, his voice edged with irritation. "What's this got to do with anything?"

"What if the item that the Strangler took from the Neal scene was a photo of their son?"

"Not possible."

"Why not? Who did the walk-through after their murder?"

"It was . . . it was a coworker. Someone Justin worked with."

The cab jerked to a halt a block from Penn Station. Josie handed the driver a tip, mouthed a thank you, and got out, dragging her bag along. To Starkey, she said, "A coworker? Not a parent or sibling? Not even a friend?"

"From what I remember, they didn't have anyone. Everyone in their lives had written them off 'cause of all the drug problems," Starkey said. "I think a friend came through after the funerals and had a look, but she said nothing was missing."

"So it's possible a photo could have been taken and no one would know," Josie pressed.

More silence. Finally, he said, "I guess so, yeah. You done?"

"No," Josie said icily. "I'm not. You also said when Devil's Blade dumped Gretchen in front of the Seattle ATF headquarters that she was 'cut up.' What did you mean?"

"What do you think I meant? I meant they sliced her up."

Josie passed through the doors of Penn Station, moving along with the throngs of people, and pressed the phone harder against her ear to hear Starkey over the din. "Where did they slice her up?"

"What kind of question is that?" Now he was sounding like an angry drunk, but Josie pressed forward.

"Where on her body, Starkey? She must have had cuts or scars. Where were they?"

"Oh," he said, the tension in his voice dimming. "Her abdomen. All over. All the way across and back. There were a lot. We had to take photos, you know? For our file. We had the hospital document everything. We had hoped to nail the Devil's Blade for what they did to her, but ultimately, she wouldn't help us."

"Right," Josie said. "How deep were the cuts?"

"I don't know. I mean, some of 'em were old, like the ones near her breasts. They must have been torturing her—like cutting her up—the whole time."

"Did she tell you that? Did she say all the scars were from her... ordeal?"

He gave an exasperated sigh. "Well, yeah, Quinn. That's what she told the doctors. I'd been over her file about a hundred times trying to convince her to testify against the Devil's Blade. How the hell do you think I know all this?"

"Did she need stitches on the newer cuts?"

"No, I don't think so. I mean, she was sliced up pretty good, but they were superficial. The newer ones. I remember that. Thinking how lucky she was but also how cruel they were to cut her up just enough that she would be scarred. A pretty young girl like that?"

Josie wanted to say something snarky about a "pretty young girl" preferring her life to being able to wear a bikini, but she kept quiet.

"What the hell's this about, Quinn?" he asked.

It's about the lies Gretchen's told, she thought. To Starkey, she said, "A hunch. We'll talk later."

CHAPTER 53

She felt the vibration of her cell phone in her pocket as she maneuvered through Penn Station, but she waited until she was seated on the train to Philadelphia to pull up Noah's message and read Omar's text messages. There were several pages of them. Some were between him and his family, mostly having to do with who was getting what for his mother's birthday, and whether or not he had the time or money to fly home for the weekend to see her. There were several between him and unknown numbers, but they had to do with class assignments and study-group meetings. Then there were the messages between Omar and his roommate, Ethan Robinson. Josie saw immediately what Noah meant. The two seemed to have their own shorthand. Some of them were innocuous, like an exchange where Omar told Ethan not to forget the "guac" when he picked up the Mexican food, and another where Ethan texted Omar to say he'd left a textbook behind.

Then there were several whose meaning Josie couldn't divine, like an exchange nearly two weeks earlier:

Ethan: *did u talk 2 him*

Omar: *yes*

Ethan: *what did he say*

Omar: *we'll talk later*

A few days later, there was another:

Omar: *where are you?*

Ethan: *getting food why*

Omar: *I talked to her. She doesn't believe me. It didn't go well. When will you be home?*

Ethan: *what did she say? Did you ask if she'll do it?*

Omar: *talk when you get home*

Josie took her notepad out and flipped through it, looking for the information she had jotted after she and Noah reviewed Omar's phone records. Omar had called Gretchen on the same day as the text exchange with Ethan. Josie was certain that Gretchen was the "she" the two referred to in their exchange.

There was nothing after that besides mundane, everyday exchanges until the day of Omar's shooting.

Omar: *this wasn't a good idea*

Ethan: *what's happening*

Omar: *we shouldn't have lied.*

Ethan: *you should abort. Turn around.*

Omar: *too late*

Several minutes elapsed, and then Ethan texted: *u there, bro?*

Then a few hours after that, around the time that Josie and Noah were arriving at Gretchen's house to find Omar dead in Gretchen's driveway, Ethan texted once more: *dude, u there????*

Two minutes later, there was a text from Omar's phone in response: *You fucked up.*

CHAPTER 54

"Are you out of your damn mind?" Bob Chitwood shouted.

He stood at the head of the conference room table facing Josie, Noah, and Detective Heather Loughlin. Josie had just briefed him on her trip to New York City and all she'd found out from Jack Starkey and the online forum that Trinity had gotten her access to.

Chitwood went on. "You're telling me that you think a serial killer from two decades ago on the opposite end of the country is here in Denton now?"

Josie said, "Yes."

"You think that Gretchen, a trained police officer, saw the guy who murdered her husband over two decades ago, and instead of arresting him, she let him shoot Omar and then went with him in her car?"

"No," Josie answered. "I mean, yes, I think this guy shot Omar and kidnapped Gretchen. I don't know what happened, but he obviously had control of the scene and of Gretchen. Otherwise, I'm certain she would have shot him on sight. I think he held her against her will."

"And then he let her go?" Chitwood said. "How did that go, exactly? He told her to take the fall for Omar's murder, and then he said, 'Oh yeah, Gretchen, if you could not mention that I was there that day, that would be great.' Do you hear this? 'Cause that's what you're telling me. Is that what you think?"

Josie put a hand on one of her hips. "I don't have it all worked out yet," she admitted.

"No shit!" Chitwood exclaimed. "This is some half-assed shit if I ever heard it."

Ignoring his barbs, Josie said, "That's exactly why I need to have a conversation with Gretchen."

"Not going to happen," Loughlin chirped without malice. She leaned back in her chair, legs kicked out in front of her. One of her feet rocked the chair back and forth. She looked almost bored. "Bowen isn't going to allow it, especially now."

"Then you have a conversation with her," Josie said. "You get in the room with her. I'll tell you the approach I would take."

Chitwood tapped the table with two fingers. "You're not listening, Quinn. None of us is getting in a room with Gretchen. Bowen thinks we're trying to pin the double homicide on her, and I'm not so sure we shouldn't be. We've got her prints inside the house. No alibi for that night."

"We don't have enough to charge her with the Wilkins murders," Noah said.

"We also don't have enough for Quinn's outlandish theory that someone else was involved in the Omar shooting, and if you think Bowen is going to let us talk to her when we tell him we think she's taking the fall for a serial killer, he's going to tell us to go pound sand," Chitwood said. "He'll think we're trying to nail her as accomplice—and if you can prove that someone else was there, I'm not so sure we shouldn't be. Quinn, you've got nothing to support your crazy, half-assed theories."

A soft knock sounded on the door, and Lamay shuffled in with a sheaf of papers, which he handed to Josie. With one finger, he pointed to something he had highlighted for her. It took only a few seconds for what she was looking at to register. "Wait a second," she said. "We might have something. A hair. A short gray hair was found in Gretchen's vehicle, on the driver's headrest, with the root still attached, which means we can get DNA from it."

Chitwood was unimpressed. "Quinn. Gretchen's got short hair and she's in her forties. You don't think she's got some gray hairs?"

Noah said, "She dyes it. She keeps it brown."

Josie stared at him with a raised brow. She hadn't suspected he'd be the one to notice such a thing, but she was glad that he had. Turning back to Chitwood, she said, "All I'm asking is that you expedite the analysis on this hair together with the DNA found on Margie Wilkins's body. If neither of them match the profile of the Seattle Soul Mate Strangler, and they don't match each other, then you can dismiss all my—what did you call them? *Outlandish* theories?"

Chitwood glared at her through narrowed eyes.

"Test my theory," Josie went on firmly. "If I'm wrong, I'll get on board with Gretchen as Omar's killer."

From the corner of her eye, Josie could see Loughlin's back had straightened and her eyes were locked on Josie with interest.

"This a hill you want to die on, Quinn?" Chitwood asked.

Josie thrust her chin forward. "Yes, sir, it is."

They stared at one another for a few seconds longer. Josie was gratified when Chitwood broke eye contact first. "Fine," he said, snatching the report out of Josie's hands as he passed by her. "I'll make some phone calls. See how fast we can get this done. But mark my words—I want some arrests in this goddamn Wilkins case. Yesterday. If I don't get arrests soon, you better believe I'm going to make your lives a living hell."

With that, he stalked out of the room.

Noah said, "That might be an improvement."

Josie laughed. Loughlin was still looking at them with interest. She said, "You think there's something I can say to Bowen to get him to let us have a crack at Gretchen?"

Josie said, "I think if we could just get to her, she would talk."

"She didn't talk before," Noah interjected.

"I know more now," Josie said. To Loughlin, she instructed, "Ask Bowen to give Gretchen a message."

"Which is?" Loughlin asked, taking out her notebook and pen.

"Ask him to tell Gretchen that I know the truth about Linc Shore and her year with Devil's Blade. Make sure he says Josie. If she thinks I've told everyone, she'll never talk."

Loughlin scribbled down her words, then looked back up. "Anything else?"

"No. Just ask him to deliver that message."

Loughlin stood up and tucked her notebook back inside her jacket. "What is the truth about Linc Shore and her year with Devil's Blade?"

Josie smiled. "I'm not sure yet. It's a bluff. I just know she lied about it, but I don't know why."

"How do you know?" Noah asked.

"Starkey said when they dumped her in front of the ATF building, she was sliced up all over, but that the newer cuts were superficial. They didn't even require stitches. He said some of them were old, and that she said the old ones were also from whatever had happened to her in the time she'd been gone. Six months ago, when we were working the Belinda Rose case, Gretchen showed me the old scars criss-crossing her upper abdomen. She told me they were from operations her mother convinced doctors to do on her when she was a kid."

"My God," Loughlin said.

"Her mother had Munchausen's by proxy," Noah explained.

"At first I thought maybe she didn't want to get into it with the medical staff—about her mother and her past. But I think she really just wanted everyone to believe that the Devil's Blade had badly tortured her."

"But she refused to press charges," Noah said. "So why would she care about anyone thinking they tortured her the whole time she was with them?"

"Because she was lying. I'm not sure why yet. I just know there is something more to the story of her year in captivity."

"How do you know Gretchen wasn't lying to you about the scars when she showed them to you?" Loughlin asked.

Because we were talking about toxic mothers, Josie thought. It was a sacred topic between them. Not something Gretchen would lie about. But this wasn't something she could explain to Loughlin, so she said, "It would be easy enough to prove. Her mother was convicted of murder and attempted murder. Gretchen's injuries would have been well-documented in the court records."

Loughlin nodded. "Excellent. I'm sure we can get our hands on them if we need to, but hopefully it won't come to that. I'll go talk to Andrew Bowen."

Noah and Josie watched her go, listening to the sound of her footsteps as they faded. Noah pulled out one of the chairs and sat down. "You read the text messages?"

"They raise more questions than they answer," she said.

Noah leaned back in his chair, lacing his hands together behind his head. "Omar and Robinson were planning something," he said. "But what?"

"I don't know," Josie answered. "But I'm assuming the 'she' is Gretchen."

"Has to be. But what did they lie about?"

"No idea. The problem is that the only two people who can answer that are Omar and Ethan Robinson. Omar is dead, and Robinson is missing," Josie said. "Did you send the messages to Philly PD?"

"Yeah, I got in touch with the detective there handling Robinson's disappearance. He had me email them. He was happy to have them, said he would shake down all of Robinson and Omar's friends on campus and find out if anyone knew what they were planning. He also told me that they searched Omar and Robinson's apartment, and that Robinson's phone and laptop are missing. Robinson doesn't have his own vehicle. He uses public transportation."

"What about bank accounts?" Josie asked. "Credit cards?"

"Philly PD says he has a bank account that his dad funds, and he keeps an ATM card. They had his dad check the balance. Apparently, he withdrew $3,000 the day Omar was shot. Not long after he got that last text message."

"So Ethan ran," Josie said. "He's hiding."

"Looks that way," Noah agreed. "Anyway, Philly PD said they'll let us know if they come up with anything."

"That's great," Josie said. She felt a small measure of relief knowing that Ethan's case was being actively handled. Still, there were so many unanswered questions, her head spun. She was wondering what Ethan was running from. And what had he and Omar wanted from Gretchen?

Noah glanced at the clock. "We've still got a little daylight. What do you want to tackle next?"

She focused her attention on him, letting the swirl of questions float to the back of her mind, where maybe her subconscious would use everything they already knew to tease out some answers. To Noah, she said, "I want to find Amy and Justin Neal's son."

CHAPTER 55

It took them an hour to track down the couple who had adopted Amy and Justin Neal's son back in 1994. Since Josie had taken trips to both Philadelphia and New York City in the last week, Noah got the job of cold-calling them and having one of the more awkward conversations that Josie had ever overheard in her life. He got through to them on their landline, and Josie could hear both the husband's and wife's voices through Noah's desktop phone. She imagined one of them talking on a phone in the kitchen while the other sat on a bed upstairs on the other phone.

Their son was now an adult, and they couldn't understand why the issue of the adoption was being brought up again. They had taken him on as a foster child when he was still an infant and raised him for several years before the adoption was finalized. That would explain why no one in the Neals' lives at the time of their murders knew about their son. He'd been taken from them as a baby. His adoptive parents told Noah that their son knew he was adopted, but they would prefer if the matter was not dragged into the light all these years later. As the discussion continued, Josie was glad that Noah had made the call. He was patient and calm, as always, and somehow managed to explain that a photo that might be of their son was found at a crime scene without sending their anxiety sky-rocketing. Finally, they agreed to receive the photo by email to see if the boy pictured was indeed their son. Noah read off his phone number to them three times before hanging up.

He ran a hand over his face. "It may take them several weeks to access their email and then actually view the photo," he complained.

Josie rubbed at the knots in the back of her neck, trying to loosen the tension that had built while Noah spoke with the couple. She had a lot riding on their answer. "Dear lord, I hope it doesn't take them that long."

Noah studied her. "You should go home, get some sleep," he said. "You look exhausted."

"I am, but if you think I'll be able to sleep while we're waiting to hear back about that photo or from Loughlin about getting a meeting with Gretchen, you're out of your mind."

Standing, Noah grabbed his jacket from the back of his chair. "Let's walk down to Komorrah's, then, and get some coffee."

The last rays of sunlight warmed the autumn air as they walked the two blocks to a nearby coffee shop. Stepping through the doors, Josie couldn't help but think of the last time she'd been there with Gretchen. They'd eaten pastries and discussed their abusive mothers, and Josie had felt comfort in the fact that Gretchen understood, on some level, what she was going through.

"I'm going to need a Danish," Josie said as they stepped up to the counter.

Noah smiled and started to order, but his cell phone rang. He took it out of his pocket and glanced at it. "It's about the photo," he said.

Josie waved him off and finished ordering, keeping one eye on Noah as he spoke softly into his phone on the other side of the shop. She paid, waited for their order, and found a table in the back of the dining area where it was quiet and they were unlikely to be bothered. Seconds later, Noah joined her, his face pale.

"I was right," she said.

He picked up his coffee but didn't drink. "Yeah," he said. "You were right. That photo—it's of their son. The mother gave it to Amy Neal after the adoption was final. She wanted Amy to know that he was happy."

"So the Seattle Soul Mate Strangler did take something from the Neal scene, and he's held on to it all this time."

"How else would it have ended up here in Pennsylvania?" Noah asked. "And in the driveway of his only surviving victim? He must have brought it with him to Gretchen's house, killed Omar, and left it there," Noah said.

"Then he kidnapped Gretchen, but he had to take something from the scene, because that's a compulsion for him, so he took her mug, which he then left at the Wilkins scene," Josie filled in. "And we never would have known had it not been for his connection to Gretchen."

"We never would have known had it not been for you pushing to unravel Gretchen's past," Noah said. "You were right about all of it. I'm sorry I didn't believe you, Josie."

"You mean you're sorry you doubted Gretchen."

"Yes, but I'm also sorry I doubted you."

Josie smiled at him. "It's okay. I'll let it slide this time. You've always had my back in the past. Of course, I just thought that was because you were secretly in love with me."

It was meant as a joke, but the seriousness in his face stopped her cold, a cheese Danish lingering halfway from the table to her mouth.

"It wasn't a secret," Noah said. "I was in love with you. I still am."

She gulped air. The Danish fell back onto the tray. "Noah."

"It's okay. I'm not asking you to say it back or anything like that. I know you need to move at your own pace. That's not even my point. I'm just saying I was wrong. I get what you were trying to say about us sticking together. I underestimated your relationship with Gretchen. When you care about someone, you have their back. I know that you and Gretchen have an understanding—something aside from what you and I have. I should have respected that."

Josie reached across and touched his hand. "Thank you."

The moment passed. Noah cleared his throat and said, "So what's next? Should we call Seattle PD?"

"We need a DNA match first," Josie said. "I don't want to go full throttle on this until we know for sure."

"What about Gretchen? Why didn't she just tell us it was him? Why did she confess to a crime she didn't commit?" Noah asked. "What is she afraid of?"

"That's where I'm stuck," Josie admitted. "I don't get it. I don't understand why she's protecting him."

"Maybe it's like a domestic violence kind of thing," Noah offered.

"Meaning what?"

"He terrorized her, right?"

Josie nodded.

"Broke into her home, killed her husband, raped her, and then he taunted her until she was kidnapped. Hell, maybe she ran off with Linc Shore to get away from this freak. Starkey said he kept finding her, right? He didn't find her while she was with Shore. But she's obviously still afraid of him. People don't put spikes on their windows unless they are terrified of something."

"And they don't keep only plastic dishes in their house twenty-five years after the crime if they're not still afraid," Josie mumbled.

"What's that?"

Josie told him about Gretchen's plastic dishes.

"Oh Jesus," he replied.

"Yeah, there's a lot of trauma there," Josie said.

"So maybe it's the trauma that's keeping her from turning him in. She's so afraid of him, and in her mind, he's so powerful—more powerful than any police department, especially if he's been able to track her down time and again even under police protection—that she feels safer not reporting him."

"That's what you meant by a domestic violence situation," Josie said. "A lot of times, women know the system fails them, and they think the only way to stay alive is to lie and not press charges."

Noah sipped his coffee. "We've seen what happens when things go wrong. A woman is brave enough to tell what's happening to her. She presses charges. Gets a restraining order."

"And then the guy violates it and kills her while she's waiting for him to go to trial," Josie filled in. "To other people she seems so irrational, but the threat is very real."

"Hey, remember last year on the West Coast that young teenage girl was abducted from her home?"

"Yeah, and everyone thought her dad killed her?"

"That's the one," Noah said. "He took her to another state, but when they got there, he didn't even bother trying to hide her. He started passing her off as his daughter, and she went along with it."

"Because she was completely terrorized."

He nodded. "Two people saw her and recognized her, but when they asked her if she was the missing girl, she said no, because she was absolutely terrified of him."

"I thought someone saw her walking down the street with the guy, and that's how she was found," Josie said.

"Because that person didn't ask her directly, and certainly not while he was standing right there—they got her away from him first, and after a lot of questioning, she finally admitted who she was."

"It was okay if someone else figured it out," Josie said. "As long as she wasn't the one to turn him in."

"Right."

Josie didn't have any trouble believing that the Soul Mate Strangler had twisted Gretchen's psyche into something unrecognizable, or that he had a strange hold over her even all this time later. Some traumas left much deeper wounds than others. But she wasn't entirely convinced that Noah's psychological reasoning was enough to account for Gretchen letting a serial killer go free.

"She said she was responsible for Omar's death," Josie said. "Maybe she's punishing herself."

"Maybe we'll get to ask her," Noah said as his phone chirped.

Josie's buzzed at the same time. It was a text from Loughlin to both of them. *Got you a sit-down with Gretchen. Bellewood County*

Jail. Tomorrow, 9 a.m. Be warned. Bowen is pissed. He advised against it. She wants to talk anyway.

Relief coursed through Josie. She typed back, *Thanks. See you then.*

Josie and Noah finished their coffees. She was wondering if he would ask to come home with her or for her to come home with him. As exhausted as she was, she wouldn't turn him down. Although they still had a few hours of work and lots of paperwork to do. "Better get me a coffee to go," she told Noah as she went to use the restroom.

The owners of Komorrah's kept a community corkboard in the small hallway leading to the restrooms. People advertised things like music lessons, dog walking services, and other random information. There were also flyers for community gatherings, and colorful pages advertising events that Komorrah's was hosting—sometimes bands, sometimes artists, and other times, authors held signings. It was the last one that caught Josie's eye—a flyer for an author event coming next month. The book was about the missing girls case that Josie herself had solved.

"Unbelievable," she muttered.

She hadn't been interviewed by the author for the book. As far as she knew, no one with direct knowledge of the case had been. Yet, here was someone with a book out about the case. She pushed her frustration back down to the dark place all her feelings about that case lived, and went to the bathroom. On the way out, she stopped again, considering whether or not to tear the flyer down and throw it away. Then her phone rang. It was Misty Derossi.

"I'm so sorry to bother you," Misty said when Josie answered. "I know you guys have a lot going on right now with these murders. I wouldn't ask unless—"

"It's fine," Josie said. "What's up?"

"It's work. They need someone to fill in overnight on the domestic violence hotline. I really want to do it. I had all those hours of training, and I hardly get to use them. But I need a sitter for Harris. Just overnight. He's really good now—"

Again, Josie cut her off. "Bring him over on your way in."

"Really?" Excitement filled Misty's voice.

"Of course. I'll be home. I just have to be out of the house by eight tomorrow."

"I can pick him up at seven thirty. Thank you so much."

Josie hung up and walked out to the counter where Noah stood, smiling, a cup of to-go coffee in his hand. So much for going home together.

CHAPTER 56

Little Harris Quinn was a year old, and now that he was mobile, Josie couldn't take her eyes off him for a second. His little toddler walk was still unsteady. He used her furniture to pull himself to standing and then walk from one end of the living room to the other. He'd been there for an hour, and every toy that Misty had brought with him, together with every toy that Josie kept for when he came over, was littered around the floor.

"You're just a little baby tornado," she told him as she scooped him up and squeezed him.

He squealed with delight, clapping his chubby little hands together. "Jo!" he cried.

Every time he said it, her heart skipped a beat. His father, her late husband, Ray, had been the only person allowed to call her Jo. Harris had only started doing it a few weeks earlier, and Josie knew it was because he couldn't get her entire name out. He called Ray's mother "Gam" instead of Grandma, and Misty "Ma," which had been his first word. Josie couldn't believe how quickly he was growing. He seemed to reach a new milestone every day, and every time he said a new word, there was a flurry of phone calls among the three of them, marveling over him.

Josie settled into her rocking chair with him in her lap. She handed him his sippy cup and found one of the board books he liked to read whenever he came over. As they rocked, she read it to him. He nestled closer to her, his blond hair tickling her chin. When she finished, he held up a finger and said, "More?" That was his signal for one more, meaning to read it again. She kissed his head and turned to the front of the book to start over. Her mouth read the words with all the appropriate inflection, on auto-pilot, as she had done hundreds of times before, but her mind was on Gretchen.

Strangely, after seeing the flyer for the true crime book about the missing girls case, something had started chafing at the corners of her mind. Something important about Gretchen and the Soul Mate Strangler case. She couldn't pry it out of her subconscious; not yet, anyway. She rocked Harris until he snored softly against her, then carried him upstairs to her room, where she had set up a co-sleeper crib next to her bed. He didn't wake when she laid him down.

Downstairs, she sat in the living room and listened to him breathing through the handheld monitor. If Ray could see her now. He would never believe it, but he would be happy. Not for the first time, Josie wished he could see his beautiful son. But if Ray was still alive, Josie would never have gotten to know Harris. Misty, Ray, and baby Harris would be one happy little family unit, and Josie would never have been involved in his life. She would never know what it felt like to love another soul so much that you would kill or die for him without any thought of self-preservation.

"Oh my God." She spoke the words aloud, jumping up and running over to her laptop in the kitchen. Her fingers worked so quickly, she got the password wrong three times. Muttering expletives under her breath, she finally got in, pulling up her internet browser and logging back on to the forum. It only took her a few minutes to find the thread she was looking for. She needed her phone. Back to the living room.

"Where the hell is it?"

Her hands scrabbled across the couch cushions, searching for her phone. Harris loved phones and always wanted to play with hers. She finally found it on the floor amid a set of soft blocks strewn about, covered in his sticky finger marks with only a five percent charge left.

She ran into the kitchen where she kept one of her chargers and plugged it in. Then she dialed Dr. Perry Larson. He answered right away.

"Detective?" he said. "Is everything okay?"

"I'm sorry, Dr. Larson," Josie said. "I know it's kind of late, but this is important. I need you to do something for me, and also, I have a few questions."

CHAPTER 57

Gretchen looked as though she had lost weight in just the few days she'd been in custody. Her skin was sallow, and large bags hung beneath her eyes. Josie wondered if she was being targeted by other prisoners because she was a police officer. Loughlin had asked that she be kept in solitary confinement for her own safety, but Josie knew that sometimes their requests weren't honored. She sat at a table in an interview room at the county jail, looking defeated. Her teeth scraped across her bottom lip.

Neither the district attorney nor Andrew Bowen would agree to let Josie interview her without Detective Heather Loughlin present, which Josie knew was going to happen. At least she knew that Loughlin was a good and fair detective who would be able to follow Josie's lead or take over the questioning depending on how things went. Bowen insisted on being present, and as they filed into the room, he sat beside Gretchen.

While Josie and Loughlin sat across from Gretchen, Bowen said, "I strongly recommended against this interview, but my client has insisted on it."

"We're not here to trick or intimidate her," Loughlin told him. "We're trying to solve a crime. Detective Quinn believes she can help your client."

Bowen shot Josie a nasty glare. "Oh yes, she's good at helping people, isn't she?"

"I want to talk to Josie in private, please," Gretchen said without looking up from the table.

"I really don't think that's a good idea," Bowen said.

"Andrew, please," Gretchen said.

"Gretchen—"

She looked over at him. "I'm the client. Please. Wait outside, would you?"

A muscle ticked in his jaw as he stood and stalked out of the room.

When the door closed behind him, Gretchen said, "Just Josie, please."

Josie said, "Gretchen, you know how this works. Heather has to be here. It's to protect you as much as it's to protect the Denton PD. This is the best I could do."

With a sigh, Gretchen sat back in her chair, looking up at the ceiling and blowing a breath out of her mouth. After a moment, she lowered her gaze to meet Josie's eyes. "Whatever you think you know, you're wrong," she said.

Josie took a folded sheaf of papers from her inside jacket pocket, smoothed them out on the table, and pushed them across to Gretchen.

"I don't have my reading glasses," Gretchen said.

Loughlin took a pair from the top of her head and handed them to Gretchen. "I'm in the over-forty club too," she joked lamely.

"Thank you," Gretchen mumbled.

She put them on, adjusted them on the bridge of her nose, and started reading. After a few moments, she looked up at Josie. "What is this?"

"An autopsy report," Josie answered.

"I don't understand."

Josie pointed to it. "That's the autopsy report of the last serial killer who thought he could murder people in my town."

"Well, Jesus," Gretchen said with a small shudder.

"I know the Seattle Soul Mate Strangler is in Denton, Gretchen."

What little color was left in her skin drained from her face. "No," she croaked.

"I know he was there the day Omar was shot in your driveway," Josie continued.

"No."

"I'm going after him."

"Oh God, no."

"I can do it on my own, or you can help me."

Something in Gretchen's face closed off. Her eyes left Josie's face, instead gazing at the wall behind Josie's head. A vacant look. "I don't know what you're talking about."

"Gretchen, I know about Ethan. I know he's your son."

Her mouth twisted as she tried unsuccessfully to suppress her gasp. Still, she didn't speak.

Josie said, "Tell me about Billy."

A long moment passed in silence. Gretchen's fingers folded and unfolded a corner of one of the pages in front of her. "Billy was my husband. We were very deeply in love, and then he died."

"The Soul Mate Strangler killed him."

Gretchen said nothing.

Josie tried going a different direction. "I know Billy didn't get patched in to Devil's Blade. Jack Starkey told me."

The surprise that flashed across Gretchen's face was so fleeting that Josie nearly missed it. Josie continued, "But he was close to getting patched in. He had some kind of relationship with Linc Shore, didn't he?"

Josie waited, and when Gretchen didn't answer, she said, "What happened between them?"

"How do you know there was something between them?" Gretchen asked, her voice so quiet, Josie strained to hear it.

"Because I know what Linc did for you, and he wouldn't have done something like that unless he felt somehow beholden to Billy. So what happened?"

More silence. Gretchen looked at Loughlin, who put her hands up. "This is all news to me, and so far, it doesn't seem very relevant to the Omar shooting."

Shifting in her chair, Gretchen turned back to Josie. "Billy saved his life. It was a long time before Billy died. He'd just been undercover for a few months, as a hang-around, trying to get someone in Devil's Blade to sponsor him. He was outside a store and Linc pulled up. Some lady in the parking lot had a stroke while she was driving and nearly ran Linc down. Billy saved him."

"That didn't get him patched in?" Josie asked.

Gretchen shook her head. "No. Getting patched in isn't that easy. But Linc never forgot it. He approved it when one of the other guys wanted to sponsor Billy, and every once in a while, he'd give Billy an easy assignment. He couldn't show favoritism, but Billy swore he never forgot it."

"Guess he didn't," Josie said. "After Billy's murder, how did you find Linc?"

"He wasn't hard to find. Those guys always hung around the same bar. Nearly got killed walking in there."

"Did you tell him you were pregnant?"

It was slow to come, but Gretchen nodded.

"You knew the baby wasn't Billy's?"

"No, I didn't know. I didn't think it was Billy's baby because Billy and I hadn't used any birth control or protection for two years, and I never got pregnant. But then one night…" She drifted off, unable to complete the sentence.

"Did you tell Linc that you thought the baby was the Soul Mate Strangler's?"

Gretchen nodded. "I didn't know what to do. I just wanted protection. The police couldn't do it, couldn't keep him away from me. I thought he was one of them. I knew that Devil's Blade could hide me. I heard the stories Billy told me. Serial killer or not, this guy wouldn't get past them."

"Whose idea was it to give the baby up for adoption?"

Gretchen licked her lips. "It was Linc's idea. After the baby came, I knew I couldn't stay with Devil's Blade forever. A lot of their people were getting pretty upset with me still being around, even though I was under Linc's protection. But I couldn't take the baby back with me. What if he found us? What if he found out the baby was his? I was afraid he'd kill—I was not ready to be a mom. I would have done it, gladly, but I couldn't be a mom and keep my baby safe from a serial killer. I had no resources, and I couldn't rely on the kindness of others forever."

"Why didn't you just take him back to your grandparents?" Josie asked.

"I was afraid he'd still find us. It was one thing if he found me and he wanted to finish the job, but I knew my child would never be safe if that monster knew he existed. You don't understand. You don't know—I thought my mother was evil. He made her look like a saint."

Josie thought of the Wilkins scene and of her own up-close-and-personal experience with a serial killer. "I think I can understand."

"I was young," Gretchen said. "Young and stupid. At the time, it didn't seem like I had many options. My only goal, the only thing I wanted to do, was protect my child."

"I believe you," Josie said.

"That's why we had to make it look like Devil's Blade had tortured me and then dumped me off. Word of that would get back to everyone involved in the Strangler case, from the ATF to Seattle PD, and he would hear it too. He would never even know I was pregnant. No one knew. No one ever knew until—"

She stopped speaking. A tear slid down her cheek.

"Until Ethan Robinson and James Omar figured it out. You thought Seth Cole was your son until the day James Omar called you, didn't you?"

Gretchen nodded, more tears streaming down her face.

"That's why you took the Shore/Cole murders to heart. Linc had helped you in your time of need, and you believed that Cole was your son," Josie said.

"I was so mad at Linc. He promised me that they—that my son would go to a normal home with a normal family. He had some court official in some other state on the take who owed him favors. He said she knew people who could help him push an adoption through for a couple who wanted a baby. Money changed hands. I never saw any of it. Was never involved. Didn't know anything besides what Linc promised me. I didn't want to know where he was, because I didn't want that information to ever be able to be tortured out of me."

"So when you caught the Shore/Cole murders, you found out during the investigation that Cole was adopted—"

"And I assumed he was mine. Why else would he be on the East Coast with Linc? I never had any proof, but I mourned my son, and I put his killers away."

"And then James Omar called you."

Gretchen didn't respond.

"Gretchen, we've confirmed that the photo found pinned to Omar's shirt came from a Soul Mate Strangler crime scene from 2004. We have his DNA. He left a hair in your car, and he killed a couple in Denton and left his DNA there as well."

This was a bluff, as they still didn't have the DNA results back, but Josie was confident they would both come back as a match for the Soul Mate Strangler.

Still, Gretchen did not speak.

"I couldn't figure out what Omar had to do with anything, but we knew he had called you twice, and that the last time he called you, you left the station to go meet him. We knew that he and his roommate had planned something involving you, because their text messages suggested that. We wanted to talk to Omar's roommate, but Ethan went AWOL right after the shooting. I kept wondering if whatever these kids were up to, was it completely unconnected to the Soul Mate Strangler? Did James Omar just show up at your house at the wrong time? Was it coincidence that he happened to be there at the very moment the Soul Mate Strangler finally tracked you down and came back to finish what he started in 1994?"

Gretchen remained silent.

Josie pushed ahead. "But even if that were true, why would you protect the Soul Mate Strangler? Why would you take the fall for this animal?"

"I'm responsible for James Omar's death," Gretchen said.

"You didn't shoot that boy," Josie said. "Why are you lying?"

"I'm responsible for his death."

"The person who pulled the trigger is responsible. I'm trying to help you here, Gretchen."

"Where's Ethan?"

"We don't know."

Gretchen shut back down. Josie waited several minutes for her to say something, ask a question, anything, but that vacant look had returned.

"Here's what I think happened," Josie said. "Ethan found out he was adopted in high school. It's bothered him ever since. In grad school, he meets James Omar, who is studying epigenetics. Maybe James said, 'Hey, I can help you track your blood relatives.' I think somehow, James and Ethan found you first. Not from DNA you submitted to any of these sites, but from DNA your cousins submitted—or some distant relatives. I think between the two of them, Ethan and James were able to find you by extrapolating the family tree of your relatives who have DNA profiles on one of these sites. I think Ethan realized you were a victim of the Soul Mate Strangler. You know, he was obsessed with serial killers even as a young teenager. He majored in criminology. He read books about serial cases. Did you know there is a book written about the Seattle Soul Mate Strangler?"

Gretchen didn't answer.

"There is. I looked on a forum devoted to the Soul Mate Strangler case. There's a thread about the book. I saw it when I went to Omar and Ethan's apartment. I didn't know what it was or that it was significant at the time, so last night I called their landlord and asked him to go over there and confirm it was there. So Ethan was already aware of the case. One of the other books in Ethan's collection? It was about a case that was cold for forty years before police used a DNA ancestry site to track down the killer through his distant relatives. I think he somehow made the connection, and then the two of them started doing the same thing on the other side of his family. I think they found the Soul Mate Strangler, and instead of contacting authorities, they came up with some plan to get mom, dad, and son together like some happy family—or maybe Ethan thought he could give you the closure you needed by showing up with the killer, having you recognize him, and since you're a police officer now, you could arrest him. You'd get to be your own hero. I'm not sure why Ethan wanted to get you two together, but it's clear that Ethan knew they were dealing with a cold-blooded killer. He got scared. He and James came up with the idea to send James in Ethan's place. This way if the guy went batshit crazy, James could say, 'I'm not your son,' and buy himself some time because this guy would want his real son."

Gretchen's lower lip trembled.

"Except something went wrong. Their plan backfired. Omar told you both he wasn't really your son, that it was Ethan. The Strangler shot Omar and took you. I don't know why he let you go. Maybe because he enjoys your terror—you always living in fear of him—maybe he likes to play games. But I think you made a deal with him. It's the only thing that makes sense. You would plead guilty to Omar's murder and pretend he wasn't even there if he left Ethan alone. He's holding Ethan over your head, and in the time it would take for you to find Ethan and get him into protective custody and then locate and arrest the Strangler, he could kill Ethan. Ethan knows his name, but Ethan's never met him. Ethan wouldn't know him if he walked right up to him, which makes this killer even more dangerous to your son. You think the only way to protect him is by keeping your end of this bargain you've made with him. You don't think you have a choice."

More tears streamed down Gretchen's face.

"He doesn't have Ethan," Josie told her. "Ethan is in the wind. No one even knows where to look for him—not the police, not his friends at school, not his dad. No one. The Strangler isn't going to find him."

No relief spread across Gretchen's face. She didn't believe Josie. Or, she didn't believe that Ethan was safe.

"I'm going after the Strangler, Gretchen. I can leave Omar out of it for now—until we get him, and Ethan is found safe—but he killed a couple in Denton, and he needs to go down for that."

"Please don't," Gretchen whimpered.

Josie's heart sank. "I will get him. No one else will be hurt."

"How?" Gretchen asked. "How will you get him? He's a ghost. I don't even know who he is—I saw his face and I don't know who he is."

"Ethan knows who he is—Ethan and James located him."

"You just said Ethan was missing," Gretchen pointed out.

"Then we put Ethan's photo out in the press and ask for help locating him. In the meantime, you'll give us a composite," Josie said.

"I can't. I can't do that. You can't expose Ethan like that. The killer will always be one step ahead of us." She leaned toward Josie, lowering her voice. "I think he's one of us."

"An officer?" Josie said. "Starkey told me that both of you thought that. But Gretchen, he's not an officer on our payroll. You know that."

"It's too risky," Gretchen said. "Please. Don't put my son at risk."

Josie held up a hand. "Okay, fine. Forget Ethan. You give us the composite. We'll say a witness saw him near the Wilkins scene."

Gretchen shook her head. "I can't. He'll know. He'll know it was me. Please."

Loughlin said, "If you don't help us, you can be charged with obstruction of justice."

Josie said, "Gretchen, we have to go after this guy. Do you really think he's going to keep his end of this bargain? He's a killer. Do you really think that he's just going to stop killing?"

"Do not do this," Gretchen said.

Josie stood up. "I have to do my job, Gretchen. Help. Don't help. I'm going after him."

She waited another tense moment, but Gretchen offered nothing. Finally, Loughlin sighed and stood, walking toward the door. Josie turned to follow. She heard the sound of Gretchen's chair scraping the tile, but before she had a chance to turn back, Gretchen's hands were on her shoulders. Josie barely had time to get her own hands up to protect her face as Gretchen slammed her into the wall. Josie pushed back, scrambling to try to get out of Gretchen's grasp. She heard shouting behind them, and within seconds, Loughlin, Bowen, and a guard were dragging Gretchen off. But not before Gretchen spoke into Josie's ear, her voice desperate and urgent.

She said, "I just need more time. Just a little more time."

CHAPTER 58

Josie sat in the county jail infirmary with an unused ice pack next to her on the gurney. Noah leaned against the wall across from her, arms crossed, as they waited for the doctor.

"This is ridiculous," Josie said. "I'm fine. I didn't hit my head."

"Just let the doctor have a look at you," he said.

"I'm not injured," Josie said. "She didn't injure me. It was an accident."

Noah laughed. "She accidentally pushed your face into the wall?"

"She didn't push my face into the wall. I didn't hit anything. I don't want her punished in any way."

"She's already in solitary. Now she'll just have to be chained when she has visitors."

Loughlin breezed in behind the doctor. As the doctor shined a small flashlight into Josie's eyes, Loughlin said, "She's not going to give you a composite."

"No shit," Josie said. The doctor asked her a series of questions, which she answered as quickly as she could. Finally, she was cleared to go.

The three detectives walked out to the parking lot together. Noah and Loughlin discussed the day's revelations while Josie's mind kept returning to the words Gretchen had hissed into her ear.

More time for what?

She waited until she was alone in the car with Noah to tell him what Gretchen had said, but he couldn't make sense of it either. "We should go back and ask her," he said. "Ask Bowen to ask her."

"No," Josie said. "She obviously only wanted me to hear, or she would have just said it in front of Loughlin. That was meant only for me."

"And you're telling me."

She swatted at his shoulder. "I need you to help me figure this out."

"Well, I don't know what she needs more time for. She's sitting in jail."

Josie's cell phone rang. She took one look at it and groaned. "It's Chitwood," she told Noah. She pressed ANSWER and barked, "Quinn."

His scratchy voice was just as loud over the phone as it was in person. "Quinn, you got your DNA match from the Wilkins scene. Nothing on your hair from Gretchen's car yet. The Wilkins DNA came up in the federal database as a match for this Strangler from Seattle. So, good work. Now get your ass in here, because we have to give a press conference, and seeing as this guy is a lady-hater, I think you should be the one to do it. That'll really get under his skin."

He hung up before she could say anything.

Noah said, "I heard every word. I can't figure out which part of that was the weirdest: when he said you did a good job, when he said 'lady-hater,' or him suggesting that you try to get under the skin of a serial killer."

Josie laughed, then Noah laughed, and then she laughed some more. It felt so good after the week they'd been having.

But in just a few minutes, all the levity in the vehicle leached away. They still had a murderer to catch.

"You know," Noah said, sensing the shift in mood, "I think Gretchen's going to get that time she wants."

"What do you mean?"

"I mean, does it make sense to have a press conference when we have absolutely zero leads? So we tell the public that this serial killer everyone thought was dead has struck here instead of his old hunting ground, fourteen years after his last-known murder. So what? Then he knows we know it's him. We still don't know who he is."

Josie groaned. "You're right. I'm not sure we should tell the world without having solid leads. He can just go back underground. No one will ever see him again."

"Unless we find Ethan. Ethan knows who he is—Ethan and James found him," Noah said.

"Yes, but I think all the research they did is on Ethan's computer, which he has with him. That doesn't help us."

"Okay, well Gretchen thinks the killer is Seattle PD. Can we track down any members out there who either moved East or are on vacation right now?" Noah suggested.

"We can," Josie said. "And we might have no choice but to do it that way, but if this guy is really in law enforcement, I'm not sure we should risk alerting him before we have a better handle on this situation. We make one phone call to Seattle PD, this guy finds out what's going on, and he's gone. Although…"

"What is it?"

"If this guy was law enforcement, his DNA would be in some database somewhere. They would have matched it by now."

"True."

"So maybe he's not. I need to have a look at the case materials again," Josie said.

Noah slowed the vehicle. Josie looked around and realized they were only a few blocks from the station house.

"What is this?" Noah muttered as they pulled to a stop behind a snarl of traffic. Ahead of them, patrol cars and an ambulance blocked one half of the residential street. Josie could see patrol officers loitering outside of a house.

"Pull over," she said. "We'll check it out."

Noah found a spot near the curb that they would probably never get out of with all the backed-up traffic. As they approached the house, Josie saw the ambulance bay doors were open. Inside, a woman sat on the gurney, her face battered and bloody. Owen leaned over her, gently wiping at the blood with a piece of folded gauze. Josie squinted at the woman and recognized her as the person who had made the domestic violence call that Josie handled the other day. She climbed into the back of the ambulance as Noah walked on, over to the uniformed officers.

The woman said, "I'm ready to press charges."

Josie nodded. "I'll do everything I can to help you." She turned to Owen. "Take her to the hospital so we can document her injuries."

"You got it," Owen said.

Josie began climbing out of the ambulance. "I'll meet you over there," she said.

She heard Owen telling the woman about the new women's center and the new shelter the city had just built. The difficulty the woman would have in staying safe until her husband was prosecuted was not lost on Josie.

"It used to be near the hospital," he was telling the woman. "But this new one is a lot nicer. It's a little out of the way. You know that road by Denton East…"

Josie didn't hear anything else. Her heart did a quick double tap.

She searched for Noah. When their eyes locked, he said something to the officers he'd been speaking to and walked over to her. "What's the matter?" he asked.

"Can you take this domestic?" she said. "I really need to go back and get another look at Omar's phone records."

"Of course," he said. "What's going on?"

"I think I know how to find the identity of the Strangler."

CHAPTER 59

"Quinn!" Chitwood shouted as soon as Josie entered the bullpen. He stood at his office door, white hairs floating over his head. He looked behind her. "Where's the other one?"

Josie riffled through the piles of paperwork on her desk. "Fraley? He caught a case on the way here. He has to go to the hospital to get a statement from the victim."

"So the vic is still alive?"

The phone records weren't on her desk. She moved around and started going through the reports on Noah's desk. "It was a domestic," Josie told him.

"We need to talk about this Strangler situation," Chitwood said. "I want to make sure we're all on the same page."

"So do I," Josie said. Finally, her fingers closed on the report of records from Omar's phone. "Give us a couple of hours."

Josie waited for him to protest—he didn't like giving them additional time for anything—but he merely stared at her a moment longer. Then he clapped a hand against the doorframe and said, "You and Fraley in my office in two hours. Have your shit together, you got it?"

Josie nodded and mumbled, "Got it," but her hands were already frantically flipping pages, searching for the call she'd seen on Omar's phone records the day they'd received them. The one she had dismissed as a wrong number because it was a one-off. The call to the Norristown volunteer ambulance company two weeks before his murder. Snatching up the pages, she moved back to her own desk and booted up her computer. She did a Google search for the name of the company, and when she was satisfied she knew who to ask for, she dialed the number.

CHAPTER 60

Two hours later, Josie stood in front of Chitwood's desk, a sheaf of papers clutched to her chest. Noah was on his way back from the hospital. Beneath his desk, the tap-tap-tap of Chitwood's loafer on the tile filled the room. Pointedly, he looked at the clock above Josie's head. "I don't have all day, Quinn," he reminded her.

"Noah will be here any second," she said. "Just another minute."

Before Chitwood could add anything else, Noah jogged through the door, slightly out of breath. He plopped into a chair and looked expectantly from Josie to Chitwood.

"Good of you to join us," Chitwood told him.

Noah ignored the barb and turned to Josie. "What've you got?"

"The Soul Mate Strangler is not in law enforcement," Josie told them. She handed them a collection of pages. "Today when we stopped for that domestic call, I overheard Owen telling the victim the location of the women's shelter."

Chitwood said, "Who the hell is Owen?"

"He's a paramedic," Noah said. "He works more shifts than anyone in his whole department."

"So?" Chitwood said. "Some local paramedic knows where the domestics go. What's that got to do with the Soul Mate Strangler?"

Josie said, "The Soul Mate Strangler was an EMS worker."

Both men stared at her, Chitwood with his typical skepticism, which Josie was beginning to think was just his normal face, and Noah with dawning realization.

Noah said, "They're at almost all crime scenes. Even if there's no living victims to treat, they take the bodies to the morgue."

"They talk to the police," Josie said. "And we tell them things. They're part of our team. They know almost as much as we do about violent crimes that go on in the city. I know that here in Denton, we have a great rapport with the paramedics that respond to all the scenes. It wouldn't be hard for one of them to eavesdrop on our conversations or even to get friendly with an officer and casually ask some questions."

"That's how he found Gretchen every time," Noah said, following her line of thinking. "All he would need to do is casually bring up the one living Strangler victim to his Seattle PD buddies at a scene, act concerned, ask some innocent questions."

Josie said, "The FBI profile said he is likely very manipulative. Envision it. He's at some random scene. Everyone's milling around. He gets to talking about the Strangler case. Maybe he even says, 'Man, I'm so glad this wasn't a Strangler call; that guy has the whole city on edge. I can't believe that last lady even survived,' and it goes from there."

"He'd start talking about how he was so glad she made it, and how was she doing, and his PD buddies probably thought nothing of it," Noah added. "I can see it. I mean, we're supposed to keep things confidential, but lines get blurred in those situations. I mean, we need emergency medical services workers. It's impossible to keep everything from them."

Chitwood folded his arms across his chest. For once, his voice was at a normal volume. "I'm buying," he said. "The Strangler is a paramedic. You get a list of paramedics who responded to Strangler scenes in Seattle in 1993 and 1994?"

"Better than that," Josie said. "I found him." She gestured to the packets in their hands. "Two weeks before his murder, James Omar made a single call to a volunteer ambulance company in Norristown, which is just outside of Philadelphia. I thought it was a wrong number. Why would a grad student from Philadelphia be calling a volunteer ambulance company? I called his mentor,

Professor Larson, and his dad, and asked them if he had been in any kind of recent accident or had any recent hospitalizations—any reason he might have needed to have contact with this ambulance company. There was nothing. So I looked them up, found the name of the supervisor, and called him."

"You sure the supervisor wasn't the Strangler?" Chitwood asked.

Josie shook her head. "I researched him. He's lived in Montgomery County in Pennsylvania his entire life, and he's too young to be the Strangler. He was very helpful. Didn't even demand a warrant—after I told him what was going on. He has one sixty-three-year-old paramedic who joined the company five years ago."

"Sixty-three," Noah said. "And he's doing that kind of work?"

"Supervisor says he mostly does the driving—he said he did a lot of training to learn the layout of the area. Not a lot of heavy lifting, although the supervisor says he is pretty fit. It's volunteer. Apparently, he retired early from Seattle and moved out here. He's an avid hunter."

"That was also on the FBI profile," Noah noted.

"Yes. He fits the bill." She pulled out a copy of his driver's license, which showed a white man with thinning white hair and a sharp-featured face. Piercing brown eyes stared defiantly at the camera. It looked more like a mug shot than a driver's license photo. Or maybe he only seemed chilling because Josie knew all the havoc he had wreaked on innocent people. "Ed O'Hara. I called Seattle PD and talked to someone who worked the case when the Neals were murdered in 2004. He didn't remember O'Hara, but a couple of the older guys did. They said he was always around, worked a lot. He got married in 1998 and had a daughter, but there were a lot of domestic issues, and eventually the wife took the daughter and left him."

"You mean domestic calls," Noah said. "He beat her."

"Yes."

"She's lucky she got away," Chitwood remarked.

Josie nodded. "The supervisor in Norristown says he hasn't been around for almost two weeks. They called him a few times to take some shifts, but he doesn't answer his phone. No one has seen him for days. Norristown PD has been alerted. They're going to go to his house. I also let Philadelphia PD know since this is all connected to Ethan Robinson's disappearance."

"Did you draw up a warrant?" Noah asked.

She shook her head. "Not yet. Right now, he's just a person of interest. We need a DNA sample from him to be sure."

"Or for someone to positively identify him," Noah pointed out, but they both knew that wouldn't happen.

"All right," Chitwood said, his voice still at a reasonable volume. Three horizontal lines creased his forehead. "This is going to be delicate. Let's see what Norristown PD turns up. Get his vehicle information out to every department in the state, make sure everyone's aware we're looking for him. But if we can't sneak up on this guy, I'm going balls to the wall. We're going to draw this guy out. Make it impossible for him to hide."

"Get under his skin?" Noah asked.

"Yeah," Chitwood said. "We'll put Quinn here in front of the cameras. Have her challenge him. Call him out for the little pissant he is, and then when he pokes his nasty little head out of the sand, we nail him."

Noah frowned. "Are you talking about using Quinn as bait?"

"No, I'm saying—"

"That's what you're saying," Josie said. "You want to dangle me out there, make him turn all his anger toward me, and then wait for him to come after me."

"No, no," Chitwood said. "I'm saying he won't be able to help himself. He'll feel the need to do something to reassert his dominance, to prove how superior he is, and as soon as he does that, he'll expose himself."

Chitwood must have been able to tell by the looks on their faces that they didn't believe him. He sighed with frustration. "Don't you remember that guy in Kansas? The police publicly challenged him, and so he sent them some computer disk that they were then able to trace back to his location."

Josie thought of Margie Wilkins's sightless eyes. "This guy isn't the type to send flash drives. If he gets riled enough, he's going to kill. We can't protect every person in this city."

"I thought you liked the aggressive approach," Chitwood said.

Josie gave him a wry smile. "I've learned over the years that the smart approach works better."

"Well, I think the smart approach is to challenge this guy. Draw him out. If you're worried about retaliation, I'll put a unit on you. Or you can stay with Fraley, and I'll put units on both your houses. You've got twenty-four hours to see if Norristown or Philly PD turns him up. Tighten everything up. Get your ducks in a row. Tomorrow, Quinn gives a press conference, and we go after this animal."

CHAPTER 61

The day was interminably long, and even after she had gone home and escaped the bustle of the station and the piles and piles of paperwork on her desk about the Omar and Wilkins murders, Josie still had the horrible feeling she was headed toward certain doom. It wasn't the press conference. As interim chief, she'd given press conferences nearly once a week. She'd been on *Dateline* with Trinity three times. It wasn't even the idea that the killer might come after her. Getting his face and name out into the press would go a long way to finding him. She was guaranteed national press coverage thanks to Trinity. There was a good chance he would be apprehended wherever he was in the country before he even thought about targeting Josie.

She just felt like she was missing something.

What had Gretchen meant when she asked for more time? Time for what?

Moving through the living room, she picked up all of Harris's toys. She had been so enthralled in her revelation and her phone call to Dr. Larson the night before, she hadn't even bothered to straighten up. She went upstairs and broke down the co-sleeper, taking a moment to smell the sheet after stripping it from the mattress. It smelled just like him. Like sunshine, fresh air, and fruit.

Back downstairs she turned on the television but didn't watch it. Her mind brimmed with thoughts about the various cases and Gretchen and her son. She wished she could get it to shut off. Normally in this situation, she would down a half bottle of Wild Turkey and fall asleep on the couch in a perfect, contented, dreamless slumber. Instead, she called Noah. When he answered, she said, "I'm home alone."

He said, "I'll be there in twenty."

He was there in ten. He wasn't even completely through the front door when she rocked up onto her toes and kissed him, hooking her arms around his neck and pulling him down to her. Their hands and mouths were frantic, as though their very lives depended on these moments. By the time they reached Josie's bedroom, they'd left a trail of discarded clothing from the foyer, up the steps, and down the hall. Noah's skin was hot against hers. As he lowered her onto the bed, he pulled his head back, looking into her eyes. There was an excruciating stillness in the air around them.

"What?" Josie asked.

"Are you sure about this?"

She had, in fact, never been more certain about anything in her life. She realized then that she hadn't called him to distract herself from dark thoughts or demons. She didn't want sex to blot out her anxiety. Sure, a distraction from work was welcome, but she had asked him over because she wanted to be with him.

"Yes," she said. "I'm sure."

CHAPTER 62

The first hint of daylight, gray and indistinct through her blinds, blanketed Josie's bedroom. Noah turned away from her to study the large bank of windows across from the bed. "We've been up all night," he said.

Josie stretched her arms over her head and turned onto her stomach, resting her face on her pillow. Beneath the tangle of sheets, Noah's hand found the small of her back and stroked up and down her spine. "Marathons aren't known for their brevity," she joked.

He laughed. His head disappeared beneath the sheets, and a moment later she felt his hot mouth against her bare shoulder, working its way down. She closed her eyes and sighed with contentment. For the first time in months, her head felt remarkably clear, and it had started already to work back through what she knew about Gretchen's case, the Strangler, and the Wilkins murders.

"He's going to kill Ethan Robinson," she said.

She felt Noah's mouth pause. His head popped up, and he pulled the sheet back so his face was exposed. "If this is your idea of pillow talk," he said, "then I think we need to reevaluate this relationship."

Josie laughed. She turned over so she could meet his gaze. "I'm sorry. Sex helps me think better."

Noah gave a deep belly laugh, his sides shaking. Josie slapped lightly at his chest. "Hey," she said. "It's not funny. You don't feel clearer-headed afterward?"

"No, I feel sleepy. Well, except for now."

His index finger traced the skin over her collarbone. She watched him for a long moment as his hands explored her. The scar on his right shoulder where she'd shot him during the missing girls case drew her eyes. She touched it gingerly.

Noah said, "Ethan knows O'Hara's identity. He has to kill him."

Their hands continued to move along each other's bodies, a slow study. Making up for lost time, she supposed. "So why would Gretchen make a deal with the Strangler to let Ethan go as long as she takes the fall for Omar's murder? She can't speak for Ethan. There's no guarantee that he won't go to the police."

"Well, he hasn't," Noah said.

"But why? Why wouldn't he? He's been studying serial killers since he was a teenager. He read the book about the Strangler. He knows exactly what O'Hara is capable of, and he must know that O'Hara killed James. Why wouldn't he go directly to the police?"

"Maybe he feels guilty. He probably convinced Omar to arrange this meeting between Gretchen and the Strangler, and if he didn't convince him, he still let Omar do it, and now his friend is dead."

"True," Josie said. She thought about what Gretchen said about being young and stupid. Ethan was only in his early twenties. Josie had no idea what kind of person he was or how he handled stress. "So let's say that Ethan is just young and dumb. But that doesn't account for why Gretchen would think that O'Hara would let Ethan live. She must know. She must realize that O'Hara knows this kid knows who he is and that he could turn him in at any time."

"I'm sure she does. But we know she asked you for more time before going public with this whole thing, so obviously she's up to something."

"Like what?"

She felt him shrug beneath her hands. She hadn't expected an answer. He had access to all the same information she did. She asked another question that she didn't expect him to answer: "What the hell could she be up to?"

"She told you that all she cared about then and all she cares about now is protecting her child," Noah reminded her.

Then.

She sprang up, nearly elbowing Noah in the face as she did.

"Hey," he said. "What's going on?"

"I know where Ethan Robinson is," Josie said.

She jumped out of bed and went to her dresser, pulling out clean clothes. "Get dressed," she told him.

"Are you serious?"

"Do you really need to ask that question?"

CHAPTER 63

The station house was relatively quiet as they entered through the lobby with coffees from Komorrah's in hand and made their way up to their desks.

"I need those phone records again," she said.

"Gretchen's or Omar's?" Noah asked, setting his coffee down and starting to thumb through the piles on his desk.

"Omar's," Josie said, searching her own desk for a copy.

"Got it," Noah said. He plucked the packet from his desk and brought it around to where Josie stood.

She flipped through until she found the call. It was the last call, made from Omar's phone to Ethan's phone in that undefined length of time between Gretchen leaving the station to meet Omar at her home and the first patrol car arriving at her home to find Omar dead in the driveway. "This was Gretchen," she told Noah, pointing to the call. "Not O'Hara. Somehow, she was able to get alone or at least out of earshot of O'Hara, gain access to Omar's phone, and call Ethan. Look, the call is four minutes long."

"How long does it take to disable the MDT?" Noah asked.

"I don't know, but if O'Hara was the one who did it, it would have taken at least that long."

"So Gretchen's alone in the car with the phones while O'Hara's prying the external antenna off and tossing the whole thing into the river," Noah said.

"Right," Josie agreed.

"What does she tell Ethan?" he asked. "She's got four minutes. What does she say?"

"She tells him to do what she did when she was his age. When she was young and stupid and needed protection from this guy. She tells him to go to Devil's Blade."

Noah stared at her for a long moment. When he didn't say anything, Josie said, "Think about it. It's the most fail-proof plan she could possibly come up with. She knows Devil's Blade will hide him. That's why she needs more time. O'Hara is so arrogant, he thinks he's getting over on her. He's probably out there looking for Ethan right now so he can kill him. As soon as she knows Ethan is safe, she'll come clean."

She watched her words sink in. His brow furrowed. "What do we do?" he asked. "We just call up the Seattle chapter of the Devil's Blade and say, 'Hey, we're looking for this kid'?"

Josie laughed. "No. I have a better idea. Ethan's way in with Devil's Blade must surely be through the man and woman who gave Gretchen the jacket. I've got to call Steve Boyd with Philly Homicide and see if he knows their names, or if he doesn't, see if he can get them. Linc's people were at the trial every day, he said. Then we find them."

CHAPTER 64

Boyd didn't know the man or the woman's name. He promised to do everything he could to find them out and get back to her as soon as possible. In the meantime, Josie went back to philly.com to read the articles about the murders and the trial that she had seen before, searching for any mention of Linc Shore's wife or girlfriend or any other Devil's Blade member. There was nothing. She called Jack Starkey to see if he or any of his ATF contacts knew Linc's old lady or anyone else particularly close to Linc. As it turned out, Linc had had several old ladies and several close associates in the gang. Josie suggested narrowing the list down to anyone who would have had a significant enough presence in Linc's life to travel to Philadelphia for his killer's trial. Starkey said he'd get to work and get back to her.

The morning had slipped past while she and Noah made phone calls and tried to follow the Devil's Blade lead to locate Ethan Robinson. It was close to noon when Chitwood appeared beside her desk. "Quinn," he said. "We're doing this press conference."

"Chief," she said, "please. Another day or two. I think we can locate Ethan Robinson. He'll be able to positively ID O'Hara as the Strangler. He's got the DNA evidence. We can issue a warrant."

"I can't give you any more time, Quinn," Chitwood told her, his voice shockingly gentle. "We need to go after this guy. He killed three people in this city in the span of a few days. The longer he's out there, the greater the odds he'll kill again. We need his face on every television and website in this country. Someone will recognize him. By that time, we'll have found the Robinson kid. We can't wait on this."

Across the desks, Noah gave her a nod. She would have liked to have Ethan Robinson in her custody before setting the media loose on Ed O'Hara, but she certainly felt better knowing they had viable leads for finding him. It was only a matter of time. The sad truth was that Ethan was probably safer under the protection of the outlaw motorcycle gang than police departments who might not have the resources to protect him long-term—or on his own.

"Okay," Josie said.

Chitwood patted her shoulder. "We'll pregame in an hour. Press will be here in two."

*

Josie hadn't been in front of cameras for months, and she didn't miss it one bit. In the twenty-four hours since Chitwood had decided to call the press conference in the first place, he had managed to alert nearly the entire world that the double murder committed in central Pennsylvania a week earlier was connected to a cold serial case. By the time the press conference rolled around two hours later, they had to move it to the municipal parking lot to make room for all the reporters. Cameras and lights pointed at Josie as she stood behind a podium with the Denton PD crest on it. She'd tried to cover the cut on her face with makeup, but she knew it would still stand out.

Still, she did as Chitwood suggested. After she went over the Wilkins murder and the evidence that connected their case to the cold Seattle Soul Mate Strangler case, and identified Ed O'Hara as their person of interest, she pulled herself up straight and tall, looked directly into the sea of cameras as if she were looking into the killer's face, and delivered a message meant for him. "Your time is up. This is the end of the road. We know your name. We know where you live. Your reign of terror is over. Make this easy on yourself and your victims: turn yourself in. Make no mistake, I will not stop until I've caught you and put the cuffs on your wrists."

She didn't take questions. As she walked back into the building, the lack of sleep from the night before caught up to her. By the time she got to her desk, she felt like she could put her head down and go right to sleep there for six hours. Lucky for her, Noah had a mug of coffee waiting. He set it down before her and she thanked him.

"You did great out there," he said. "We'll wait until the press clears out, and then we can grab a bite to eat and get out of here."

"Sounds perfect," Josie said, smiling.

"My place tonight?"

She realized he hadn't gone home to change the entire day. "Absolutely."

CHAPTER 65

They called it a day early, went to Noah's house, and collapsed into his bed. Too exhausted to fool around, they both fell deeply asleep. When she woke, it was dark outside, and a glance at the clock showed they'd been sleeping for four hours. Beside her, Noah lay flat on his back, snoring lightly. She leaned over and traced the line of his jaw, then ran her fingers through his thick brown hair. It was something she wanted to do often but, of course, never could because they were work colleagues. Now, everything had changed.

Smiling, she woke him with a kiss.

An hour later they were showered and dressed in sweats, sitting at Noah's kitchen table together, a smorgasbord of Chinese takeout spread before them.

"This," Noah said, stabbing a piece of sweet-and-sour chicken with his fork. "This is nice."

"The food?" Josie teased.

"No," he replied, waving his fork around. "This. Us. Together with no interruptions. Finally."

He was right, of course, but Josie knew it was only a temporary reprieve. At any moment one or both of their phones would ring—hopefully with a lead or good news about Ethan Robinson. Gretchen's whispered words about needing more time still pricked at the back of her mind. It was like gravel in her shoe. Every time she thought she got it out, she'd start walking again, only to be stabbed in the sole of her foot once more.

"I know that look," Noah said.

She blinked and focused on his face, on the sexy stubble that had grown in that day. "What look is that?"

"You're thinking about work." He took a bite of rice. He wasn't angry or even annoyed, and she loved him for that.

"I'm sorry," she said.

He smiled. "Don't be. I know you can't help it. So, tell me, what's on your mind?"

She sighed and selected an egg roll, picking at its flaky skin. "I feel like I'm missing something."

"Still?"

"Shouldn't Ethan be with the Devil's Blade by now?" she asked. "It's been a week."

"Hard to say," Noah said. "We're assuming he had to go to the Seattle chapter. We don't know how much instruction Gretchen was able to give him. Maybe it was just a name. He had to get to Seattle and locate some man or some woman and then convince them not to let Devil's Blade kill him. Gretchen asked for more time. She must be expecting some sort of notification either from this kid or from Devil's Blade."

"I still think there's something, something important, that we haven't figured out yet."

"I'm not sure there's anything we need to figure out. We know who killed Omar. We know why Gretchen lied. We know who killed the Wilkins couple. We know the identity of the Soul Mate Strangler, and we even have a damn good idea where to find Ethan Robinson."

Josie put her egg roll back down. He was right, of course, but she was still bothered. Noah put his fork on the table, stood, and walked over to her, extending a hand. "Come on," he said. "Let me help clear your head."

Josie laughed. She took his hand and let him lead her upstairs.

CHAPTER 66

Josie woke to the sound of her cell phone beeping. She reached across Noah's sleeping form to snag it from his bedside table. The screen cast a blue glow across the entire room. The time read midnight. It was Trinity. *I think we should do the twin study with Larson. It might give us access to whatever programs and techniques these kids used to track down a serial killer. Btw, good job on solving the case.*

Josie sighed. She typed back, *It's late. I'm not doing the twin study. And thanks.*

A minute later, a reply came back. *I've never known you to sleep.*

Josie glanced at Noah. *I'm going to start trying.*

Think about the twin study. Larson says it's extremely hard to find twins separated at birth. We can really help and all it requires is doing some interviews.

Josie tapped back: *You're just looking for a story on using DNA to find killers.*

Trinity: *I'm always looking for a story.* Followed with a smiley face emoji with its tongue sticking out. *Let's just do the study.*

Josie typed: *NO!!!*

Trinity: *Ok, we'll talk later.*

"Oh for God's sake," Josie muttered.

She read back over the exchange, smiling in spite of herself, and the piece of the puzzle lodged in the back of her mind loosened and fell into place. Epigenetics. The twin study. Twins separated at birth. "Holy shit," she said aloud. How had she missed it? It had been there the entire time, right in front of her face.

"Noah," she said, shaking his shoulder.

He moaned in his sleep.

"Noah, I figured it out. I know what Gretchen was hiding."

He mumbled a few sleepy words and turned over onto his stomach. She thought about waking him so she could tell him, so they could discuss it, but decided against it. As shocking as the revelation was, there wasn't a damn thing she could do about it until the morning anyway. But now her adrenaline coursed through her veins, setting her whole body on fire. She tried to go back to sleep, listening to Noah's even breaths, feeling the warmth of his body radiate toward her. After twenty minutes, she gave up and padded downstairs. She'd stayed at his house during the Belinda Rose case enough times that she didn't need to flip on the lights. The overhead light outside on the front stoop illuminated the foyer just enough, and the clock on the cable box in the living room gave off enough glow for her to make her way through the rooms and into the kitchen.

She had just stepped into the doorway of Noah's kitchen, her fingers on the light switch, when alarm bells sounded in her head. In her mind, she traced her steps back past the living room, then the foyer. The foyer. In the dull lamplight from outside, she had seen the table where they normally deposited their keys. Tonight, they had been so exhausted they'd discarded their holsters with their service weapons there as well. Noah had also left his phone. But when she had passed by it in the dark, the only thing that lay there was an old leather jacket.

Her breath froze in her body. Her throat constricted. Her fingertips trembled against the light switch.

A leather jacket. Gretchen's jacket.

Which meant that Ed O'Hara, the Seattle Soul Mate Strangler, was inside Noah's house.

CHAPTER 67

Her mind worked frantically, going over all the things she had learned from the forum and from Jack Starkey. Even the Wilkins scene. The flashlight. He would have a flashlight. Disorienting his victims in the dark using the beam was part of his MO.

Josie flipped on the kitchen light. She wasn't going to let him have the element of surprise. In her chest, her heart raced so fast it set her entire body to vibrate. Slowly, she walked across the room and opened a cabinet, taking out a glass, still trying to act natural while she figured out what the hell to do. She could leave. She could climb out a kitchen window, run out the back door. But she couldn't leave Noah inside the house. She couldn't leave him behind. Noah's phone was gone, as were their guns. Her phone was upstairs in the bedroom. She thought about the unit that Chitwood had promised. Were they still out there? Had the killer hurt them, or had he snuck in through the back of the house without them noticing? She had to assume that O'Hara had done something to them and that they would not be able to come to the rescue. Squeezing the glass in her hand, she thought about how she would do it—if she wanted to render two police officers powerless without actually discharging a weapon. There were plenty of ways to do it if someone was ruthless enough or manipulative enough—and Josie knew that O'Hara was both of those things.

Loosening her grip on the glass, she dropped it on the tile. It shattered, the sound like a gunshot in the small room. She felt a piece of glass lodge in her calf. Reaching into the cabinet, she took out two more glasses and dropped those as well. Shards of glass flew everywhere, more lodging in the skin of her feet and legs. When she had shattered every drinking glass, she went for the plates.

"Josie?" It was Noah's voice.

With bloody bare feet, she edged around the corner of the room to avoid the glass as much as she could. At the doorway she could see that he had turned on the hall light that illuminated the upstairs hall, the steps, and a portion of the downstairs.

Barefoot and bare-chested in boxer shorts, he trudged down the steps, eyes bleary with sleep. He stopped three steps from the bottom. "What's going on?"

Josie smiled. "I'm so sorry," she said. "I was trying to get something from the back of the cabinet, and there was an avalanche of dishes."

He scratched his head, still looking at her in the low light.

Silently, hoping his lip-reading was as good as always, she mouthed, *He's here. He took our guns. My phone is upstairs.*

She saw his shoulders tense, watched the fatigue in his face recede and every line of his posture sharpen with the realization. "Oh," he said. "Well, let me help you clean it up."

He mouthed, *Where?*

"No," she said, holding up a hand. "I've got this. You go back to bed."

I don't know, she responded silently. Wherever he was—the foyer, the living room, or perhaps even the dining room that Noah never used—he was listening to their entire exchange, this she knew. Would he wait until he had them both together to strike? Were they putting themselves at risk even standing here this long, talking?

"Are you sure?" he asked.

You go, Noah mouthed.

He wanted her to leave. To go out the back door, a kitchen window. To get out.

I'm not leaving you, she responded.

"Yes," she said. "I've got this."

My phone is upstairs, she urged him.

She couldn't leave him behind. She'd never walked away from a fight in her life. She wasn't about to run from this one and leave the man she loved behind to face a monster who killed as easily as he breathed.

"Okay," he told her. "I'll see you up there."

He made the shape of a gun with his right hand, the barrel pointed toward the ceiling. There was another gun upstairs. He just had to get to it.

Go, she mouthed seconds before she felt the cold, hard barrel of a gun pressed against the base of her neck and a meaty hand clamp down on her shoulder. Noah's face registered shock and a fleeting panic before hardening into anger.

The voice behind her said, "Why don't we invite Noah to join us?"

The sound of Noah's name on O'Hara's lips sent a shiver through Josie's body. Her heart stopped and kicked on, stopped and kicked on again. How long had he been there? What had he heard? Had he been hiding in the house when they were making love? Discussing the case? He had been perfecting his stealth for decades.

"Get away from her," Noah snarled, moving down a step.

O'Hara laughed. Josie felt his breath against her hair. "I don't think so, son. Your lady and I are gonna have a good time together. I'm gonna show you how it's done. So why don't you just stick around?"

Josie was making calculations. She had to assume that the unit outside was not in a position to come help them. Still, this was a residential neighborhood, and Noah's nearest neighbors would very likely hear a gunshot if he was to start shooting them. Then again, he had shot James Omar in the back in broad daylight on a residential street, and no one had even come to investigate.

But he hadn't used a gun in any of his crimes, except for when he murdered Billy Lowther, and that was because things didn't go according to plan. That was over twenty years ago, when he still wore a cloak of anonymity. His back was against the wall now. The whole country was looking for him. If he wanted to kill them and get away, he would have to keep some of his impulses in check. Plus, he would have limited time. When the unit outside failed to check in with dispatch within an hour, the Denton PD would send another unit out to investigate. Josie had no doubt O'Hara would use the gun, but hopefully only as a last resort. Still, she wasn't about to let him assume control of the situation.

She met Noah's eyes. *Get down*, she mouthed.

CHAPTER 68

O'Hara pushed her forward, closer to Noah. "Now, what we're gonna do is stick together. You'll get something that your girlfriend here can tie you up with, and we're gonna come with you so you don't get any ideas about being a hero. You try anything, anything at all, and this bitch is dead. You got that?"

Josie kept her eyes locked on Noah. He gave her a small nod, barely perceptible. Silently, she counted down for him: *Three, two, one.*

Noah dove off the steps onto the floor, and rolled out of sight into the living room. At that instant, she felt O'Hara's grasp on her shoulder loosen and the barrel of the gun slip to one side just a fraction. The outside of her right heel ran up along his jeans as she lifted her foot, using it as a guide so she didn't miss when she brought it down hard on the top of his foot. With the sneakers he wore, it wasn't enough to cause any pain, but it surprised him for just a second. In one fluid movement, she reached across her chest and seized his hand, clasping the pinky side and twisting his wrist. He cried out in pain, and she lifted his hand off her shoulder and slipped her body beneath it, twisting it violently up his back as he stumbled. The gun fell from his other hand, and Josie kicked it away. She slammed him into the wall, but he was strong, and he bucked back against her. His head flew back, striking her in the forehead so hard, she saw stars. She lost her grip on his hand, and he used the wall as leverage, pushing back against her.

She flew, her back striking the opposite wall before she slid down to the floor, dizzy and disoriented. He was on her then, pushing her onto the floor, straddling her, his hands closing around her throat. She clutched at his fingers. A hazy darkness hovered at the edges of her vision. Her lungs screamed, and the pressure on her windpipe was unbearable. As O'Hara squeezed harder, Josie felt her hold on consciousness slip. Although it was probably only seconds since he'd climbed on top of her, it felt like an eternity. As her body struggled to draw air, to break his grip, fear prickled over every inch of her skin. Where the hell was Noah? Then, suddenly, O'Hara was completely still. His grip loosened. Josie sucked in a breath. She saw Noah standing behind O'Hara, a gun pointed at the man's head.

"Get away from her," Noah said.

O'Hara put his hands in the air. Josie gulped the air and rubbed her bruised windpipe. She wriggled, trying unsuccessfully to get out from under him.

"Stand up," Noah instructed. "Keep your hands where I can see them."

O'Hara didn't move.

Normally, they would be telling a suspect to get on the ground, but Josie was underneath O'Hara, and try as she might, she could not get out from under him. His hips pinned hers to the floor.

Noah's voice rose to a shout. "I said, stand up! Right now, O'Hara. Stand up, keep your hands in the air."

O'Hara remained motionless. Finally, Noah said, "That's it." He took one hand off his weapon, grabbed O'Hara by the back of his collar, and started to push him over, off Josie and onto his right side. O'Hara seemed compliant at first, but with lightning speed, one of his hands balled into a fist and flew backward, striking Noah's wrist.

A gunshot exploded in the small hallway. The muzzle flash burst across the semidarkness. Josie felt a release of the pressure on her pelvis and scrambled to her feet. Noah and O'Hara were a shadowy lump rolling toward the living room, bodies locked in battle. Stumbling down the hall after them, her head fuzzy and her vision still gray, Josie's eyes searched the floorboards for the gun. Blood streamed from the cuts in her legs, making a slick along the hallway. Her fingers scrabbled over the wall, trying to find the light switch. From the living room came the sound of glass breaking, wood splintering, and a guttural grunting. Josie found the light switch for the living room and flipped it on. The coffee table was on its side, one of its legs broken completely off. A lamp from one of the end tables lay shattered on the carpet. In front of the small entertainment center, O'Hara straddled Noah, raining down punches at his head. Noah had his forearms over his face, blocking most of the blows.

Josie took another look around but still didn't see the gun O'Hara had discarded. She tried to shake off her disorientation. A scream rose up from deep in her diaphragm, and she ran, throwing the full weight of her body into O'Hara. Together, they toppled. Josie heard a crack as the side of his head hit the wall. She took advantage of his momentary daze to climb to her feet and knee his head into the wall once more. His arms flailed and jerked, reaching for her. She kicked at his chest, knocking him onto the floor, flat on his back.

"Noah," she called breathlessly.

She squatted down and tried to turn O'Hara onto his stomach so she could pin his hands behind his back, but he fought, one fist flying out and knocking her on the cheek just where Gretchen had split her skin only days earlier, knocking her off-balance and onto her ass. The howl of pain came out as a blunt gasp as her body tried to right itself. She saw him coming at her, and her hands reached up toward his head, grabbing for his throat or his eyes. Then she saw the flash of metal, and O'Hara's head whipped to the side.

Noah stepped between them, turning the gun in his hands so that he could point the barrel at O'Hara's head. "Don't you fucking touch her," he said.

Before O'Hara could fully recover from the pistol-whipping Noah had given him, Josie and Noah pushed him onto his stomach.

They had no cuffs and no plastic zip ties. Noah pinned the man's wrists together high up on his back and then put one knee on his wrists and one knee on his neck. He held O'Hara's gun to his head.

"Upstairs," Noah said. "Get your phone. Call 911. Then go outside and check on the patrol unit."

CHAPTER 69

For the third time in just over a week, Josie sat on a hospital gurney, sucking in sharp breaths every time the nurse tweezed a particularly large shard of glass from her legs and feet. Between that and the sting of the antiseptic they'd used to clean off all the blood before they started taking the glass out, both of Josie's lower legs felt like they were on fire. Noah stood across the room, arms folded over his chest, grimacing every time Josie did. "It's fine," she told him. "Really. This is nothing."

"It was a lot of blood."

"All the wounds are very superficial," the nurse mumbled without looking up from her work. "So far, only two of these will require stitches." Her eyes snapped up to Josie's face. "You were very lucky."

Yes, Josie thought. *I was.*

She laid her head back on the pillow and concentrated on taking deep, slow breaths. One of her hands reached out, and a second later, she felt Noah's hand slide into it. "You have to talk," she said. "Distract me."

"How did you know he was there? Did he make noise when he broke in? I didn't hear a thing."

"I was awake," Josie explained. She opened her eyes but focused them on Noah's face instead of her shredded legs. "Trinity texted me. It woke me up. Then I figured out what else Gretchen was hiding. I tried to go back to sleep, but I couldn't."

"Why didn't you wake me?" he asked.

"I tried. You were so out of it, and I thought you'd be mad if I woke you up to tell you something that could wait until the morning."

"It would have been better than waking up to you smashing every glass I owned and finding a serial killer in my house."

Josie laughed. Noah gave her hand a squeeze. "So?" he asked. "What was it? What was Gretchen hiding?"

"Ethan Robinson has a twin. When Gretchen got pregnant after the assault by O'Hara and went into hiding with Devil's Blade, she had two babies. That's why Ethan wasn't in Seattle yet. Gretchen told him to go get his twin and take him or her with him."

CHAPTER 70

ONE WEEK LATER

Gretchen sat at the conference room table in the station house. She had twisted the cap off the bottle of water Noah had given her and was now pushing it around the table between her index fingers until it pinged off one of her fingers and went flying across the table toward where Josie sat. Gretchen jumped up, trying to catch it before it hit Josie, but only succeeded in knocking over her bottle of water. A pool spread across the table. Josie caught the cap expertly, righted the bottle, and said, "Just a minute."

She returned with a roll of paper towels and helped Gretchen sop up the mess.

Gretchen said, "I'm really sorry."

Josie smiled at her. "It's water."

Instead of sitting back down, Gretchen paced the room. Josie sat down again and watched her friend move back and forth across the room, her own head swinging like a metronome.

"It's going to be okay," Josie told her.

"Is it?" Gretchen asked.

Josie tapped the glass top of the table. "Hey," she said, stopping Gretchen in place to meet her eyes. "It is. It's going to be okay."

Gretchen put both hands on the back of one of the chairs and leaned in toward Josie. "How did you know? How did you figure it out?"

Talking, putting the puzzle pieces together, always helped both of them with their anxiety. Josie said, "The study—well, one of the studies—that Dr. Larson and James Omar were working on was one about twins separated at birth. That was the one that seemed to be of the most interest to Larson when I met him. He asked if Trinity and I would join the study, and when I said no, he called her and tried to sell her on it."

"Pushy," Gretchen said.

"No, I think committed," Josie replied. "I mean, yeah, pushy, but I think his heart is in the right place. I think he wants to help people with this research. Anyway, at first I thought Ethan was just curious about his birth parents, and that James helped him find them through the genetic profiles of their distant relatives. You know there are all kinds of sites out there now."

"Yeah," Gretchen said. "I see the commercials all the time. Pay ninety-nine bucks and get your ancestry profile."

"Right," Josie said. "I think that Ethan took one of those tests and found that he had a twin. I think he approached him—"

"Her," Gretchen corrected.

"What?"

"Ethan has a sister, not a brother. They are fraternal twins—a boy and a girl. One of each." Her smile was sad.

"Her," Josie said. "I think Ethan approached her and asked her to be part of James's twin study. The separated-at-birth study. I think that's how it started. He probably didn't realize until he actually spoke to James about it that they had to be identical twins. His field was criminology, not genetics or epigenetics."

"She agreed? That means Larson has her name and address somewhere in his files," Gretchen said, urgency pitching her voice an octave higher.

"No," Josie said. "Like I said, they wouldn't have been eligible for the study since they were fraternal and not identical. I don't think that she would have agreed to it anyway. I think she was interested in finding you and... her father. I think Ethan started doing more research. I think he figured out you were his mother, and when he dug into your life, he realized you were a victim of the Strangler."

"Oh God," Gretchen said, closing her eyes. "Why didn't he just call the police?"

"You were the police," Josie said.

Gretchen opened her eyes. They glistened with tears. "I wasn't ready. When James called me—well, he told me he was Ethan—but when he called, he never told me that . . . that . . ."

"That he was bringing O'Hara with him?" Josie filled in.

Gretchen nodded. "When he called me and said they were at my house, I thought he meant him and his sister. I got freaked out. I wasn't ready to meet. I snuck up on them from the back because I just wanted to look at them first. I just wanted to see them. I didn't know how it would be. I didn't know if they would look like . . . O'Hara . . ."

Josie could tell trying his real name on for once was disconcerting to Gretchen. "That would have been distressing, I bet," Josie murmured.

"Yes. I admit it. It would. But still, they were my children. I always wanted those babies. I always wondered if I should have made different choices. Maybe I wasn't strong enough, wasn't smart enough . . . I've spent twenty-three years going over it in my head. But, what's done is done."

"When did you realize he had brought O'Hara with him?"

"I came around the corner from the back of the house. I was walking down the driveway. James saw me, smiled. He looked so nervous. I had just reached the front of the house when I heard O'Hara's voice."

A shudder ran the length of her body. Again, she closed her eyes and took several deep breaths. Then she opened them and continued. "He said, 'Hello, sweetheart. I've missed you.' You don't know how many times I've heard that voice in my head, in my nightmares. It never went away. As long as he was out there, I was afraid he'd come back. He always said he would. It got better when I moved back here, but it never went away. The fear. No, the terror."

"When did James realize that something wasn't right?"

"Oh, I think he knew before I showed up, but it was too late. He had picked O'Hara up and brought him to Denton. Then when he saw my reaction, he seemed to get more nervous. O'Hara said to me, 'You never told me we had a son.' That was when I realized James—well, I still thought he was Ethan—that he hadn't brought my daughter and that O'Hara didn't know about her. Anyway, O'Hara was angry. So angry. The coldness in his eyes—it was like nothing I'd ever seen except the night he killed Billy. He called me every name in the book. I told James to go into the house. I hoped he would get the idea—you know, call 911—and he started to walk up onto the porch, but O'Hara grabbed me. We tussled; he hit me, hard. He got my gun and put it to my head. He told James that if he took another step, he'd kill him."

"Jesus."

"Yeah, so James went back to the driveway. He looked like he was slowly trying to step away. I could see he was itching to run. O'Hara dragged me up onto the porch and tossed me onto the ground. He had the gun on me. He said something like, 'We've got a real problem here,' and that's when James started babbling. He told us everything. That he wasn't Ethan Robinson. His name was James Omar. He was Ethan's roommate. That Ethan had tracked us down, and Ethan had some idea of getting his parents together—making it a surprise and having me arrest O'Hara. The only surviving Strangler victim now a police officer and gets to arrest him. He said it was all Ethan's idea. O'Hara asked him where Ethan was, and James said he didn't know, but he could find out. He mumbled something about going to call Ethan and turned to go, and that's when O'Hara shot him. Just like that. He went right down. I was so shocked and so stunned. It's like I wasn't me anymore. I was that twenty-year-old girl again, and this man had just shot my husband."

"I know," Josie said softly.

"Then he took my keys. He kept the gun on me and made me go into the house. I thought...I thought he was going to hurt me again. Like he did all those years ago, but all he wanted was that stupid Wawa mug. Then he made me take him to my car, and no one saw us because we went through the back. He had zip ties, although he didn't need them really because he hit me. He stopped at the bridge when he realized that the car was department-issued. He had to disable the MDT. That took a while. Then he pulled me out of the car, hit me again." She pointed to her forehead. "And stuffed me in the trunk. I don't remember much after that. Waking up in the dark, tied, my head pounding. At some point he took me out of the trunk. We were in the woods. He said things—so many horrible things. He went on for hours about what he was going to do to me and Ethan when he found him. He kept talking about how he had stopped, how he hadn't killed in fourteen years, and now I made him kill again. He kept calling Ethan names and talking about how Ethan figured out who he was, and so Ethan had to die. On and on he went. It was almost like he was possessed. At some point it was like he didn't even notice I was there anymore, he just circled and circled, muttering to himself. It got dark. Eventually he left. When he came back, it was daytime. I actually felt relieved to see him. I was afraid some wild animal would come along and eat me. Maybe that would have been better."

"Did he let you go then?" Josie asked.

"Not precisely then. When he came back, he was like a completely different person. He was calm. It was almost like someone gave him a drug—he was so different. He brought me something to eat and drink, untied me, tossed me a blanket. Let me relieve myself. When he talked, he sounded so reasonable. I imagined this was what he must be like in his 'real' life. This must be what most people saw. Then I realized..."

She broke off.

"What?" Josie prompted softly.

"The night he killed Billy, he was wound up. Not crazy like he was this time, but he was...agitated. Angry. Mean. Once he had finished with me, he was so much calmer. Even when he heard the dishes topple, he wasn't as high-alert as he was when he first broke in. It was like he needed to hurt us to satisfy some overwhelming urge. Like how a drug addict will be climbing out of their own skin for more of whatever they need, and then once they get it, it's like this relaxed feeling takes over. That's what it was like with him. It was subtle back in 1994, but still, I recognized it this time."

"You thought he had killed someone?"

Gretchen nodded. "I asked him, 'What did you do?' and he said, 'What your shit-stain of a kid made me do.' Then he said he wasn't going to get caught. That cops were stupid, and he hadn't been caught in over twenty years—he wasn't about to go down now."

"So you tried to work out a deal with him?"

"I had to. He was going to kill me. No doubt. I knew once I was dead, he'd go after Ethan. I had told Ethan what to do, but I had no way of knowing if he would do it or if he would do it before O'Hara found him. I just knew I had to stall for time. Like I said, I didn't care if he killed me, but my children..."

"You had to protect them," Josie said. "I understand."

"I didn't know his name, but Ethan did. His name, where he lived, everything. I knew if he ever found Ethan, he'd find out about my daughter, and she'd be dead too. My only chance to buy my kids some time was to work out some kind of deal with him. Anything. I thought even if Ethan doesn't do what I told him to do, maybe he'll have the good sense to go to the police. To find my daughter and go to the police. That's why I told O'Hara I would take the fall for James's murder. That everyone would believe it was me anyway because he was so smart, he hadn't left any evidence behind. He loved that."

"He was arrogant, just like the FBI profile said."

"Yes, very arrogant. He liked to have his ego stroked. I told him instead of killing me, he could put me in prison for the rest of my life. Like the cops have wanted to do to him for over twenty years. I said imagine that. Imagine getting away with that. Turning the so-called justice system on its head. I could tell by the look on his face that he was really liking the idea. It really appealed to his sense of egotism. Like the crime-scene tokens he always took and left. He didn't have to do that to commit the crimes. He liked to fuck with people—that was his thing. That was always his thing. I think that's why he attacked couples. He liked the idea of the husband having to listen while his wife was tortured in the next room."

Gretchen stopped, a pallor coming over her features.

"Sit," Josie said softly. "Drink some water."

She pushed a fresh water bottle across the table, and Gretchen took it, gulping it down. Then she sat down again. This time she was more fatigued than nervous. "Anyway," she continued, "he seemed to think me getting life in prison—especially now that I was a cop—was like the ultimate mind-fuck. I said I would do it, but he had to leave Ethan alone. He told me I was crazy, that Ethan knew his identity, and I couldn't make a deal with him based on what Ethan might or might not do. I said if Ethan had wanted to turn him in, he would have already, that Ethan clearly just wanted to know his dad."

"Did he buy that?"

Gretchen shrugged. "I don't know. I mean it's true though, isn't it? Ethan knew O'Hara was a serial killer, or at least, he had a damn good idea, and he didn't tell the authorities. I like to think he would have eventually."

"Maybe it wasn't real to him," Josie said. "It was more like a game to him. Then when Omar started sending texts implying he was in over his head, Ethan got scared."

"I think you're right. Well, O'Hara and I went back and forth, and I agreed he could put a scare into Ethan, but he couldn't kill him. If I found out Ethan had been killed, I would sing. I told him if he couldn't convince Ethan, then I would try. It took hours. So many hours. Going round and round, trying to talk him into it. I think he was going to kill Ethan all along, and that he figured my confession would fall on deaf ears since there was no physical evidence he was at the Omar scene, and I didn't know his actual identity. He didn't think the cops would figure out the big clue he left at the Wilkins scene. He also didn't even care if the police figured out the Seattle Soul Mate Strangler killed them. No one had ever solved a Strangler crime. It was his crowning achievement. I was the one who ruined all of that when I got away. He told me that he had spent years trying to track me down, and that he finally had about ten years ago. That was why he moved out to the East Coast. He liked the idea of spying on me, of always being within striking distance if the need took him. I often felt like I was being watched, but he never made himself known as far as I can tell. I'm not sure he wanted to kill me, because if he did, the game would be over once and for all."

"It might have been that game that kept him from killing all this time. He was getting older, the murders were getting riskier, and knowing he had that power over you might have been enough to satisfy his urges."

"Yes," Gretchen agreed.

"O'Hara agreed to your deal then," Josie said. "But you had already called Ethan."

"It was a miracle, really. O'Hara was driving my car. Apparently, he had come to Denton with James in a rental, and he didn't want to take that because it could be traced. I was lying in the back seat and had seen him toss the phones onto the front passenger seat. I knew I had to try. He had tied my hands in front of me, thank God, so there was a chance I could get Omar's phone and make a call. If it had been password protected, I would have been screwed. I told him he had to take the MDT out of the car or the police would find him in minutes. I made sure to send him out to get the antenna off, and I was purposely vague about where it was so it would take him longer."

Josie smiled. "It worked."

"Yes. I got Ethan right away, and I just talked. I really had no idea if he'd take any of what I said to heart, but he said he already knew where my daughter was. I made him repeat back to me my instructions, the name of my contact in the Devil's Blade. I told him that when he and my daughter were safe, to tell her to find a way to let me know. Then, once I knew they were safe, I was going to tell the truth."

"Well, your plan worked," Josie said.

"Josie," Gretchen said, her eyes mournful. "I'm sorry I didn't trust you to help me."

"No apologies necessary. You thought the killer was in law enforcement. That complicated things. I don't know if I would have done anything differently. In the heat of the moment, we make decisions we might not make otherwise. When your world narrows down to surviving, everything changes."

"Thank you," Gretchen said. Another moment ticked by. A small smile curved Gretchen's lips. "I'm sorry I hit you."

Josie laughed and gave her a wink. "You may have to buy me a few Danishes to make up for that."

A moment passed between them in silence. There was one last piece of the puzzle that Josie hadn't yet figured out. "You gave birth to twins," she said. "Why didn't anyone pick up on that when the Devil's Blade dropped you off in front of the ATF building? I know they did medical examinations. At the very least, you would have had lots and lots of stretch marks."

A sad smile spread across Gretchen's face. "Twenty-three years ago, at a hospital in San Diego, a young mother named Anne Carson went into labor prematurely. She gave birth to twins seven weeks early. Carson Baby A and Baby B. I called them Billy and

Agnes—after my husband and my grandmother. They were barely three pounds each. They spent two months in the NICU. I stayed with them as long as possible, and then Linc set me up nearby in one of his safe houses. He was the one who got me the fake identity before the babies came, so that when I went into labor, there were no questions at the hospital. I didn't worry about the bills, because I wasn't really Anne Carson. But that was the first time I knew I couldn't really hide forever, and I sure as hell couldn't give those babies the care they needed. Linc cut me up real good before they left me at the ATF building, so what stretch marks I did have weren't really noticeable. I hadn't had a C-section, so there was no scar from that. It was a risk, certainly, but no one ever questioned me."

A dull roar rumbled outside. Gretchen and Josie went still, their ears pricked to the sound. It got closer, sounding like a jet taking off. The chair Josie sat in seemed to vibrate as the noise got louder, closer, and rose to a deafening crescendo.

Gretchen's eyes bulged. "Devil's Blade. They're here."

CHAPTER 71

Outside the Denton Police Station was a sea of Harley Davidsons as far as the eye could see. They filled up the street, blocking off traffic in every direction. Josie didn't even try to count how many there were. All of them wore the Devil's Blade bandanna on their heads. Most looked like stereotypical bikers: heavy, rough leather jackets; long, scraggly hair; lengthy beards; tattoos on any exposed skin; and a look of menace that would make even a seasoned officer squirm. Except no one was squirming today. Gretchen, Josie, Noah, Dan Lamay, Heather Loughlin, and several other curious officers stood on the front steps of the station house, waiting as the sea of bikes parted down the middle and two people got off the backs of bikes driven by someone else.

Josie could tell by the awkward way the two of them dismounted that they were Gretchen's children. Each of them tugged off a helmet and handed it to the biker who had driven them. Ethan looked exactly as he had in the photo of him and James on their fridge, but he was taller and skinnier than she had anticipated. His sister was equally as tall and thin, with long, dark hair that flowed down her back. When she turned her face toward the building, Josie was stunned by her resemblance to Gretchen. In fact, both of them looked a lot like their mother. Josie studied them as they approached slowly. She could see O'Hara in their faces, but his imprint was faint compared to Gretchen's.

Gretchen stepped down to meet them at the bottom of the steps. The three of them stood around in awkward silence for a long moment. Finally, the girl stuck her hand out in Gretchen's direction. "Hi, I'm Paula," she said.

From where she stood, Josie could see the tears spill over and stream down Gretchen's cheeks as she took the hand of her daughter for the first time. "Gretchen," she croaked.

Ethan threw his arms around Gretchen, and slowly, she responded, wrapping her own arms around him and talking quietly into his ear.

The engines of the motorcycles roared once more. As each motorcycle departed, the biker gave Gretchen a small wave, almost a salute. Gretchen held one palm up in a constant wave back until every last one of them was gone.

Josie walked down to the pavement and introduced herself. "Let's go inside," she told them. "There's a lot to talk about."

CHAPTER 72

Josie stood in front of the hotel window. Below her, the lights of New York City shimmered and glowed like something alive. Now that she was here on a vacation instead of a case, she could appreciate the view, which was similar to—but a little better than—the one from Trinity's apartment. Of course, the room was Trinity's doing. Josie told her that she and Noah wanted to get away for a few days, and Trinity had made all kinds of arrangements for them. Josie suspected that Trinity was trying to get her to fall in love with the city so that she would visit more.

Behind her, the door creaked open, and Noah walked through. In his hands he held a collection of brochures and maps. His phone was pressed to his ear.

"Yeah, okay," he said into it. "That's good news. Yeah, I'll tell her."

He hung up and tossed his phone onto the dresser. "That was Loughlin. She said the DA decided not to press obstruction charges against Gretchen. They felt it would be too much of a public-relations nightmare to prosecute the Strangler's only surviving victim now that he's been caught and the press is following his case so intensely."

"That's great," Josie said.

"Yes," he said. "It is." He waved the brochures in the air. "I got a map of Manhattan." He walked to the table in the corner of the room and spread them out. "Here's one for the tour of Rockefeller Center. Horse carriage rides in Central Park, the 9/11 Museum... oh, and it looks like Trinity got us tickets to a Broadway show tomorrow."

From behind him, Josie wrapped her arms around his waist and buried her face between his shoulder blades. He turned in her embrace, smiling down at her and smoothing her hair away from her face. "This is great," he said. "But to tell you the truth, the only thing I want to see in New York City is you."

Grinning, Josie stood on her tiptoes and kissed him. "Same."

A LETTER FROM LISA

Thank you so much for choosing to read *Her Final Confession*. If you enjoyed it, and want to keep up-to-date with all my latest releases, just sign up at the following link. Your email address will never be shared, and you can unsubscribe at any time.

lisaregan.com

Thank you so much for returning to the fictional Pennsylvania city of Denton to follow Josie Quinn on her latest adventure! I hope you'll stick around for more as Josie takes on more intriguing and exciting cases.

I love hearing from readers. You can get in touch with me through any of the social media outlets below, including my website and Goodreads page. Also, if you are up for it, I'd really appreciate it if you'd leave a review and perhaps recommend *Her Final Confession* to other readers. Reviews and word-of-mouth recommendations go a long way in helping readers discover my books for the first time. As always, thank you so much for your support. It means the world to me. I can't wait to hear from you, and I hope to see you next time!

Thanks,
Lisa Regan

 LisaReganCrimeAuthor

 @LisaIRegan

 www.lisaregan.com

ACKNOWLEDGMENTS

As always, first and foremost, I must thank my wonderful readers and loyal fans! Thank you so much for your relentless enthusiasm and passion, and for sticking with me on this wonderful journey. I deeply appreciate every message, email, and tweet. You are the best! Thank you to my husband, Fred, and daughter, Morgan, for your constant encouragement and for answering all my crazy questions—and for generally making life worth living. Thank you to my first readers: Nancy S. Thompson, Dana Mason, and Katie Mettner and Torese Hummel. Thank you to my Entrada readers. Thank you to my parents—William Regan, Donna House, Rusty House, Joyce Regan, and Julie House—for your constant support and for never getting tired of hearing good news. Thank you to the following "usual suspects"—people in my life who support and encourage me, spread the word about my books, and generally keep me going: Carrie Butler, Ava McKittrick, Melissia McKittrick, Andrew Brock, Christine & Kevin Brock, Laura Aiello, Helen Conlen, Jean & Dennis Regan, Sean & Cassie House, Marilyn House, Tracy Dauphin, Michael Infinito Jr., Jeff O'Handley, Susan Sole, the Funk family, the Tralies family, the Conlen family, the Regan family, the House family, the McDowells, and the Kays. Thank you to the lovely people at Table 25 for your wisdom, support, and good humor. I'd also like to thank all the lovely bloggers and reviewers who read the first three Josie Quinn books for so enthusiastically spreading the word!

Thank you so very much to Sgt. Jason Jay for answering all my law-enforcement questions so quickly and in such great detail that I can get things as close to authentic as fiction will allow.

As always, I must thank Jessie Botterill for her brilliance, her unmatched support, her enthusiasm, her encouragement, and her faith in me, as well as the entire team at Bookouture. No one works harder for their authors than all of you. You are miracle workers, all of you, and I feel so blessed and grateful to be working with you.

A huge thank you to Kirsiah McNamara and the entire team at Grand Central Publishing for taking a chance on this book, for being so thorough in editing, and for being so supportive and enthusiastic. I am so grateful to all of you!